"MERAU VARAGAN, YOU ARE UNDER ARREST BY THE TIME PATROL!"

Varagan shrugged, as a were-cat might have shrugged. "Concede me this much," he said, "that my empire would have had a certain dark magnificence."

The hopper flashed into being and hovered twenty feet aloft. Its rider grinned and aimed the firearm he carried. From the saddle of his horse, Merau Varagan waved at his time-traveling self.

Everard never quite knew what happened next. Somehow he made it out of the stirrups and onto the ground. Then the blaster-bolt struck.

POUL ANDERSON
TIME PATROLMAN

A JIM BÆN PRESENTATION:

A TOM DOHERTY ASSOCIATES BOOK

TIME PATROLMAN

This is a work of fiction. All the characters and events portrayed in this book are fictional, and any resemblance to real people or incidents is purely coincidental.

A TOR Book

Published by:

Tom Doherty Associates, Inc.
8–10 West 36th Street
New York, New York 10018

First TOR printing, October, 1983

ISBN: 53-076-4
CAN. ED.: 812-53-077-2
Cover art by Kevin Eugene Johnson

Printed in the United States of America

Distributed by:
Pinnacle Books
1430 Broadway
New York, New York 10018

To
Víctor Fernández-Dávila

IVORY, AND APES, AND PEACOCKS

While Solomon was in all his glory and the Temple was a-building, Manse Everard came to Tyre of the purple. Almost at once, he was in peril of his life.

That mattered little in itself. An agent of the Time Patrol was expendable, the more so if he or she enjoyed the godlike status of Unattached. Those whom Everard sought could destroy an entire reality. He had come to help rescue it.

One afternoon, 950 B.C., the ship that bore him approached his destination. The weather was warm, nearly windless. Sail furled, the vessel moved under manpower, creak and splash of sweeps, drumbeat of a coxswain posted near the sailors who had the twin steering oars. Around the broad seventy-foot hull, wavelets glittered blue, chuckled, swirled. Farther out, dazzlement off the water blurred sight of other craft upon it. They were numerous, ranging from lean warships to tublike rowboats. Most were Phoenician, though many hailed from different city-states of that society. Some were quite foreign, Philistine, Assyrian, Achaean, or stranger yet; trade through the known world flowed in and out of Tyre.

"Well, Eborix," said Captain Mago genially, "there you have her, queen of the sea like I told you she is, eh? What d'you think of my town?"

He stood in the bows with his passenger, just behind a fishtail ornament that curled upward and aft toward its mate at the stern. Lashed to that figurehead and to the latticework rails which ran down either side was a clay jar as big as himself. The oil was still within it; there had been no need to calm any billows, as easily as the voyage from Sicily had gone.

Everard glanced down at the skipper. Mago was a typical Phoenician, slender, swarthy, hook-nosed, eyes large and a bit slant, cheekbones high; neatly bearded, he wore a red-and-yellow kaftan, conical hat, sandals. The Patrolman towered over him. Since he would be conspicuous whatever guise he assumed, Everard took the part of a Celt from central Europe, complete with breeches, tunic, bronze sword, and sweeping mustache.

"A grand sight, indeed, indeed," he replied in a diplomatic, heavily accented voice. The electrocram he had taken, uptime in his native America, could have given him flawless Punic, but that wouldn't have fitted his character; he settled for fluency. "Daunting, almost, to a simple backwoodsman."

His gaze went forward again. Truly, in its way Tyre was as impressive as New York—perhaps more, when you recalled how much King Hiram had accomplished in how short a span, with only the resources of an Iron Age that was not yet very old.

Starboard the mainland rose toward the Lebanon Mountains. It was summer-tawny, save where orchards and woodlots spotted it with green or villages nestled. The appearance was richer, more inviting than when Everard had seen it on his future travels, before he joined the Patrol.

Usu, the original city, lay along the shore. Except for its size, it was representative of the milieu, adobe buildings blocky and flat-roofed, streets narrow and twisty, a few vivid façades indicating temple or palace. Battlemented walls and towers ringed three sides of it. Along the docks, gates between warehouses let those double as defenses. An aqueduct ran in from heights beyond Everard's view.

The new city, Tyre itself—Sor to its dwellers, meaning "Rocks"—was on an island half a mile offshore. Rather, it covered what had been two skerries until men filled in between and around them. Later they dug a canal straight through, from north to south, and flung out jetties and breakwaters to make this whole region an incomparable haven. With a burgeoning population and a bustling commerce thus crowded together, houses climbed upward, story upon story until they loomed over the guardian walls like small skyscrapers. They seemed to be less often of brick than of stone and cedarwood. Where earth and plaster had been used, frescos or inlaid shells ornamented them. On the eastward side, Everard glimpsed a huge and noble structure which the king had had built not for himself but for civic uses.

Mago's ship was bound for the outer or southern port, the Egyptian Harbor as he called it. Its piers bustled, men loading, unloading, fetching, bearing off, repairing, outfitting, dickering, arguing, chaffering, a tumble and chaos that somehow got its jobs done. Dock wallopers, donkey drivers, and other laborers, like the seamen on this cargo-cluttered deck, wore merely loincloths, or kaftans faded and patched. But plenty of brighter garments were in sight, some flaunting the costly colors that were produced here. Occasional women passed among the men, and Everard's preliminary education told him that they weren't all hookers. Sound rolled out to meet him, talk, laughter, shouts, braying, neighing, footfalls, hoofbeats, hammerbeats, groan of wheels and cranes, twanging music. The vitality was well-nigh overwhelming.

Not that this was any prettified scene in an Arabian Nights movie. Already he made out beggars crippled, blind, starveling; he saw a lash touch up a slave who toiled too slowly; beasts of burden fared worse. The smells of the ancient East roiled forth, smoke, dung, offal, sweat, as well as tar, spices, and savory roastings. Added to them was a stench of dyeworks and murex-shell middens on the mainland; but sailing along the coast and camping ashore every night, he had gotten used to that by now.

He didn't take the drawbacks to heart. His farings through history had cured him of fastidiousness and case-hardened him to the cruelties of man and nature—somewhat. For their era, these Canaanites were an enlightened and happy people. In fact, they were more so than most of humanity almost everywhere and everywhen.

His task was to keep them that way.

Mago hauled his attention back. "Aye, there are those who'd shamelessly swindle an innocent newcomer. I don't want that to happen to you, Eborix, my friend. I've grown to like you as we traveled, and I want you to think well of my town. Let me show you to an inn that a brother-in-law of mine has—brother of my junior wife, he is. He'll give you a clean doss and safe storage for your valuables at a fair exchange."

"It's thankful to you I am," Everard replied, "but my thought was I'd seek out that landsman I've bespoken. Remember, 'twas his presence emboldened me to fare hither." He smiled. "Sure, and if he's died or moved away or whatever, glad I'll be to take your offer." That was mere politeness. The impression he had gathered along the way was that Mago was as cheerfully rapacious as any other merchant adventurer, and hoped to get him plucked.

The captain regarded him for a moment. Everard counted as big in his own era, which made him gigantic here. A dented nose in the heavy features added to the impression of toughness, while blue eyes and dark-brown hair bespoke the wild North. One had better not push Eborix too hard.

At the same time, the Celtic persona was no great wonder in this cosmopolitan place. Not only did amber come from the Baltic littoral, tin from Iberia, condiments from Arabia, hardwoods from Africa, occasional wares from farther still: men did.

Engaging passage, Eborix had told of leaving

his mountainous homeland because of losing out in a feud, to seek his fortune in the South. Wandering, he had hunted or worked for his keep, when he didn't receive hospitality in return for his tales. He fetched up among the Umbrians of Italy, who were akin to him. (The Celts would not begin overrunning Europe, clear to the Atlantic, for another three centuries or so, when they had become familiar with iron; but already some had won territory far from the Danube Valley that was the cradle of their race.) One of them, who had served as a mercenary, described opportunities in Canaan and taught Eborix the Punic tongue. This induced the latter to seek a bay in Sicily where Phoenician traders regularly called and buy passage with goods he had acquired. A man from his area of birth was said to be living in Tyre, after an adventurous career of his own, and probably willing to steer a compatriot in a profitable direction.

This line of bull, carefully devised by Patrol specialists, did more than slake local curiosity. It made Everard's trip safe. Had they supposed the foreigner to be a waif with no connections, Mago and the crew might have been tempted to set upon him while he slept, bind him, and sell him for a slave. As was, the journey had been interesting, yes, rather fun. Everard had come to like these rascals.

That doubled his wish to save them from ruin.

The Tyrian sighed. "As you wish," he said. "If you do need me, my home is on the Street of Anat's Temple, near the Sidonian Harbor." He brightened. "In any case, do come look me up, you and your host. He's in the amber trade, you mentioned? Maybe we can work out a little deal of some kind. . . . Now, stand aside. I've got to bring us in." He shouted profane commands.

Deftly, the sailors laid their vessel along a quay, got it secured, put out a gangplank. Folk swarmed close, yelling for news, crying for stevedore work, chanting the praises of their wares or of their masters' business establishments. None boarded, however. That prerogative belonged initially to the customs officer. A guard, helmeted, scale-mailed, armed with spear and shortsword, went before him, pushing a way through the crowd, leaving a wake of fairly good-natured curses. At the officer's back trotted a secretary, who bore a stylus and waxed tablet.

Everard went below decks and fetched his baggage, which he had stowed among the blocks of Italian marble that were the ship's principal cargo. The officer required him to open the two leather sacks. Nothing surprising was in them. The whole purpose of traveling all the way from Sicily, instead of time-hopping directly here, was to pass the Patrolman off as what he claimed to be. It was well-nigh certain that the enemy was keeping watch on events, as they neared the moment of catastrophe.

"You can provide for yourself a while, at least." The Phoenician official nodded his grizzled head when Everard displayed some small ingots of bronze. Coinage would not be invented for several centuries, but the metal could be swapped for whatever he wanted. "You must understand that we cannot let in one who might feel he has to turn robber. In fact—" He looked dubiously at the barbarian sword. "What is your purpose in coming?"

"To find honest work, sir, as it might be a caravan guard. I'll be seeking out Conor the amber factor." The existence of that resident Celt had been a major reason for Everard's adoption of his specific disguise. The chief of the local Patrol base had suggested it.

The Tyrian reached a decision. "Very well, you may go ashore, your weapon too. Remember that we crucify thieves, bandits, and murderers. If you fail to get other work, seek out Ithobaal's hiring house, near the Hall of the Suffetes. He can always find something in the way of day labor for a husky fellow like you. Good luck."

He returned to dealing with Mago. Everard lingered, awaiting a chance to bid the captain farewell. Discussion went quickly, almost informally, and the tax to be paid in kind would be modest. This race of businessmen had no use for the ponderous bureaucracy of Egypt or Mesopotamia.

Having said what he wanted to, Everard picked up his bags by the cords around them and went ashore. The crowd surged about him, staring, chattering. At first he was amazed; after a couple of tentative approaches, nobody begged alms or beset him to buy trinkets. Could this be the Near East?

He recalled the absence of money. A newcomer wouldn't likely have anything corresponding to small change. Usually you made a bargain with an innkeeper, food and lodging for so-and-so much of the metal, or whatever else of value, you carried. For lesser purchases, you sawed a piece off an ingot, unless some different trade was arranged. (Everard's fund included amber and nacre beads.) Sometimes you called in a broker, who made your transaction part of a complicated one involving several other individuals. If you felt charitable, you'd carry around a little grain or dried fruit and drop it in the bowls of the indigent.

Everard soon left most of the people behind. They were mainly interested in the crew. A few idle curiosity-seekers, and many stares, trailed him. He strode over the quay toward an open gate.

A hand plucked his sleeve. Startled enough to miss a step, he looked down.

A brown-skinned boy grinned back. He was sixteen or so, to judge from the fuzz on his cheeks, though small and scrawny even by local standards. Nonetheless, he moved lithely, barefoot, clad only in a ragged and begrimed kilt at which hung a pouch. Curly black hair fell in a queue behind a sharp-nosed, sharp-chinned face. His smile and his eyes — big, long-lashed Levantine eyes — were brilliant.

"Hail, sir, hail to you!" he greeted. "Life, health, and strength be yours! Welcome to Tyre! Where would you go, sir, and what can I do for you?"

He didn't burble, but spoke very clearly, in hopes the stranger would understand. When he got a response in his own language, he jumped for joy. "What do you want, lad?"

"Why, sir, to be your guide, your advisor, your helper, and, yes, your guardian. Alas, our otherwise fair city is afflicted with scoundrels who like nothing better than to prey on innocent newcomers. If they do not outright steal everything you have, the first time you blink, they'll at least wish the most worthless trash on you, at a cost which'll leave you paupered almost as fast—"

The boy broke off. He had spied a seedy-looking young man approach. At once he sped to intercept, windmilling his fists, yelling too quickly and shrilly for Everard to catch more than a few words. "—louse-bitten jackal! . . . I saw him first. . . . Begone to the latrine that spawned you—"

The young man stiffened. He reached for a knife hung at his shoulder. Hardly had he moved before the stripling snatched a sling from his pouch and a rock to load it. He crouched, leered, swung the leather strap to and fro. The man spat, said something nasty, turned on his heel, and stalked off. Laughter barked from such passersby as had paid attention.

The boy laughed too, gleefully, loping back to Everard. "Now that, sir, was a prime example of what I meant," he crowed. "I know yon villain well. He's a runner for his father—maybe his father—who keeps the inn at the Sign of the Blue Squid. There you'd be lucky to get a rotten piece of goat's tail for your dinner, the single wench is a shambling farm of diseases, the pallets hang together only because the bedbugs hold hands, and as for the wine, why, I think the wench must have infected somebody's horse. You'd soon be too sick to notice that grandsire of a thousand hyenas when he plundered your baggage, and if you sought to complain, he'd swear by every god in the universe that you gambled it away. Little does he fear hell after this world is rid of him; he knows they'd never demean themselves there by letting him in. That is what I've saved you from, great lord."

Everard felt a grin tug at his lips. "Well, son, you might be stretching things just a trifle," he said.

The boy smote his thin breast. "No more than needful to give your magnificence the proper impression. Surely you are a man of the widest experience, a judge of the best as well as a generous rewarder of faithful service. Come, let me bring you to lodgings, or whatever else you may desire, and then see for yourself whether or not Pummairam has led you aright."

Everard nodded. The map of Tyre was engraved in his memory; he had no need of a guide. However, it would be natural for a yokel to engage one. Also, this kid would keep others from pestering him, and might give him a few useful tips.

"Very well, lead me whither I would go. Your name is Pummairam?"

"Yes, sir." Since the youth didn't mention his father, as was customary, he probably didn't know who that had been. "May I ask how my noble master should be addressed by his humble servant?"

"No title. I am Eborix, son of Mannoch, from a country beyond the Achaeans." With none of Mago's folk listening, the Patrolman could add: "He whom I seek is Zakarbaal of Sidon, who deals for his kin in this city." That meant Zakarbaal represented his family firm among the Tyrians, and handled its affairs here in between visits by its ships. "I've heard tell his house is on, uh, the Street of the Chandlers. Can you be showing me the way?"

"Indeed, indeed." Pummairam took Everard's bags. "Only deign to accompany me."

Actually, it wasn't hard to get around. As a

planned city, rather than one which had grown organically through centuries, Tyre was laid out more or less on a gridiron pattern. The thorough-fares were paved, guttered, and reasonably wide, considering how short of acreage the island was. They lacked sidewalks, but that didn't matter, because except for a few trunk routes, beasts of burden were not allowed on them outside the wharf areas; nor did people dump stuff on them. They also lacked signs, of course, but that didn't matter either, since almost anybody would have been glad to give directions for the sake of some words with an outlander and perhaps a deal to propose.

Walls rose sheer to right and left, mostly win-dowless, enclosing the inward-looking houses that would prevail in Mediterranean countries for mil-lennia to come. They shut off breezes and radi-ated back the heat of the sun. Noise echoed off them, odors rolled thick between. Yet Everard found himself enjoying the place. Still more than at the waterfront, crowds moved, jostled, gestured, laughed, talked at machine-gun speed, chanted, clamored. Porters beneath their yokes, litter-bearers conveying the occasional wealthy burgher, forced a way among sailors, artisans, vendors, laborers, housewives, entertainers, mainland farmers and shepherds, foreigners from end to end of the Midworld Sea, every variety and condition of life. If most clothes were of dull hue, many were gaudy, and none seemed to cover a body that was not overflowing with energy.

Booths lined the walls. Everard couldn't resist lingering now and then, to look at what they offered. That did not include the famous purple dye; it was too expensive, sought after by garmentmakers everywhere, destined to become the traditional color of royalty. But there was no dearth of bright fabrics, draperies, rugs. Glassware abounded, anything from beads to beakers; it was another specialty of the Phoenicians, their own invention. Jewelry and figurines, often carved in ivory or cast in precious metals, were excellent; this culture originated little or nothing artistic, but copied freely and skillfully. Amulets, charms, gewgaws, food, drink, utensils, weapons, instruments, games, toys, endlessness—

Everard remembered how the Bible gloated (would gloat) over the wealth of Solomon, and whence he got it. *"For the king had at sea a navy of Tharshish with the navy of Hiram: once in three years came the navy of Tharshish, bringing gold, and silver, ivory, and apes, and peacocks.—"*

Pummairam was quick to switch off conversations with shopkeepers and start Everard onward. "Let me show my master where the really good stuff is." Doubtless that meant a commission for Pummairam, but what the hell, the youngster had to live somehow, and didn't seem ever to have lived terribly well.

For a while they followed the canal. To a bawdy chant, sailors towed a laden ship along. Its officers stood on deck, wrapped in the dignity that behooved businessmen. The Phoenician bourgeoisie tended to be a sober lot . . . except in their religion, some of whose rites were orgiastic enough to compensate.

The Street of the Chandlers led off from this waterway. It was fairly long, being hemmed in by massive buildings that were warehouses as well as offices and homes. It was quiet, too, despite its far end giving on a thronged avenue; no shops crouched against the high, hot walls, and few people were in sight. Captains and shipowners came here for supplies, merchants came to negotiate, and, yes, two monoliths flanked the entrance of a small temple dedicated to Tanith, Our Lady of the Waves. Several little children who must belong to resident families—boys and girls together, naked or nearly so—darted about at play while a gaunt, excited mongrel dog barked.

A beggar sat, knees drawn up, by the shady entrance to an alley. His bowl rested at his bare feet. A kaftan muffled his body and a cowl obscured his face. Everard did see the rag tied over the eyes. Poor, blind devil; ophthalmia was among the countless damnations that made the ancient world not so glamorous after all. . . . Pummairam darted past the fellow, to overtake a man in a priestly robe who was leaving the temple. "Hoy, sir, your reverence, if you please," he called, "which is the door of Zakarbaal the Sidonian? My master condescends to visit him—" Everard, who already knew the answer, lengthened his stride to follow.

The beggar rose. His left hand plucked away his bandage, to reveal a lean, thick-bearded visage and a pair of eyes that had surely been watching through the cloth. From that flowing sleeve, his right hand drew something that gleamed.

A pistol!

Reflex flung Everard aside. Pain whipped through his own left shoulder. Sonic gun, he realized, from futureward of his home era, soundless, recoilless. If that invisible beam got him in the head or heart, he'd be dead, and never a mark upon him.

No place to go but forward. "Haaa!" he roared, and plunged zigzag to the attack. His sword hissed forth.

The other grinned, drifted back, took careful aim.

A *smack!* resounded. The assassin lurched, yelled, dropped his weapon, grabbed at his ribs. Pummairam's spent slingstone clattered over the cobbles.

Children scattered, screaming. The priest returned prudently through his temple door. The stranger whirled and ran. He vanished down the lane. Everard was too slow. His injury wasn't serious, but for the moment it hurt abominably. Half dazed, he stopped at the alley mouth, stared down the emptiness before him, panted, and rasped in English, "He's escaped. Oh, God damn it, anyway."

Pummairam darted to him. Anxious hands played over the Patrolman's form. "Are you wounded, my master? Can your servant help? Ah, woe, woe, I'd no time for a proper windup, nor to aim right, else I'd have spattered the evildoer's brains for yon dog to lick up."

"You . . . did mighty well . . . just the same." Everard drew shuddering breaths. Strength and steadiness began to return, agony to recede. He was still alive. That was miracle enough for one day.

He had work to do, though, and urgent it was. Having obtained the gun, he laid a hand on Pummairam's shoulder and made their gazes meet. "What did you see, lad? What d'you think happened this while?"

"Why, I—I—" Ferret-fast, the youth collected his wits. "It seemed to me that the beggar, though such he scarcely was, threatened my lord's life with some talisman whose magic did inflict harm. May the gods pour abominations on the head of him who would have extinguished the light of the universe! Yet, naturally, his wickedness could not prevail against the valor of my master—" the voice dropped to a confidential whisper: "—whose secrets are assuredly locked away safe in the bosom of his worshipful servant."

"Good," Everard grunted. "Sure, and these be matters about which common folk should never dare talk, lest they be stricken with palsy, deafness, and emerods. You've done well, Pum." *Saved my life, probably,* he thought, and stooped to untie the cord on a fallen bag. "Here, small reward it is, but this ingot ought to buy you something you'd like. And now, before the brannigan started, you did learn which is the house I want, did you not?"

Underneath the business of the minute, fading pain and shock from the assault, exhilaration of survival, grimness rose. After all his elaborate precautions, within an hour of arrival, his cover was blown. The enemy had not only had Patrol headquarters staked out, somehow their agent had instantly seen that it was no ordinary wanderer come into this street, and had not hesitated a second before trying to kill him.

This was a hairy mission for sure. And more was at stake than Everard liked to think about—first the existence of Tyre, later the destiny of the world.

Zakarbaal closed the door to his inner chambers and latched it. Turning around, he held out his hand in the manner of Western civilization. "Welcome," he said in Temporal, the Patrol language. "My name, you may remember, is Chaim Zorach. May I present my wife Yael?"

They were both of Levantine appearance and in Canaanite garb, but here, shut away from office staff and household servants, their entire bearing changed, posture, gait, facial expressions, tone of voice. Everard would have recognized them as being of the twentieth century even if he had not been told. The atmosphere was as refreshing to him as a wind off the sea.

He introduced himself. "I am the Unattached agent you sent for," he added.

Yael Zorach's eyes widened. "Oh! An honor. You . . . you are the first such I have met. The others who've been investigating, they are just technicians."

Everard grimaced. "Don't be too awe-struck. I'm afraid I haven't made much of a showing so far."

He described his journey and the contretemps at its end. She offered him some painkiller, but he said he was pretty well over hurting, and her husband thereupon produced what was better anyway, a bottle of Scotch. Presently they were seated at their ease.

The chairs were comfortable, not unlike those of home—a luxury in this milieu, but then, Zakarbaal was supposed to be a wealthy man, with access to every kind of imported goods. Otherwise the apartment was austere by future standards, though frescos, draperies, lamps, furnishings were tasteful.

It was cool and dim; a window opening on a small cloister garden had been curtained against the heat of the day.

"Why don't we relax a while and get acquainted before we buckle down to duty?" Everard suggested.

Zorach scowled. "You can do that right after you almost got killed?"

His wife smiled. "I think he might need to all the more, dear," she murmured. "We too. The menace can wait a little longer. It's been waiting, hasn't it?"

From the pouch at his belt, Everard drew anachronisms he had permitted himself, hitherto used only in solitude: pipe, tobacco, lighter. Zorach's tension eased a trifle, he chuckled and fetched cigarettes out of a locked coffer which held various such comforts. His language changed to Brooklyn-accented English: "You're American, aren't you, Agent Everard?"

"Yes. Recruited in 1954." How many years of his lifespan had passed "since" he answered an ad, took certain tests, and learned of an organization that guarded a traffic through the epochs? He hadn't added them up lately. It didn't matter much, when he and his fellows were the beneficiaries of a treatment that kept them unaging. "Uh, I thought you two were Israelis."

"We are," Zorach explained. "In fact, Yael's a *sabra*. Me, though, I didn't immigrate till I'd been doing archaeology there for a spell and had met her. That was in 1971. We got recruited into the Patrol four years later."

"How'd that happen, if I may ask?"

"We were approached, sounded out, finally told

the truth. Naturally, we jumped at the chance.
The work's often hard and lonesome—twice as
lonesome, in a way, when we're home on furlough
and can't tell our old friends and colleagues what
we've been up to—but it's totally fascinating."
Zorach winced. His words became a near mumble.
"Also, well, *this* post is special for us. We don't
just maintain a base and its cover business, we
manage to help local people now and then. Or we
try to, as much as we can without causing anybody to suspect there's anything peculiar about
us. That makes up, somehow, a little bit, for . . . for
what our countrymen will do hereabouts, far
uptime."

Everard nodded. The pattern was familiar to
him. Most field agents were specialists like these,
passing their careers in a single milieu. They had
to be, if they were to learn it thoroughly enough
to serve the Patrol's purposes. What a help it
would be to have native-born personnel! But such
were very rare before the eighteenth century A.D.,
or still later in most parts of the world. How
could a person who hadn't grown up in a scientific-
industrial society even grasp the idea of auto-
matic machinery, let alone vehicles that jumped
in a blink from place to place and year to year?
An occasional genius, of course; however, most
identifiable geniuses carved niches for themselves
in history, and you didn't dare tell them the facts
for fear of making changes. . . .

"Yeah," Everard said. "In a way, a free operative like me has it easier. Husband-and-wife teams,
or women generally—Not to pry, but what do you
do about children?"

"Oh, we have two at home in Tel Aviv," Yael

Zorach answered. "We time our returns so we've never been gone from them for more than a few days of their lives." She sighed. "It is strange, of course, when to us months have passed." Brightening: "Well, when they're of age, they're going to join the outfit too. Our regional recruiter has examined them already and decided they'll be fine material."

If not, Everard thought, *could you stand it, watching them grow old, suffer the horrors that will come, finally die, while you are still young of body?* Such a prospect had made him shy away from marriage, more than once.

"I think Agent Everard means children here in Tyre," Chaim Zorach said. "Before traveling from Sidon—we took ship, like you, because we were going to become moderately conspicuous—we quietly bought a couple of infants from a slave dealer, took them along, and have been passing them off as ours. They'll have lives as good as we can arrange." Unspoken was the likelihood that servants had the actual raising of those two; their foster parents would not dare invest much love in them. "That keeps us from appearing somehow unnatural. If my wife's womb has since closed, why, it's a common misfortune. I do get twitted about not taking a second wife or at least a concubine, but on the whole, Phoenicians mind their own business pretty well."

"You like them, then?" Everard inquired.

"Oh, yes, by and large, we do. We have excellent friends among them. We'd better—as important a nexus as this is."

Everard frowned and puffed hard on his pipe. The bowl had grown consolingly warm in his clasp, aglow like a tiny hearthfire. "You think that's correct?"

The Zorachs were surprised. "Of course!" Yael said. "We *know* it is. Didn't they explain to you?"

Everard chose his words with care. "Yes and no. After I'd been asked to look into this matter, and agreed, I got myself crammed full of information about the milieu. In a way, too full; it became hard to see the forest for the trees. However, my experience has been that I do best to avoid grand generalizations in advance of a mission. It could get hard to see the trees for the forest, so to speak. My idea was, once I'd been dropped off in Sicily and taken ship for Tyre, I'd have leisure to digest the information and form my own ideas. But that didn't quite work out, because the captain and crew were infernally curious about me; my mental energy went into answering their questions, which were often sharp, without letting any cat out of the bag." He paused. "To be sure, the role of Phoenicia in general, and Tyre in particular, in Jewish history—that's obvious."

On the kingdom that David had cobbled together out of Israel, Judah, and Jerusalem, this city soon became the main civilizing influence, its principal trading partner and window on the outside world. Now Solomon continued his father's friendship with Hiram. The Tyrians were supplying most of the materials and nearly all the skilled hands for the building of the Temple, as well as structures less famous. They would embark on joint exploratory and commercial ventures with the Hebrews. They would advance an immensity of goods to Solomon, a debt which he could only pay off by ceding them a score of his villages . . .

with whatever subtle long-range consequences
that had.

The subtleties went deeper, though. Phoenician
customs, thoughts, beliefs permeated the neigh-
boring realm, for good or ill; Solomon himself
made sacrifices to gods of theirs. Yahweh would
not really be the sole Lord of the Jews until the
Babylonian Captivity forced them to it, as a means
of preserving an identity that ten of their tribes
had already lost. Before then, King Ahab of Israel
would have taken the Tyrian princess Jezebel as
his queen. Their evil memory was undeserved;
the policy of foreign alliance and domestic religious tolerance which they strove to carry out
might well have saved the country from its even-
tual destruction. Unfortunately, they collided with
fanatical Elijah—"the mad mullah from the mountains of Gilead," Trevor-Roper would call him.
And yet, had not Phoenician paganism spurred
them to fury, would the prophets have wrought
that faith which was to endure for thousands of
years and remake the world?

"Oh, yes," Chaim said. "The Holy Land's
aswarm with visitors. Jerusalem Base is chroni-
cally swamped, trying to regulate the traffic. We
get a lot fewer here, mostly scientists from different eras, traders in artwork and the like, the
occasional rich tourist. Nevertheless, sir, I maintain that this place, Tyre, is the real nexus of the
era." Harshly: "And our opponents seem to have
reached the same conclusion, right?"

The starkness took hold of Everard. Precisely
because the fame of Jerusalem, in future eyes,
overshadowed that of Tyre, this station was still
worse undermanned than most; therefore it was

terribly vulnerable; and if indeed it was a root of the morrow, and that root was cut away—

The facts passed before him as vividly as if he had never known them before.

When humans built their first time machine, long after Everard's home century, the Danellian supermen had arrived from farther yet, to organize the police force of the temporal lanes. It would gather knowledge, furnish guidance, aid the distressed, curb the wrongdoer; but these benevolences were incidental to its real function, which was to preserve the Danellians. A man has not lost free will merely because he has gone into the past. He can affect the course of events as much as ever. True, they have their momentum, and it is enormous. Minor fluctuations soon even out. For instance, whether a certain ordinary individual has lived long or died young, flourished or not, will make no noticeable difference several generations later. Unless that individual was, say, Shalmaneser or Genghis Khan or Oliver Cromwell or V. I. Lenin; Gautama Buddha or Kung Fu-Tze or Paul of Tarsus or Muhammad ibn Abdallah; Aristotle or Galileo or Newton or Einstein—Change anything like that, traveler from tomorrow, and you will still be where you are, but the people who brought you forth do not exist, they never did, it is an entirely other Earth up ahead, and you and your memories bespeak the uncausality, the ultimate chaos, which lairs beneath the cosmos.

Before now, along his own world line, Everard had had to stop the reckless and the ignorant before they worked that kind of havoc. They weren't too common; after all, the societies which possessed time travel screened their emissaries pretty carefully as a rule. However, in the course of a million years or more, mistakes were bound to happen.

So were crimes.

Everard spoke slowly: "Before going into detail about that gang and its operation—"

"What pitiful few details we have," Chaim Zorach muttered.

"—I'd like some idea of what their reasoning was. Why did they pick Tyre for the victim? Aside from its relationship to the Jews, that is."

"Well," Zorach began, "for openers, consider political events futureward of today. Hiram's become the most powerful king in Canaan, and that strength will outlive him. Tyre will stand off the Assyrians when they come, with everything that that implies. It'll push seaborne trade as far as Britain. It'll found colonies, the main one being Carthage." (Everard's mouth tightened. He had cause to know, far too well, how much Carthage mattered in history.) "It'll submit to the Persians, but fairly willingly, and among other things provide most of their fleet when they attack Greece. That effort will fail, of course, but imagine how the world might have gone if the Greeks had not faced that particular challenge. Eventually Tyre will fall to Alexander the Great, but only after a siege of months—a delay in his progress that also has incalculable consequences.

"Meanwhile, more basically, as the leading Phoenician state, it will be in the forefront of spreading Phoenician ideas abroad. Yes, to the Greeks themselves. There are religious concepts— Aphrodite, Adonis, Herakles, and other figures originate as Phoenician divinities. There's the alphabet, a Phoenician invention. There's the knowledge of Europe, Africa, Asia that Phoenician navigators will bring back. There's the progress in shipbuilding and seamanship."

Enthusiasm kindled in his tone: "Above everything else, I'd say, there's the origin of democracy, of the worth and rights of the individual. Not that the Phoenicians have any such theories; philosophy, like art, never will be a strong point of theirs. Just the same, the merchant adventurer—explorer or entrepreneur—he's their ideal, a man out on his own, deciding for himself. Here at home, Hiram's no traditional Egyptian or Oriental godking. He inherited his job, true, but essentially he presides over the suffetes—the magnates, who must approve every important thing he does. Tyre is actually quite a bit like the medieval Venetian republic in its heyday.

"We don't have the scientific personnel to trace the process out step by step, no. But I'm convinced that the Greeks developed their democratic institutions under strong Phoenician influence, mainly Tyrian—and where will your country or mine get those ideas from, if not the Greeks?"

Zorach's fist smote the arm of his chair. His other hand brought the whisky to his lips for a long and fiery gulp. "That's what those devils have learned!" he exclaimed. "They're holding Tyre up for ransom because that's how to put the future of the whole human race at gunpoint!"

Having broken out a holocube, he showed Everard what would happen, a year hence.

He had taken pictures with a sort of minicamera, actually a molecular recorder from the twenty-second century, disguised as a gem on a ring. ("Had" was the ludicrous single way to express in English how he doubled back and forth in time. The Temporal grammar included appropriate tenses.) Granted, he was not a priest or acolyte, but as a layman who made generous donations so that the goddess would favor his ventures, he had access.

The explosion took place (would take place) along this very street, in the little temple of Tanith. Occurring at night, it didn't hurt anybody, but it wrecked the inner sanctum. Rotating the view, Everard studied cracked and blackened walls, shattered altar and idol, strewn relics and treasures, twisted scraps of metal. Horror-numbed hierophants sought to placate the divine wrath with prayers and offerings, on the site and everywhere else in town that was sacred.

The Patrolman selected a volume of space within the scene and magnified. The bomb had fragmented its carrier, but there was no mistaking the pieces. A standard two-seat hopper, such as plied the time lanes in untold thousands, had materialized, and instantly erupted.

"I collected some dust and char when nobody was looking, and sent it uptime for analysis," Zorach said. "The lab reported the explosive had been chemical—fulgurite-B, the name is."

Everard nodded. "I know that stuff. In common use for a rather long period, starting a while after the origin span of us three. Therefore easy to obtain in quantity, untraceably—a hell of a lot easier than nuke isotopes. Wouldn't need a large amount to do this much damage, either. . . . I suppose you've had no luck intercepting the machine?"

Zorach shook his head. "No. Or rather, the Patrol officers haven't. They went downtime of the event, planted instruments of every kind that could be concealed, but—Everything happens too fast."

Everard rubbed his chin. The stubble felt almost silky; a bronze razor and a lack of soap didn't make for a close shave. He thought vaguely that he would have welcomed some scratchiness, or anything else familiar.

What had happened was plain enough. The vehicle had been unmanned, autopiloted, sent from some unknown point of space-time. Startoff had activated the detonator, so that the bomb arrived exploding. Though Patrol agents could pinpoint the instant, they could do nothing to head off the occurrence.

Could a technology advanced beyond theirs do so—Danellian, even? Everard imagined a device planted in advance of the moment,generating a forcefield which contained the violence when it smote. Well, this had not happened, therefore it might be a physical impossibility. Likelier, though, the Danellians stayed their hand because the harm *had* been done—the saboteurs could try again— all by itself, such a cat-and-mouse game might warp the continuum beyond healing—He shivered and asked roughly: "What explanation will the Tyrians themselves come up with?"

"Nothing dogmatic," Yael Zorach replied. "They don't have our kind of *Weltanschauung*, remember. To them, the world isn't entirely governed by laws of nature, it's capricious, changeable, magical."

And they're fundamentally right, aren't they?
The chill struck deeper into Everard.

"When nothing else of the kind occurs, excitement will die down," she went on. "The chronicles that record the incident will be lost; besides, Phoenicians aren't especially given to writing chronicles. They'll think that somebody did something wrong that provoked a thunderbolt from heaven. Not necessarily any human; it could have been a quarrel among the gods. Therefore nobody will become a scapegoat. After a generation or two, the incident will be forgotten, except perhaps as a bit of folklore."

Chaim Zorach fairly snarled: "That's if the extortionists don't do more and worse."

"Yeah, let's see their ransom note," Everard requested.

"I have a copy only. The original went uptime for study."

"Oh, sure, I know. I've read the lab report. Sepia ink on a papyrus scroll, no clue there. Found at your door, probably dropped from another unmanned hopper that just flitted through."

"Certainly dropped in that way," Zorach reminded him. "The agents who came in set up instruments for that night, and detected the machine. It was present for about a millisecond. They might have tried to capture it, but what would have been the use? It was bound to be devoid of clues. And in any case, the effort would have entailed making a racket that could have brought the neighbors out to see what was going on."

He fetched the document for Everard to examine. The Patrolman had pored over a transcript as part of his briefing, but hoped that sight of the actual hand would suggest something, anything to him.

The words had been formed with a contemporary reed pen, rather skillfully used. (This implied that the writer was well versed in the milieu, but that was obvious already.) They were printed, not cursive, though certain flamboyant flourishes appeared. The language was Temporal.

"To the Time Patrol from the Committee for Aggrandizement, greeting." At least there was none of the cant about being a people's army of national liberation, such as nauseated Everard in the later part of his home century. These fellows were frank bandits. Unless, of course, they pretended to be, in order to cover their tracks the more thoroughly. . . .

"Having witnessed the consequences when one small bomb was delivered to a carefully chosen location in Tyre, you are invited to contemplate the results of a barrage throughout the city."

Once more, heavily, Everard nodded. His opponents were shrewd. A threat to kill or kidnap individuals—say, King Hiram himself—would have been nugatory, if not empty. The Patrol would mount guard on any such person. If somehow an attack succeeded, the Patrol would go back in time and arrange for the victim to be elsewhere at the moment of the assault; it would make the event "unhappen." Granted, that involved risks which the outfit hated to take, and at best would require a lot of work to make sure that the future did not get altered by the rescue operation itself. Nevertheless, the Patrol could and would act.

But how did you move a whole islandful of

buildings to safety? You could, perhaps, evacuate
the population. The town would remain. It wasn't
physically large, after all, no matter how large it
loomed in history—about 25,000 people crowded
into about 140 acres. A few tons of high explosive
would leave it in ruins. The devastation needn't
even be total. After such a terrifying manifesta-
tion of supernatural fury, no one would come
back here. Tyre would crumble away, a ghost
town, while all the centuries and millennia, all
the human beings and their lives and civilizations,
which it had helped bring into existence . . . those
would be less than ghosts.

Everard shivered anew. *Don't tell me there is
no such thing as absolute evil*, he thought. *These
creatures*—He forced himself to read on:

"—The price of our forbearance is quite reasonable, merely a little information. We desire the
data necessary for the construction of a Trazon
matter transmuter—"

When that device was being developed, during
the Third Technological Renaissance, the Patrol
had covertly manifested itself to the creators,
though they lived downtime of its own founding.
Forever afterward, its use—the very knowledge of
its existence, let alone the manner of its making—
had been severely restricted. True, the ability to
convert any material object, be it just a heap of
dirt, into any other, be it a jewel or a machine or a
living body, could have spelled unlimited wealth
for the entire species. The trouble was, you could
as easily produce unlimited amounts of weapons,
or poisons, or radioactive atoms. . . .

"—You will broadcast the data in digital form
from Palo Alto, California, United States of

America, throughout the 24 hours of Friday 13 June 1980. The waveband to employ . . . the digital code. . . . Your receipt will be the continued reality of your time line. — "

That was smart, too. The message wasn't one that would be picked up accidentally by some native, yet electronic activity in the Silicon Valley area was so great as to rule out any possibility of tracking down a receiver.

" — We will not use the device upon the planet Earth. Therefore the Time Patrol need not fear that it is compromising its Prime Directive by this helpfulness to us. On the contrary, you have no other way to preserve yourselves, do you?

"Our compliments, and our expectations."

No signature.

"The broadcast won't be made, will it?" Yael asked low. In the shadows of the room, her eyes glimmered enormous. *She has children uptime,* Everard remembered. *They would vanish with their world.*

"No," he said.

"And yet our reality remains!" burst from Chaim. "You came here, out of it, starting uptime of 1980. So we must have caught the criminals."

Everard's sigh seemed to leave a track of pain through his breast. "You know better than that," he said tonelessly. "The quantum nature of the continuum — If Tyre explodes, why, here we'll be, but our ancestors, your kids, everything we knew, they won't. It'll be a whole different history. Whether whatever is left of the Patrol can restore it — somehow head off the disaster — that's problematical. I'd call it unlikely."

"But what would the criminals have gained,

then?" The question was raw, almost a screech.

Everard shrugged. "A certain wild satisfaction, I guess. The temptation to play God slinks around in the best of us, doesn't it? And the temptation to play Satan isn't unrelated. Besides, they'd be careful to lurk downtime of the destruction; they'd stay existent. They'd have a good chance of making themselves overlords of a future where nothing but bits and pieces of the Patrol were left to oppose them. Or at a minimum, they'd have a lot of fun trying."

Sometimes I myself have chafed at the restrictions on me. "Ah, Love! could thou and I with Fate conspire To grasp this sorry Scheme of Things entire —"

"Besides," he added, "conceivably the Danellians will countermand the decision and order us to release the secret. I could return home to find that feature of my world wasn't the same any longer. A trivial variation as far as the twentieth century is concerned, affecting nothing noticeable."

"But later centuries?" the woman gasped.

"Yeah. We've only the gang's word that it'll confine its attentions to planets in the far future and beyond the Solar System. I'll bet whatever you like that that word is worthless. Given the capabilities of the transmuter, why shouldn't they play fast and loose with Earth? It'll always be *the* human globe, and I don't see how the Patrol can stop them."

"Who are they?" Chaim whispered. "Have you any idea?"

Everard drank whisky and smoke, as if warmth could seep through his tongue into his spirit. "Too early to say, on my personal world line . . . or yours, hm? Plain to see, they're from far uptime, though short of the Era of Oneness that precedes the Danellians. In the course of many millennia, information about the transmuter was bound to leak out—enough to give somebody a clear notion of the thing and of what he might do with it. Certainly he and his buddies are rootless desperados; they don't give a damn that their action threatens to eliminate the society that begot them, and everybody living in it whom they ever knew. But I don't think they are, say, Neldorians. This operation is too sophisticated. The enemy's got to have spent a lot of lifespan, a lot of effort, getting to know the Phoenician milieu well and establishing that it is in fact a nexus.

"The organizing brain must be of genius level. But with a touch of childishness—did you notice that Friday the thirteenth date? Likewise, performing the sabotage practically next door to you. The M.O.—and my being recognized as a Patrolman—those do suggest—Merau Varagan?"

"Who?"

Everard didn't reply. He went on mumbling, mostly to himself: "Could be, could be. Not that that's much help. The gang did its homework, downtime of today, surely—yes, they'd want an informational baseline covering quite a few years. And this post is undermanned. The whole goddamn Patrol is." *Regardless of agents' longevity. Sooner or later, something or other will get each and every one of us. And we don't go back to cancel the deaths of our comrades, nor to see them again while they lived, because that could start an eddy in time, which might grow into a maelstrom; or if not, it would at least rack us too cruelly.* "We can detect time vehicles arriving and departing, if we know where and when to aim our instruments. That may be how the gang discovered this is Patrol HQ, if they didn't learn it routinely in the guise of honest visitors. Or they could have entered this era elsewhere and come by ordinary transportation, looking like any of countless legitimate contemporary people, the same way I tried to.

"We can't ransack every bit of local space-time. We haven't the manpower, nor dare we risk the disruption that so much activity of ours could cause. No, Chaim, Yael, we've got to find ourselves some clues, to narrow down our search. But how? Where do I start?"

His disguise being penetrated, Everard accepted the Zorachs' offer of a guestroom. He'd be more comfortable here than in an inn, and handier to whatever gadgets he might need. However, he'd also be cut off from the real life of the city.

"I'll arrange an interview with the king for you," his host promised. "No difficulty; he's a brilliant man, bound to be interested in an exotic like you." He chuckled. "Therefore it will be very natural for Zakarbaal the Sidonian, who needs to cultivate the friendship of the Tyrians, to inform him of a chance meeting with you."

"That's fine," Everard replied, "and I'll enjoy paying the call. Maybe he can even be some help to us. Meanwhile, uh, we've got several hours of daylight left. I think I'll stroll around town, start getting the feel of it, pick up a scent if I'm lucky."

Zorach scowled. "You might be what's picked up. The killer is skulking yet, I'm sure."

Everard shrugged. "A chance I take; and could be him that comes to grief. Lend me a gun, please. Sonic."

He set the weapon to stun, not slay. A live prisoner was at the top of his birthday list. Since the enemy would be aware of that, he didn't really expect another attempt on him — today, at any rate.

"Take a blaster, too," Zorach urged. "I wouldn't put it past them to come after you from the air. Bring a hopper to an instant where you are, hover on antigravity, and potshoot, hm? They don't have our motivation to stay inconspicuous."

Everard holstered the energy gun opposite the other. Any Phoenician who noticed would take them for charms or something of the kind, and besides, he'd let a cloak fall over them. "I scarcely think I'd be worth that much effort and risk," he said.

"You were worth trying for earlier, weren't you? How did that guy know you for an agent, anyway?"

"He may have had a description. Merau Varagan would realize that just a few Unattached operatives, me among them, were likely choices for this assignment. Which inclines me more and more to think he is behind the plot. If I'm right, we've got a mean and slippery opponent."

"Stay in public view," Yael Zorach pleaded. "Be sure to get back before dark. Violent crime is rare here, but there are no lights, the streets grow nearly deserted, you'd become easy prey."

Everard imagined himself hunting his hunter through the night, but decided not to attempt provoking such a situation unless he became desperate. "Okay, I'll return for dinner. I'm interested in what Tyrian food is like—ashore, not ship rations."

She mustered a smile. "Not awfully good, I'm afraid. The natives aren't sensualists. However, I've taught our cook several uptime recipes. Do you like gefilte fish for an appetizer?"

Shadows had lengthened and air cooled somewhat when Everard stepped forth. Traffic bustled along the street crossing Chandlers, though no more than earlier. Situated on the water, Tyre and Usu were generally free of the extreme midday heat that dictated a siesta in many countries, and no true Phoenician would waste hours asleep in which he might turn a profit.

"Master!" warbled a joyful voice.

Why, it's my little wharf rat. "Hail, uh, Pummairam," Everard said. The boy bounced up from his squat. "What are you waiting for?"

The slight brown form bowed low, albeit eyes and lips held as much merriment as reverence. "What but the fervently prayed-for hope that I might again be of service to his luminosity?"

Everard stopped and scratched his head. The kid had been almighty quick, had possibly saved his bacon, but—"Well, I'm sorry, but I've no further need of help."

"Oh, sir, you jest. See how I laugh, delighted by your wit! A guide, an introducer, a warder off of rogues and . . . certain worse persons—surely a lord of your magnanimity will not deny a poor sprig the glory of his presence, the benefit of his wisdom, the never-to-be-forgotten memory in after years of having trotted at his august heels."

While the words were sycophantic, that was conventional in this society, and the tone was anything but. Pummairam was having fun, Everard saw. Doubtless he was curious, too, as well as eager to earn more. He fairly quivered where he stood looking straight up at the huge man.

Everard made his decision. "You win, you rogue," he said, and grinned when Pummairam whooped and danced. It wasn't a bad idea to have such an attendant, anyway. Wasn't his purpose to get to know the city, rather than merely its sights? "Now tell me what it is you are thinking you can do for me."

The boy poised, cocked his head, laid finger to chin. "That depends upon what my master's desire may be. If business, what kind and with whom? If pleasure, likewise. My lord has but to speak."

"Hm-m. . . ." *Well, why not level with him, to the extent that is allowable? If he proves unsatisfactory, I can always fire him, though I expect he'd cling like a tick.* "Then hear me, Pum. I do have weighty matters to handle in Tyre. Yes, they may well concern the suffetes and the king's self. You saw how a magician tried to stop me. Aye, you aided me against him. That may happen anew, and I not so lucky next time. It's barred I am from saying more about that. Yet I think you'll understand my need to learn a great deal, to meet people of many kinds. What would you suggest? A tavern, maybe, and I buying drinks for the house?"

Pum's quicksilver mood froze to seriousness. He frowned and stared into space for a few heartbeats, before he snapped his fingers and cackled. "Ah, indeed! Well, excellent master, I can recommend no better beginning than a visit to the High Temple of Asherat."

"Hey?" Startled, Everard flipped through the information planted in his brain. Asherat, whom the Bible would call Astarte, was the consort of Melqart, the patron god of Tyre—Baal-Melek-Qart-Sor. . . . She was a mighty figure in her own right, goddess of fruitfulness in man, beast, and land, a female warrior who had once dared hell itself to recall her lover from the dead, a sea queen of whom Tanith might be simply an avatar . . . yes, she was Ishtar in Babylon, and she would enter the Grecian world as Aphrodite. . . .

"Why, the vast learning of my lord surely includes the fact that it would be foolish for a visitor, most especially a visitor as important as he, *not* to pay homage to her, that she may smile upon his enterprise. Truly, if the priests heard of such an omission, they would set themselves against you. That has, indeed, caused difficulties with some of the emissaries from Jerusalem. Also, is it not a good deed to release a lady from bondage and yearning?" Pum leered, winked, and nudged Everard. "Besides being a pleasurable romp."

The Patrolman remembered. For a moment, he was taken aback. Like most other Semites of this era, the Phoenicians required that every freeborn woman sacrifice her virginity in the fane of the goddess, as a sacred prostitute. Not until a man had paid for her favor might she marry. The custom was not lewd in origin, it traced back to Stone Age fertility rites and fears. To be sure, it also attracted profitable pilgrims and foreign visitors.

"I trust my lord's folk do not forbid such an act?" the boy inquired anxiously.

"Well. . . . They do not."

"Good!" Pum took Everard by the elbow and steered him off. "If my lord will allow his servant to accompany him, quite likely I shall recognize someone whom he would find it useful thus to get acquainted with. In all abasement, let me say that I do get around and I do keep eyes and ears open. They are utterly at the service of my master."

Everard grinned, on one side of his mouth, and strode along. Why shouldn't he? To be honest with himself, after his sea voyage he felt damnably horny; and it was true, patronizing the holy whorehouse was, in this milieu, not an exploitation but a kindness; and he might even get some lead in his mission. . . .

First I'd better try to find out how reliable my guide is. "Tell me something about yourself, Pum. We may be together for, well, several days if not more."

They came out on the avenue and threaded their way through jostling, shouting, odorous throngs. "There is little to tell, great lord. The annals of the poor are short and simple." That coincidence startled Everard too. Then, as Pum talked, he realized that the phrase was false in this case.

Father unknown, presumably one of the sailors and laborers who frequented a certain low-life hostel while Tyre was under construction and had the wherewithal to enjoy its serving wench, Pum was a pup in a litter, raised catch-as-catch-

can, a scavenger from the time he could walk
and, Everard suspected, a thief, and whatever
else might get him the local equivalent of a buck.
Nonetheless, early on he had become an acolyte
at a dockside temple of the comparatively un-
important god Baal Hammon. (Everard harked
back to tumbledown churches in the slums of
twentieth-century America.) Its priest had been a
learned man once, now gentle and drunken; Pum
had garnered considerable vocabulary and other
knowledge from him, like a squirrel garnering
acorns in a wood, until he died. His more respectable successor kicked the raffish postulant out.
Despite that, Pum went on to make a wide circle
of acquaintances, which reached into the palace
itself. Royal servants came down to the waterfront in search of cheap fun. . . . Still too young to
assume any kind of leadership, he was wangling
a living however he could. His survival to date
was no mean accomplishment.

Yes, Everard thought, *I may have lucked out,
just a little.*

The temples of Melqart and Asherat confronted
each other across a busy square near the middle
of town. The former was the larger, but the latter
was amply impressive. A porch of many columns,
with elaborate capitals and gaudy paint, gave on
a flagged courtyard wherein stood a great brass
basin of water for ritual cleansing. The house
rose along the farther side of the enclosure,
its squareness relieved by stone facing, marble,
granite, jasper. Two pillars flanked the doorway,

overtopping the roof and shining. (In Solomon's Temple, which copied Tyrian design, these would be named Jachin and Boaz.) Within, Everard knew, was a main chamber for worshippers, and beyond it the sanctuary.

Some of the forum crowd had spilled into the court and stood about in little groups. The men among them, he guessed, simply wanted a quiet place to discuss business or whatever. Women outnumbered them—housewives for the most part, often balancing loads on their scarved heads, taking a break from marketing to make a brief devotion and indulge in a bit of gossip. While the attendants of the goddess were male, here females were always welcome.

Stares followed Everard as Pum urged him toward the temple. He began to feel self-conscious, even abashed. A priest sat at a table, in the shade behind the open door. Except for a rainbow-colored robe and a phallic silver pendant, he looked no different from a layman, his hair and beard well-trimmed, his features aquiline and lively.

Pum halted before him and said importantly, "Greeting, holy one. My master and I wish to honor Our Lady of Nuptials."

The priest signed a blessing. "Praises be. A foreigner confers double fortune." Interest gleamed in his eyes. "Whence come you, worthy stranger?"

"From north across the waters," Everard replied.

"Yes, yes, that's clear, but it's a vast and unknown territory. Might you be from a land of the Sea Peoples themselves?" The priest waved at a stool like that which he occupied. "Pray be seated, noble sir, take your ease for a while, let me pour you a cup of wine."

Pum jittered about for several minutes in an agony of frustration, before he hunkered down under a column and sulked. Everard and the priest conversed for almost an hour. Others drifted up to listen and join in.

It could easily have lasted all day. Everard was finding out a lot. Probably none of it was germane to his mission, but you never knew, and anyway, he enjoyed the gab session. What brought him back to earth was mention of the sun. It had dropped below the porch roof. He remembered Yael Zorach's warning, and cleared his throat.

"Och, how I regret it, my friends, but time passes and I must soon begone. If we are first to pay our respects—"

Pum brightened. The priest laughed. "Aye," he said, "after so long a faring, the fire of Asherat must burn hotly. Well, now, the free-will donation is half a shekel of silver or its value in goods. Of course, men of wealth and rank are wont to give more."

Everard paid over a generous chunk of metal. The priest repeated his blessing and gave him and Pum each a small ivory disc, rather explicitly engraved. "Go in, my sons, seek whom you will do good, cast these in their laps. Ah . . . you understand, do you not, great Eborix, that you are to take your chosen one off the sacred premises? Tomorrow she will return the token and receive the benison. If you have no place of your own nigh to here, then my kinsman Hanno rents clean rooms at a modest rate, in his inn just down the Street of the Date Sellers. . . . "

Pum fairly zoomed inside. Everard followed with what he hoped was more dignity. His talk-

mates called raunchy good wishes. That was part of the ceremony, the magic.

The chamber was large, its gloom not much relieved by oil lamps. They picked out intricate murals, gold leaf, inset semiprecious stones. At the far end shimmered a gilt image of the goddess, arms held out in a compassion which somehow came through the rather primitive sculpturing. Everard sensed fragrances, myrrh and sandalwood, and an irregular undertone of rustles and whispers.

As his pupils widened, he discerned the women. Perhaps a hundred altogether, they sat on stools, crowded along the walls to right and left. Their garb ranged from fine linen to ragged wool. Some slumped, some stared blankly, some made gestures of invitation as bold as the rules permitted, most looked timidly and wistfully at the men who strolled by them. Those visitors were few, at this hour of an ordinary day. Everard thought he identified three or four mariners on shore leave, a fat merchant, a couple of young bucks. Their deportment was reasonably polite; it *was* a church here.

His pulses pounded. *Damnation*, he thought, irritated, *why am I making such a production in my head? I've been with enough women before.*

Sadness touched him. *Only two virgins, though.*

He walked along, watching, wondering, avoiding glances. Pum sought him and tugged his sleeve. "Radiant master," the youth hissed, "your servant may have found that which you require."

"Huh?" Everard let his attendant drag him out to the center of the room, where they could murmur unheard.

"My lord understands that this child of poverty could never hitherto enter these precincts," spilled from Pum. "Yet, as I said earlier, I do have acquaintanceship reaching into the royal palace itself. I know of a lady who has come each time her duties and the moon allow, to wait and wait, these past three years. She is Sarai, daughter of shepherd folk in the hills. Through an uncle in the guard, she got a post in the king's household, at first only as a scullery maid, but now working closely with the chief steward. And she is here today. Since my master wishes to make contacts of that sort—"

Bemused, Everard followed his guide. When they halted, he gulped. The woman who, low-voiced, responded to Pum's greeting, was squat, big-nosed—he decided to think of her as homely—and verging on spinsterhood. But the gaze she lifted to the Patrolman was bright and unafraid. "Would you like to release me?" she asked quietly. "I would pray for you for the rest of my life."

Before he could change his mind, he pitched his token onto her skirt.

Pum had found himself a beauty, arrived this same day and engaged to the scion of a prominent family. She was dismayed when such a raga-muffin picked her. Well, that was her problem. And perhaps his too, though Everard doubted it.

The rooms in Hanno's inn were tiny, equipped with straw mattresses and little else. Slit windows, giving on the inner court, admitted a trickle of evening light, also smoke, street and kitchen smells, chatter, plaintiveness of a bone flute. Everard drew the reed curtain that served as a door and turned to his companion.

She knelt before him as if huddling into her garments. "I do not know your name or your country, sir," she said, low and not quite steadily. "Do you care to tell your handmaiden?"

"Why, sure." He gave her his alias. "And you are Sarai from Rasil Ayin?"

"Did the beggar boy send my lord to me?" She bowed her head. "No, forgive me, I meant no insolence, I was thoughtless."

He ventured to push back her scarf and stroke her hair. Though coarse, it was abundant, her best physical feature. "No offense taken. See here, shall we get to know each other a bit? What would you say to a cup or two of wine before— Well, what would you say?"

She gasped, astounded. He went out, found the landlord, made the provision.

Presently, as they sat side by side on the floor with his arm around her shoulders, she was talking freely. Phoenicians had scant concept of personal privacy. Also, while their women got more respect and independence than those of most societies, still, a little consideration on a man's part went a long ways.

"—no, no betrothal yet for me, Eborix. I came to the city because my father is poor, with many other children to provide for, and it did not seem anybody in our tribe would ever ask my hand for his son. You wouldn't possibly know of someone?" He himself, who would take her maidenhead, was debarred. In fact, her question bent the law that forbade prearrangement, as for example with a friend. "I have won standing in the palace, in truth if not in name. I wield some small power among servants, purveyors, entertainers. I have scraped together a dowry for myself, not large, but . . . but it may be the goddess will smile on me at last, after I have made this oblation—"

"I'm sorry," he answered in compassion. "I'm a stranger here."

He understood, or supposed he did. She wanted desperately to get married: less to have a husband and put an end to the barely veiled scorn and suspicion in which the unwedded were held, than to have children. Among these people, few fates were more terrible than to die childless, to go doubly into the grave. . . . Her defenses broke apart and she wept against his breast.

The light was failing. Everard decided to forget Yael's fears (and—a chuckle—Pum's exasperation) and take his time, treat Sarai like a human being simply because that was what she in fact was, wait for darkness and then use his imagination. Afterward he'd see her back to her quarters.

The Zorachs were mainly upset because of the anxiety their guest caused them, not returning until well past sunset. He didn't tell them what he had been doing, nor did they press him about it. After all, they were agents in place, able persons who coped with a difficult job often full of surprises, but they were not detectives.

Everard did feel obliged to apologize for spoiling their supper. That was to have been an unusual treat. Normally the main meal of the day occurred about midafternoon, and folk had little more than a snack in the evening. A reason for this was the dimness of lamplight, which made it troublesome to prepare anything elaborate.

Nonetheless, the technical accomplishments of the Phoenicians deserved admiration. Over breakfast, which was also a sparse meal, lentils cooked with leeks and accompanied by hardtack, Chaim mentioned the waterworks. Rain-catching cisterns were helpful but insufficient. Hiram didn't want Tyre dependent on boats from Usu, nor linked to the mainland by an extended aqueduct that could serve an enemy as a bridge. Like the Sidonians before him, he had a project in train that would draw fresh water from springs beneath the sea.

And then, of course, there was the skill, the accumulated knowledge and ingenuity, behind dyeworks and glassworks, not to mention ships less frail than they looked, since in the future they would ply as far as Britain. . . .

"The Purple Empire, somebody in our century called Phoenicia," Everard mused. "Almost makes me wonder if Merau Varagan has a thing for that color. Didn't W. H. Hudson call Uruguay the Purple Land?" His laugh clanked. "No, I'm being foolish. The murex dyes generally have more red than blue in them. Besides, Varagan was doing his dirty work a lot farther north than Uruguay when we collided 'earlier.' And so far I've no proof he's involved in this case; only a hunch."

"What happened?" asked Yael. Her glance sought him across the table, through sunlight that slanted in a doorway open to the garden court.

"No matter now."

"Are you certain?" Chaim persisted. "Conceivably your experience will call something to our minds that will be a clue. Anyhow, we do get starved for outside news in a post like this."

"Especially adventures as wonderful as yours," Yael added.

Everard smiled wryly. "To quote still another writer, adventure is somebody else having a hell of a tough time a thousand miles away," he said. "And when the stakes are high, like here, that really makes a situation feel bad." He paused. "Well, no reason not to spin you the yarn, though in very sketchy form, because the background's complicated. Uh, if a servant isn't going to come in soon, I'd like to light my pipe. And is any of that lovely clandestine coffee left in the pot?"

— He settled himself, rolled smoke across his tongue, let the rising warmth of the day bake his bones after the night's nippiness. "My mission was to South America, the Colombia region, late in the year 1826. Under Simón Bolívar's leadership, the patriots had cast off Spanish rule, but they still had plenty troubles of their own. That included worries about the Liberator himself. He'd put through a constitution for Bolivia that gave him extraordinary powers as lifetime president; was he going to turn into a Napoleon and bring all the new republics under his heel? The military commander in Venezuela, which was then a part of Colombia, or New Granada as it called itself — he revolted. Not that this José Páez was such an altruist; a harsh bastard, in fact.

"Oh, never mind details. I don't remember them well myself any more. Essentially, Bolívar, who was a Venezuelan by birth, made a march from

Lima to Bogotá. Only took him a couple of months, which was *fast* in those days over that terrain. Arriving, he assumed martial-law presidential powers, and moved on into Venezuela against Páez. Bloodshed was becoming heavy there.

"Meanwhile Patrol agents, monitoring the history, turned up indications that all was not kosher. (Um-m, pardon me.) Bolívar wasn't behaving quite like the selfless humanitarian that his biographers, by and large, described. He'd acquired a friend from . . . somewhere . . . whom he trusted. This man's advice had, on occasion, been brilliant. Yet it seemed as if he might be turning into Bolívar's evil genius. And the biographies never mentioned him. . . .

"I was among the Unattached operatives dispatched to investigate. This was because I, before ever hearing of the Patrol, had kicked around some in those boonies. That gave me a slight special sense for what to do. I could never pass myself off as a Latin American, but I could be a Yankee soldier of fortune, in part starry-eyed over the liberation, in part hoping somehow to cash in on it—and, mainly, though *macho* enough, free of the kind of arrogance that would have put those proud people off.

"It's a long and generally tedious story. Believe me, my friends, 99 percent of an operation in the field amounts to patient collection of dull and usually irrelevant facts, in between interminable periods of hurry-up-and-wait. Let's say that, aided by a good deal of luck, I managed to infiltrate, make my connections, pass out my bribes, gather my informers and my evidence. At last there was no reasonable doubt. This obscurely originating

Blasco López had to be from the future.

"I called in our troops and we raided the house where he was staying in Bogotá. Most of those we collared were harmless local people, hired as servants, though what they had to tell proved useful. López's mistress, accompanying him, turned out to be his associate. She told us a lot more, in exchange for comfortable accommodations when she'd go to the exile planet. But the ringleader himself had broken free and escaped.

"One man on horseback, headed for the Cordillera Oriental that rises beyond the town — one man like ten thousand genuine Creoles — we couldn't go after him on time hoppers. The search could too damn easily get too damn noticeable. Who knew what effect that might have? The conspirators had already made the timestream unstable. . . .

"I grabbed a horse, a couple of remounts, some jerky and vitamin pills for myself, and set off in pursuit."

Wind boomed hollowly down the mountainside. Grass and low, scattered shrubs trembled beneath its chill. Up ahead, they gave way to naked rock. Right, left, behind, peaks reared into a blue bleakness. A condor wheeled huge, on watch for any death. Snowfields on the heights above glowed beneath a declining sun.

A musket cracked. At its distance, the noise it made was tiny, though echoes flew. Everard heard the bullet buzz. Close! He hunched down in the saddle and spurred his steed onward.

Varagan can't really expect to drop me at this range, passed through him. *What, then? Does he hope I'll slow down? If so, if he gains a little on me, what use is that to him? What goal has he got?*

His enemy still led him by half a mile, but Everard could see how yonder animal lurched along, exhausted. To get on Varagan's trail had taken some while, going from this peon to that sheepherder and asking if a man of the given description had ridden by. However, Varagan had only the single horse, which he must spare if it was not to collapse under him. After Everard found the traces, a wilderness-trained eye had readily been able to follow them, and the pace of the hunt picked up.

It was also known that Varagan had fled bearing no more than a muzzle-loader. He'd been spending powder and balls pretty freely ever since the Patrolman hove in view. Since he was a fast recharger and an excellent shot, it did have its delaying effect. But what refuge was in these wastes? Varagan appeared to be making for a particular crag. It was conspicuous, not only high but its shape suggestive of a castle tower. It was no fortress, though. If Varagan took shelter behind it, Everard could use the blaster he carried to bring the rock molten down upon his head.

Maybe Varagan wasn't aware the agent had such a weapon. Impossible. Varagan was a monster, yes, but not a fool.

Everard pulled down his hatbrim and drew his poncho tight against the wind. He didn't reach for the blaster, no point in that yet, but as if by instinct, his left hand dropped to the flintlock pistol and saber at his hip. They were mainly part of his costume, intended to make him an authority figure to the inhabitants, but there was an odd comfort in their massiveness.

Having reined in to shoot, Varagan continued straight on uphill, this time without lingering to reload. Everard brought his own horse from trot to canter and closed the gap further. He kept alert—not tensed, but alert against contingencies, ready to swing aside or even jump down behind the beast. Nothing happened, just that lonesome trek on through the cold. Could Varagan have fired his last ammunition? *Have a care, Manse, old son.* The sparse alpine grass ended, save for tufts between boulders, and rock rang beneath hoofs.

Varagan halted near the crag and sat waiting. The musket was sheathed and his hands rested empty on the saddlebow. His horse quivered and swayed, neck a-droop, utterly blown, lather swept freezingly off its hide and out of its mane.

Everard took forth his energy gun and clattered nigh. Behind him, a remount whickered. Still Varagan waited.

Everard stopped three yards off. "Merau Varagan, you are under arrest by the Time Patrol," he called in Temporal.

The other smiled. "You have the advantage of me," he replied in a soft tone that, somehow, carried. "May I request the honor of learning your name and provenance?"

"Uh . . . Manson Everard, Unattached, born in the United States of America about a hundred years uptime. No matter. You're coming back with me. Hold on while I call a hopper. I warn you, at the least suspicion you're about to try something, I'll shoot. You're too dangerous for me to be squeamish."

Varagan made a gentle gesture. "Really? How much do you know about me, Agent Everard, or think you know, to justify this violent an attitude?"

"Well, when a man takes potshots at me, I reckon he's not a very nice person."

"Might I perhaps have believed you were a bandit, of the sort who haunt these uplands? What crime am I alleged to have committed?"

Everard's free hand paused on its way to get out the little communicator in his pocket. For a moment, eerily fascinated, he stared through the wind at his prisoner.

Merau Varagan seemed taller than he actually was, as straight as he held his athletic frame. Black hair tossed around a skin whose whiteness the sun and the weather had not tinged at all. There was no sign of beard. The face might have been a young Caesar's, were it not too finely chiseled. The eyes were large and green, the smiling lips cherry-red. His clothes, down to the boots, were silver-trimmed black, like the cape that flapped about his shoulders. Seen against the turreted crag, he made Everard remember Dracula.

Yet his voice remained mild: "Evidently your colleagues have extracted information from mine. I daresay you have been in touch with them as you fared. Thus you know our names and somewhat of our origin—"

Thirty-first millennium. Outlaws after the failure of the Exaltationists to cast off the weight of a civilization grown older than the Old Stone Age was to me. During their moment of power, they possessed themselves of time machines. Their genetic heritage—

Nietzsche might have understood them. I never will.

"—But what do you truly know of our purpose here?"

"You were going to change events," Everard retorted. "We barely forestalled you. At that, our corps has a lot of tricky restoration work ahead. Why did you do it? How could you be so . . . so selfish?"

"I think 'egoistic' might be a better word," Varagan gibed. "The ascendancy of the ego, the unconfined will—But think. Would it have been altogether bad if Simón Bolívar had founded a true empire in Hispanic America, rather than a gaggle of quarrelsome successor states? It would have been enlightened, progressive. Imagine how much suffering and death would have been averted."

"Come off that!" Everard felt anger rise and rise within himself. "You must know better. It's impossible. Bolívar hasn't the cadre, the communications, the support. If he's a hero to many, he's at least got many others furious with him: like the Peruvians, after he detached Bolivia. He'll cry on his deathbed that he 'plowed the sea' in all his efforts to build a stable society.

"If you meant it about unifying even part of the continent, you'd have tried earlier and elsewhere."

"Indeed?"

"Yes. The only chance. I've studied the situation. In 1821 San Martín was negotiating with the Spanish in Perú, and playing with the idea of setting up a monarchy under somebody like Don

Carlos, King Ferdinand's brother. It could have included the territories of Bolivia and Ecuador, maybe later Chile and Argentina, because it would have had the advantages Bolívar's inner sphere lacks. But why am I telling you this, you bastard, except to prove I know you're lying? You must have done your own homework."

"What then do you suppose my real objective was?"

"Obvious. To make Bolívar overreach himself. He's an idealist, a dreamer, as well as a warrior. If he pushes too hard, everything hereabouts will break up in a chaos that could well spread to the rest of South America. And there would be your chance for seizing power!"

Varagan shrugged, as a were-cat might have shrugged. "Concede me this much," he said, "that such an empire would have had a certain dark magnificence."

The hopper flashed into being and hovered twenty feet aloft. Its rider grinned and aimed the firearm he carried. From the saddle of his horse, Merau Varagan waved at his time-traveling self.

Everard never quite knew what happened next. Somehow he made it out of the stirrups and onto the ground. His horse screamed as an energy bolt struck. Smoke and a stench of seared flesh spurted forth. Even while the slain animal crumpled, Everard shot back from behind it.

The enemy hopper must veer. Everard skipped clear of the falling mass and maintained fire, upward and sideways. Varagan leaped from his own horse, behind the rock. Lightnings blazed and crackled. Everard's free hand yanked forth his communicator and thumbed the Mayday spot.

The vehicle dropped, rearward of the crag. Displaced air made a popping noise. Wind blew away the stinging ozone.

A Patrol machine appeared. It was too late. Merau Varagan had already borne his earlier self away to an unknowable point of space-time.

Everard nodded heavily. "Yeah," he finished, "that was his scheme, and it worked, God damn it. Reach an obvious landmark and note the time on his watch. That meant he'd know, later along his world line, where-when to go, in mounting his rescue operation."

The Zorachs were appalled. "But, but a casual loop of that sort," Chaim stammered, "didn't he have any idea of the dangers?"

"Doubtless he did, including the possibility that he would make himself never have existed," Everard replied. "But then, he'd been quite prepared to wipe out an entire future, in favor of a history where he could have ridden high. He's totally fearless, the ultimate desperado. That was built into the genes of the Exaltationist princes."

He sighed. "They lack loyalty, also. Varagan, and whatever associates he had left, made no attempt to save those we'd captured. They just vanished. We've been wary of their reappearance ever 'since then,' and this new caper does bear similarities to that one. But of course—time loop hazard again—I can't go read whatever report I'll have filed at the conclusion of the present affair. If it has a conclusion, and if I don't."

Yael patted his hand. "I'm sure you'll prevail,

Manse," she said. "What happened next in South America?"

"Oh, once the bad counsel, which he hadn't recognized was bad—once that stopped, Bolívar went back to his natural ways," Everard told them. "He made a peaceful settlement with Páez and issued a general amnesty. More troubles broke out later, but he handled them capably and humanely, too, while fostering both the interests and the culture of his people. When he died, most of the great wealth he'd inherited was gone, because he'd never taken a centavo of public money for himself. A good ruler, one of the few that humankind will ever know.

"So's Hiram, I gather—and now his rule is threatened likewise, by whatever devil is loose in the world."

When Everard emerged, sure enough, there was Pum waiting. The boy skipped to meet him.

"Where would my glorious master go today?" he caroled. "Let his servant conduct him whithersoever he wills. Perhaps to visit Conor the amber factor?"

"Huh?" In slight shock, the Patrolman goggled at the native. "What makes you think I've aught to do with . . . any such person?"

Pum returned a look whose deference failed to mask its shrewdness. "Did not my lord declare this was his intention, while aboard Mago's ship?"

"How do you know that?" Everard barked.

"Why, I sought out men of the crew, engaged them in talk, lured forth their memories. Not that your humble servant would pry into that which he should not hear. If I have transgressed, I abase myself and beg forgiveness. My aim was merely to learn more of my master's plans in order that I might think how best to assist them." Pum beamed in undiminished cockiness.

"Oh. I see." Everard tugged his mustache and peered around. Nobody else was in earshot. "Well, then, know that that was a pretense. My true business is different." *As you must have guessed already, from the fact of my going straight to Zakarbaal and lodging with him,* he added silently. This was far from the first time that experience reminded him that people in any given era could be intrinsically as sharp as anybody futureward of them.

"Ah, indeed! Business of the greatest moment, assuredly. The lips of my master's servant are sealed."

"Understand that my aims are in no way hostile. Sidon is friendly to Tyre. Let's say I'm involved in an effort to organize a large joint venture."

"To increase trade with my master's people? Ah, but then you do want to visit your country-man Conor, no?"

"I do not!" Everard realized he had shouted. He curbed his temper. "Conor is not my country-man, not in the way that Mago is yours. My folk have no single country. Aye, most likely Conor and I would not be understanding each other's languages."

That was more than likely. Everard had too much intellectual baggage to carry as was, infor-mation about Phoenicia, to pile on a heap about the Celts. The electronic educator had simply taught him enough to pass for one among out-siders who didn't know them intimately—he hoped.

"What I've in mind," he said, "is just to stroll about the city today, whilst Zakarbaal seeks to get me an audience with the king." He smiled. "Sure, and for this I could well put myself in your hands, lad."

Pum's laughter pealed. He clapped his palms together. "Ah, my lord is wise! Come evening, let him deem whether or not he was led to pleasure and, yes, knowledge such as he seeks, and per-haps he . . . will in his magnanimity see fit to bestow largesse on his guide."

Everard grinned. "Give me the grand tour, then."

Pum assumed shyness. "May we first seek the Street of the Tailors? Yesterday I took it upon myself to order new garb that should be ready now. The cost will bear hard on a poor youth, despite the munificence his master has already shown, for I must pay for speed as well as fine material. Yet it is not fitting that a great lord's attendant should go in rags like these."

Everard groaned, though he didn't really mind. "I catch your drift. Och, how I do! 'Tis unsuited to my dignity that you buy your own garments. Well, let's go, and 'tis I will be standing you your coat of many colors."

Hiram did not quite resemble his average sub-ject. He was taller, lighter-complexioned, hair and beard reddish, eyes gray, nose straight. His ap-pearance recalled the Sea Peoples—that bucca-

neer horde of displaced Cretans and European
barbarians, some of them from the far North,
who raided Egypt a couple of centuries before,
and eventually became the principal ancestors of
the Philistines. A lesser number, ending up in
Lebanon and Syria, interbred with certain Bed-
ouin types who were themselves getting interested in nautical things. From that cross arose
the Phoenicians. The invader blood still showed
in their aristocrats.

Solomon's palace, of which the Bible was to
boast, would when finished be a cut-rate imita-
tion of the house in which Hiram already dwelt.
The king himself, though, usually went simply
clad, in a white linen kaftan with purple trim,
slippers of fine leather, a gold headband and a
massive ruby ring to signify royalty. His manner,
likewise, was direct and unaffected. Middle-aged,
he looked younger, and his vigor remained un-
abated.

He and Everard sat in a room broad, gracious,
and airy, that opened on a cloister garden and
fish pond. The carpet was of straw, but dyed in
fine patterns. Frescos on the plaster walls had
been done by an artist imported from Babylonia,
depicting arbors, flowers, and winged chimeras.
A low table between the men was of ebony inlaid
with mother-of-pearl. It held unwatered wine in
glass cups, and dishes of fruit, bread, cheese,
sweets. A pretty girl in a diaphanous gown knelt
nearby and strummed a lyre. Two manservants
awaited orders in the background.

"You are being right mysterious, Eborix," murmured Hiram.

"Sure, and 'tis not my wish to withhold aught

from your highness," Everard replied carefully. A
word of command could bring in guardsmen to
kill him. No, that was unlikely; a guest was sacred.
But if he offended the king, his whole mission
was compromised. "Aye, vague I am about certain things, but only because my knowledge of
them is slight. Nor would I risk laying baseless
charges against anyone, should my information
prove in error."

Hiram bridged his fingers and frowned. "Still,
you claim to bear word of danger—word which
contradicts what you have said elsewhere. You
are scarcely the bluff warrior you pass yourself
off as."

Everard constructed a smile. "My lord in his
wisdom knows well that an unlettered tribesman
is not necessarily a fool. To him I admit having,
ah, earlier shaded the truth a wee bit. 'Twas
because I had to, even as any Tyrian tradesman
does in the normal course of business. Is that not
so?"

Hiram laughed and relaxed. "Say on. If you are
a rogue, you are at least an interesting one."

Patrol psychologists had invested considerable
thought in Everard's yarn. There was no way for
it to be immediately convincing, nor was that
desirable; the king should not be stampeded into
actions that might change known history. Yet the
tale must be sufficiently plausible that he would
cooperate in the investigation which was Everard's
real purpose.

"Know, then, O lord, that my father was a
chieftain in a mountain land far over the waves—"
the Hallstatt region of Austria.

Eborix went on to relate how various Celts who

had been among the Sea Peoples fled back there
after the shattering defeat which Rameses III
inflicted on those quasi-vikings in 1149 B.C. Their
descendants had maintained tenuous connection,
mostly along the amber route, with the descendants of kinsmen who settled in Canaan by leave
of victorious Pharaoh. Old ambitions were unfor-
gotten; Celts have always had a long racial memory.
Talk went on about reviving the great Mediterranean push. That dream strengthened as wave
after wave of barbarians came down into Greece,
over the wreckage of Mycenaean civilization, and
chaos spread through the Adriatic and far into
Anatolia.

Eborix knew of spies who had also served as
emissaries to the kings of the Philistine city-states.
Tyre's amicability toward the Jews did not exactly endear it to the Philistines; and of course
the riches of Phoenicia provided ever more temptation. Schemes developed fitfully, slowly, over a
period of generations. Eborix himself was not
sure how far along arrangements might be, to
bring south an army of Celtic adventurers.

To Hiram he admitted frankly that he would
have considered joining such a troop, his handfast men at his back. However, a feud between
clans had ended in the overthrow and slaying of
his father. Eborix had barely escaped alive. Wanting revenge as much as he wanted to mend his
fortunes, he made the trek hither. A Tyre grateful
for his warning might, if nothing else, give him
the means to hire soldiers of his own and bring
them home to reinstate him.

"You offer me no proof," said the king slowly,
"naught but your naked word."

Everard nodded. "My lord sees clearly as Ra, the Falcon of Egypt. Did I not agree beforehand that I could be mistaken, that there may in truth be no real menace, just the scutterings and chatterings of vainglorious apes? Nonetheless I do urge that my lord have the matter looked into as closely as may be, for safety's sake. In that effort, 'tis I his servant that could be of help. Not only do I know my folk and their ways, but in wandering across their continent I met many different tribes, aye, and civilized nations too. I might therefore be a better hound than most, upon this particular scent."

Hiram tugged his beard. "Perhaps. Such a conspiracy must needs involve more than a few wild mountaineers and Philistine magnates. Men of several origins — But foreigners come and go like vagrant breezes. Who shall track the wind?"

Everard's heart slugged. Here was the moment toward which he had striven. "Your highness, I've thought much upon this, and the gods have sent me some ideas. I'm thinking we should first search not for common merchants, skippers, and seamen, but for strangers from lands which Tyrians have seldom or never visited, strangers who ask questions that often do not pertain to trade, or even to ordinary inquisitiveness. They would be inserting themselves into high places as well as low, seeking to learn everything. Does my lord recall any such?"

Hiram shook his head. "No, none unaccountable like that. And I would have heard about them and wanted to see them. My followers are aware of how I always hunger for new knowledge, fresh news." He chuckled. "As witness the fact I was willing to receive you."

Everard swallowed his disappointment. It tasted sour. *But I shouldn't have imagined the enemy would be openly active now, this close to the time when he's going to strike. He'd know the Patrol would be busy. No, he'd do his preliminary research, acquire his detailed information about Phoenicia and its vulnerabilities, earlier. Maybe quite a bit earlier.*

"My lord," he said, "if there is indeed a menace, it must have been a long while in the egg. Dare I ask your highness to think back? The king in his omniscience might recollect something from years agone."

Hiram lowered his gaze and concentrated. Sweat prickled Everard's skin. He forced himself to sit still. Finally, softly, he heard:

"Well, late in the reign of my illustrious father King Abibaal . . . yes . . . he had certain guests for a spell, about whom rumors flew. They were not of any land familiar to us. . . . Seekers of wisdom from the Far East, they said. . . . What was the name of their country? Shee-an? No, belike not." Hiram sighed. "Memory fades. Especially memory of mere words."

"My lord did not meet them himself, then?"

"No, I was gone, spending some years in travel through our hinterlands and abroad, so as to prepare myself for the throne. And now Abibaal sleeps with his fathers. As, I fear, do well-nigh all who may have encountered those men."

Everard suppressed a sigh of his own and struggled to ease off. The lead was fog-tenuous, if it was a lead. But what could he expect? The enemy wouldn't have left engraved announcements.

Nobody here kept journals or saved letters, nor did anybody number years in the manner of later civilizations. Everard would not be able to learn precisely when Abibaal entertained his curious visitors. The Patrolman would be lucky to find one or two individuals who remembered them well. Hiram had reigned for two decades now, and life expectancy was not great.

I've got to try, though. It's the single lonely clue I've turned up. Or else it's a false scent, of course. Those could have been legitimate contemporaries — explorers from Chou Dynasty China, maybe.

He cleared his throat. "Does my lord grant permission for his servant to ask questions, in the royal household as well as in the city? I'm thinking that humble folk might speak a little more free and open before a plain fellow like me, than they would in the awe of his highness' presence."

Hiram smiled. "For a plain fellow, Eborix, you've a smooth tongue. But — yes, you may try. Abide for a while as my guest, with your young footman whom I noticed outside. We'll talk further. If nothing else, you are a fanciful talker."

A page conducted Everard and Pum through corridors to their quarters, as evening closed in. "The noble visitor will dine with the guards officers and men of like rank, unless he is bidden to the royal board," he explained obsequiously. "His attendant is welcome at the freeborn servants' mess. If aught be desired, let him only inform a butler or steward; his highness' generosity knows no bounds."

Everard resolved not to try that generosity too far. The household seemed more status-conscious than Tyrians generally were—no doubt the presence of many out-and-out slaves reinforced that—but Hiram was probably not above thrift.

Yet when the Patrolman reached his room, he found that the king was a thoughtful host. Hiram must have issued orders after their discussion, while the newcomers were shown the sights of the palace and given a light supper.

The chamber was large, well-furnished, lit by several lamps. A window, which could be shuttered, overlooked a court where flowers and pomegranates grew. Doors were solid wood on bronze hinges. The interior one stood open on an adjacent cubicle, sufficient for a straw tick and a pot, where Pum would sleep.

Everard halted. Lamplight fell soft over carpet, draperies, chairs, a table, a cedar chest, a double bed. Shadows stirred as a young woman rose and genuflected.

"Does my lord wish more?" asked the page. "If not, let this lowly person bid him a good night." He bowed and departed.

Breath hissed between Pum's teeth. "Master, she's beautiful!"

Everard's cheeks smoldered. "Uh-huh. Goodnight to you, too, lad."

"Noble sir—"

"Goodnight, I said."

Pum rolled eyes toward the ceiling, shrugged elaborately, and trudged to his kennel. The door slammed behind him.

"Stand straight, my dear," Everard mumbled. "Don't be afraid. I'd never hurt you."

The woman obeyed, arms crossed over bosom and head meekly lowered. She was tall for this milieu, slender, stacked. The wispy gown decked a fair skin. The hair knotted loosely at her nape was ruddy-brown. Feeling almost diffident, he laid a finger beneath her chin. She lifted a face that was blue-eyed, pert-nosed, full-lipped, piquantly freckled.

"Who are you?" he wondered. His throat felt tight.

"Your handmaiden sent to attend you, lord." Her words bore a lilting foreign accent. "What is your pleasure?"

"I . . . I asked who you are. Your name, your people."

"They call me Pleshti, master."

"Because they can't pronounce your real name, I'll be bound, or won't bother to. What is it?"

She swallowed. Tears glimmered. "I was Bronwen once," she whispered.

Everard nodded to himself. Glancing around, he saw a jug of wine as well as water on the table, plus a beaker and a bowl of fruit. He took her hand. It lay small and tender in his. "Come," he said, "let's sit down, take refreshment, get acquainted. We'll share yon glass."

She shuddered and half shrank away. Sadness touched him afresh, though he achieved a smile. "Don't be afraid, Bronwen. I'm not leading up to anything that could hurt you. I simply wish us to be friends. You see, macushla, I think you're of my folk."

She fought off the weeping, squared her shoulders, and gulped, "My lord is, is g-godlike in his kindness. How shall I ever thank him?"

Everard led her to the table, got her seated, and poured. Before long her story came forth.

It was all too ordinary. Though her concepts of geography were vague, he deduced that she belonged to a Celtic tribe which had migrated south from the Danubian *Urheimat*. Hers was a village at the head of the Adriatic Sea, and she had been the daughter of a well-to-do yeoman, as Bronze Age primitives reckoned prosperity.

She hadn't counted birthdays before nor years after, but he figured she was about thirteen when the Tyrians came, about a decade ago. They were in a single ship, boldly questing north in search of new trade possibilities. They camped on the shore and dickered in sign language. Evidently they decided there was nothing worth coming back for, because when they left, they kidnapped several children who had wandered near to look at the marvelous foreigners. Bronwen was among them.

The Tyrians hadn't raped their female captives, nor mistreated any of either sex more than they found necessary. A virgin in sound condition was worth too much on the slave market. Everard admitted that he couldn't even call the sailors evil. They had just done what came naturally in the ancient world, and most subsequent history for that matter.

Bronwen lucked out, everything considered. She was acquired for the palace: not the royal harem, though the king had had her unofficially a few times, but for him to lend to such house guests as he would favor. Men were seldom deliberately cruel to her. The pain that never ended lay in being captive among aliens.

That, and her children. She had borne four over the years, of whom two died in infancy — a good record, especially when they hadn't cost her much in the way of teeth or health. The surviving pair were still small. The girl would probably become a concubine too when she reached puberty, unless she was passed on to a brothel. (Slave women did not get deflowered as a religious rite. Who cared about their fortunes in later life?) The boy would probably be castrated at that age, since his upbringing at court would have made him a potential harem attendant.

As for Bronwen, when she lost her looks she'd be assigned to labor. Not having been trained in skills such as weaving, she'd likeliest end in the scullery or at a quern.

Everard had to coax all this out of her, piece by harsh little piece. She didn't lament nor beg. Her fate was what it was. He remembered a line Thucydides would pen centuries hence, about the disastrous Athenian military expedition whose last members ended their days in the mines of Sicily. "Having done what men could, they suffered what men must."

And women. Especially women. He wondered if, way down inside, he had Bronwen's courage. He doubted it.

About himself he was short-spoken. After avoiding one Celt and then getting another thrust upon him, so to speak, he felt he'd better play very close to his vest.

Nonetheless, at last she looked at him, flushed, aglow, and said in a slightly wine-slurred voice, "Oh, Eborix—" He couldn't follow the rest.

"I fear my tongue is too unlike yours, my dear," he said.

She returned to Punic: "Eborix, how generous of Asherat that she brought me to you for, for whatever time she grants. How wonderful. Now come, sweet lord, let your handmaiden give you back some of the joy—" She rose, came around the table, cast her warmth and suppleness into his lap.

He had already consulted his conscience. If he didn't do what everybody expected, word was bound to reach the king. Hiram might well take umbrage, or wonder what was wrong with his guest. Bronwen herself would be hurt, bewildered; she might get in trouble. Besides, she was lovely, and he'd been much deprived. Poor Sarai scarcely counted.

He gathered Bronwen to him.

Intelligent, observant, sensitive, she had well learned how to please a man. He hadn't figured on more than once, but she changed his mind about that, more than once. Her own ardor didn't seem faked, either. Well, he was probably the first man who had ever tried to please *her*. After the second round, she whispered brokenly into his ear: "I've . . . borne no further . . . these past three years. How I am praying the goddess will open my womb for you, Eborix, Eborix—"

He didn't remind her that any such child would be a slave also.

Yet before they slept she murmured something else, which he thought she might well not have let slip if she were fully awake: "We have been one flesh tonight, my lord, and may we be so often again. But know that I know we are not of one people."

"What?" An iciness stabbed him. He sat bolt upright.

She snuggled close. "Lie down, my heart. Never, never will I betray you. But . . . I remember enough things from home, small things, and I do not believe Geyils in the mountains can be that different from Geyils by the sea. . . . Hush, hush, your secret is safe. Why should Bronwen Brannoch's daughter betray the only person here who ever cared about her? Sleep, my nameless darling, sleep well in my arms."

At dawn a servant roused Everard—apologizing, flattering all the while—and took him away to a hot bath. Soap was for the future, but a sponge and a pumice stone scrubbed his skin, and afterward the servant gave him a rubdown with fragrant oil and a deft shave. He met the guards officers, then, for a meager breakfast and lively conversation.

"I'm going off duty today," proposed a man among them. "What say we ferry over to Usu, friend Eborix? I'll show you around. Later, if daylight remains, we can go for a ride outside the walls." Everard wasn't sure whether that would be on donkeyback or, more swiftly if less comfortably, in a war chariot. To date, horses were almost always draught animals, too valuable for any purposes but combat and pomp.

"Many thanks," the Patrolman answered. "First, though, I've need to see a woman called Sarai. She works in the steward's department."

Brows lifted. "What," scoffed a soldier, "do you

Northerners prefer grubby housekeepers to the king's choice?"

What a gossipy village the palace is, Everard thought. *I'd better restore my reputation fast.* He sat straight, cast a cold look across the table, and growled, "I am present at the king's behest, to conduct inquiries that are no concern of anybody else's. Is that clear, gossoon?"

"Oh, yes, oh, yes! I did but jest, noble sir. Wait, I'll go find somebody who'll know where she is." The man scrambled from his bench.

Guided to an offside room, Everard had a few minutes alone. He spent them reflecting upon his sense of urgency. Theoretically, he had as much time as he wanted; if need be, he could always double back, provided he took care to keep people from seeing him next to himself. In practice, that entailed risks acceptable only in the worst emergencies. Besides the chance of starting a causal loop that might expand out of control, there was the possibility of something going wrong in the mundane course of events. The likelihood of that would increase as the operation grew more long-drawn and complex. Then too, he had a natural impatience to get on with his job, complete it, nail down the existence of the world that begot him.

A dumpy figure parted the door curtain. Sarai knelt before him. "Your adorer awaits her lord's bidding," she said in a slightly uneven voice.

"Rise," Everard told her. "Be at ease. I want no more than to ask a question or two of you."

Her eyelids fluttered. She blushed to the end of her large nose. "Whatever my lord commands, she who owes him so much shall strive to fulfill."

He understood she was being neither slavish nor coquettish. She neither invited nor expected forwardness on his part. Once she had made her sacrifice to the goddess, a pious Phoenician woman stayed chaste. Sarai was simply, humbly grateful to him. He felt touched.

"Be at ease," he repeated. "Let your mind roam free. On behalf of the king, I seek knowledge of certain men who once visited his father, late in the life of glorious Abibaal."

Her gaze widened. "Master, I can scarcely have been born."

"I know. But what of older attendants? You must know everybody on the staff. A few might remain who served in those days. Would you inquire among them?"

She touched brow, lips, bosom, the sign of obedience. "Since my lord wills it."

He passed on what scant information he had. It disturbed her. "I fear—I fear naught will come of this," she said. "My lord must have seen how much we make of foreigners. If any were as peculiar as that, the servants would talk about them for the rest of their days." She smiled wryly. "After all, we've no great store of newness, we menials within the palace walls. We chew our gossip over and over again. I think I would have heard about those men, were anybody left who remembered them."

Everard cursed to himself in several languages. *Looks like I'll have to go back to Usu in person, twenty-odd years ago, and scratch around—regardless of the danger of my machine getting detected by the enemy and alerting him, or me getting killed.* "Well," he said, strained, "ask anyway, will you? If you learn nothing, that won't be your fault."

"No," she breathed, "but it will be my sorrow, kind lord." She knelt again before she departed.

Everard went to join his acquaintance. He had no real hope of discovering a clue on the mainland today, but the jaunt should work some tension out of him.

The sun was low when they came back to the island. A thin mist lay over the sea, diffusing light, making the high walls of Tyre golden, not altogether real, like an elven castle that might at any moment glimmer away into nothingness. Landing, Everard found that most dwellers had gone home. The soldier, who had a family, bade farewell, and the Patrolman made his way to the palace through streets that, after their daytime bustle, seemed ghostly.

A dark shape stood beside the royal porch, ignored by the sentries. Those climbed to their feet and hefted their spears as Everard approached, prepared to check his identity. Standing at attention had never been thought of. The woman scuttled to intercept him. As she bent the knee, he recognized Sarai.

His heart sprang. "What do you want?" ripped from him.

"Lord, I have been awaiting your return much of this day, for it seemed you were anxious to get whatever word I might bear."

She must have delegated her regular duties.

The street had been hot, hour after hour. "You . . . have found something?"

"Perhaps, master; perhaps a scrap. Would it were more."

"Speak, for—for Melqart's sake!"

"For yours, lord, yours, since you did ask this of your servant." Sarai drew breath. Her gaze met his, and stayed. Her tone became strong, matter-of-fact:

"As I feared, of those few retainers who are old enough, none had the knowledge you seek. They had not yet entered service, or if they had, they worked elsewhere for King Abibaal than at the palace—on a farm or a summer estate or some such place. At best, a man or two said he might have heard a little talk once; but what he remembered about that was no more than what my lord had already conveyed to me. I despaired, until I thought to seek a shrine of Asherat. I prayed that she be gracious unto you who had served her through me, when for so long no other man would. And lo, she answered. Praises be unto her. I recalled that an under-groom named Jantin-hamu has a father alive, who was formerly on the steward's staff. I sought Jantin-hamu out, and he brought me to Bomilcar, and, aye, Bomilcar can tell about those strangers."

"Why, that, that is splendid," he blurted. "I don't believe I myself could ever have done what you did. I wouldn't have known."

"Now I pray that this may prove to be in truth helpful to my lord," she said mutedly, "he who was good to an ugly hill-woman. Come, I will guide you."

In filial piety, Jantin-hamu gave his father a place in the one-room apartment he shared with his wife and a couple of children still dependent on them. A single lamp picked out, through monstrous shadows, the straw pallets, stools, clay jugs, brazier that were about all the furniture. The woman cooked in a kitchen shared with other tenants, then brought the food here to eat; the air was close and greasy. Everybody else squatted, staring, while Everard interrogated Bomilcar.

The old man was bald except for white remnants of beard, toothless, half deaf, gnarled and crippled by arthritis, eyes turned milky by cataracts. (His chronological age must be about sixty. So much for the back-to-nature crowd in twentieth-century America.) He hunched on a stool, hands weakly clasped around a stick. His mind worked, though—reached forth out of the ruin where it was trapped like a plant reaching for sunlight.

"Aye, aye, they come and stand before me as I speak, as if 'twere yesterday. Could I but remember that well what happened in the real yesterday. Well, nothing did, nothing ever does any more. . . .

"Seven, they were, who said they had come on a ship from the Hittite coast. Now young Matinbaal got curious, he did, and went down and asked around, and never found a skipper who'd carried any such passengers. Well, maybe 'twas a ship that went right onward, toward Philistia or Egypt. . . . Sinim they called themselves, and told of faring thousands upon thousands of leagues from the Sunrise Lands, that they might bring home an account of the world to their king. They spoke fair Punic, albeit with an accent like none else I ever heard. . . . Taller than most, well-built;

they walked like wildcats, and were as mannerly
and, I guessed, as dangerous if aroused. No beards;
'twasn't that they shaved, their faces were hairless,
like women's. Not eunuchs, however, no, the
wenches lent 'em were soon sitting down careful,
heh, heh. Their eyes were light, their skins whiter
even than a yellow-haired Achaean's, but *their*
straight locks were raven-black. . . . Ever there was
an air of wizardry about them, and I heard tales
of eldritch things they'd shown the king. Be that
as it may, they did no harm, they were only
curious, oh, how curious about every least thing
in Usu, and about the plans that were then being
drawn up for Tyre. They won the king's heart; he
commanded they see and hear whatever they
liked, though it be the deepest secrets of a sanctuary or a merchant house. . . . I did often wonder,
afterward, if this was what provoked the gods
against them."

Judas priest! slashed through Everard. *That's
almost got to be my enemies. Yes, them, Exaltationists, Varagan's gang. "Sinim"—Chinese? A red
herring, in case the Patrol stumbled onto their
trail? No, I suspect not, I think probably they just
used that alias so as to have a readymade story to
hand Abibaal and his court. For they didn't bother
to disguise their appearance. As in South America,
Varagan must have felt sure his cleverness would
be too much for the plodding Patrol. Which it
might well have been, except for Sarai.*

Not that I'm very far along on the trail yet.

"What became of them?" he demanded.

"Ah, that was a pity, unless it was punishment
for something wrong they did, like maybe poking
into a Holy of Holies." Bomilcar clicked his tongue

and wagged his head. "After several weeks, they asked leave to go. 'Twas late in the season, most ships were already put away for the winter, but against advice they offered a rich payment for passage to Cyprus, and got a daring skipper to agree. I went down to the wharf myself to watch them depart, I did. A cold, blustery day, 'twas. I watched that ship dwindle away under the racing clouds till she vanished in the brume, and something made me stop by the temple of Tanith on my way back and put oil in a lamp—not for them, understand, but for all poor mariners, on whom rests the well-being of Tyre."

Everard restrained himself from shaking that withered frame. "And then? Anything?"

"Aye, my feeling was right. My feelings have always been right, haven't they, Jantin-hamu? Always. I should've been a priest, but too many boys were trying for what few acolytes' berths there were. . . . Ah, yes. That day a gale sprang up. The ship foundered. Everybody lost. I heard about that, I did, because we naturally wanted to know what'd happened to those strangers. Her figurehead and some other bits and pieces drifted onto the rocks where this city now is."

"But—wait, gaffer—are you sure everybody drowned?"

"No, I suppose I couldn't swear to that, no. I suppose a man or two could've clung to a plank and been borne ashore likewise. They'd've made landfall elsewhere and trudged home unremarked. Who in the palace cares about a common sailor? Certain is, the ship was lost, and the Sinim—for if *they'd* returned, we'd know, wouldn't we, now?"

Everard's mind whirred. *Time travelers might*

*well have arrived here by machine, directly. The
Patrol base, with instruments to detect it, wasn't
yet established. (We can't man every instant of
the millennia. At best, at need, we send agents
back and forth within a milieu, out of those stations we do keep.) If they weren't to cause a
sensation that would endure, though, they would
have to depart in contemporary wise, by land or
sea. But surely, before embarking, they'd have
checked out what the weather was going to be
like. Ships in this age practically never sail during
the winter; they're too fragile.*

*Could this be a false scent regardless? Bomilcar's
memory may not be as clear as he claims. And
the visitors could* have *been from one of those
odd, short-lived little civilizations that history
and archaeology afterward lost sight of, and time-
traveling scientists discover mainly by accident. For
instance, a city-state off in the Anatolian mountains somewhere, which'd learned things from the
Hittites, and whose aristocracy is so inbred that
its members have a unique physiognomy —*

*On the other hand, of course, this could be the
real means of breaking the trail, this shipwreck.
That would explain why enemy agents didn't
trouble to make themselves look Chinese.*

How to find out, before Tyre explodes?

"When did this happen, Bomilcar?" he asked
as gently as he was able.

"Why, I told you," the old man said. "Back in
the days of King Abibaal, when I worked for his
steward in the palace in Usu."

Everard felt acutely, annoyingly conscious of
the family around and their eyes. He heard them
breathe. The lamp guttered, shadows thickened,

the air was cooling fast. "Could you tell me more closely?" he pursued. "Do you recall which year of Abibaal's reign it was?"

"No. No. Nor anything else special. Let me think. . . . Was it two years, or three, after Captain Rib-adi brought back such a treasure trove from—from—where was it? Somewhere beyond Tharshish. . . . No, wasn't that later? . . . My first wife died in childbed a while afterward, that I remember, but 'twas several years before I could arrange a second marriage, and meanwhile I had to make do with harlots, heh, heh. . . . " With the abruptness of the aged, Bomilcar's mood changed. Tears trickled forth. "And my second wife, my Batbaal, she died too, of a fever. . . . Crazed, she was, didn't know me any longer. . . . Don't plague me, my lord, don't plague me, leave me in peace and darkness and the gods will bless you."

I'll get nothing further here. What did I get? Maybe nothing.

Before he went, Everard made Jantin-hamu a present of metal which should allow the family to live in more comfort. The ancient world had some few advantages over his; it was free of gift and income taxes.

A couple of hours past sunset, Everard returned to the palace. That was late in local eyes. The sentries raised rushlights, squinted at him, and summoned their officer. When Eborix had been identified, they let him in with apologies. His indulgent laugh was better than a large tip would have been.

He didn't really feel like laughing. Lips gone tight, he followed a lamp bearer to his room.

Bronwen lay asleep. A single flame still burned. He undressed and stood for a minute or three looking down at her through the flickery dimness. Unbound, her hair glowed across the pillow. One arm, out of the blanket, didn't quite cover a bare young breast. It was her face he regarded, though. How innocent she looked, childlike, woundable even now, even after everything she had endured.

If only. No. We may be a little bit in love already. But no possible way could it last, could we ever really live together, unless as a mere pair of bodies. Too much time sunders us.

What shall become of her?

He started to get into bed, intending simply slumber. She roused. Slaves learn to sleep alertly. He saw joy blossom in her. "My lord! Welcome, a thousand welcomes!"

They held each other close. Just the same, he found he wanted to talk with her. "How did your day go?" he asked into the warmth where her jaw met her ear.

"What? I—O master—" She was surprised that he would ask. "Why, it was pleasant, surely because your dear magic lingered. Your servant Pummairam and I chatted a long while." She giggled. "He's an engaging scoundrel, isn't he? Some of his questions struck too near the bone, but have no fear, my lord; those I refused to answer, and he backed off at once. Later I sallied forth, leaving word where I could be found should my lord return, and spent the afternoon in the nursery where my children are. They are such darlings." She didn't venture to inquire if he would care to meet them.

"Hm." A thought nudged Everard. "What did Pum do meanwhile?" *I can't see him sitting idle all day, that squirrel.*

"I know not. Well, I glimpsed him twice, on his errands down the corridors, but took it for given that my lord must have commanded — My lord?"

Alarmed, she sat straight as Everard left the bed. He flung open the door to the cubicle. It stood empty. What in hell was Pum up to?

Perhaps nothing much. Yet a servant who got into mischief might cause trouble for his master.

Standing there in a brown study, the floor cold beneath his feet, Everard grew aware of arms around his waist, and a cheek stroking across his shoulderblades, and a voice that crooned: "Is my lord overly weary? If so, let his handmaiden sing him a lullaby from her homeland. But if not—"

To hell with my worries. They'll keep. Everard turned his attention elsewhere, and himself.

The boy was still missing when the man awoke. Discreet questions revealed that he had spent hours the day before, talking with various members of the staff. They agreed he was inquisitive and amusing. Finally he had gone out, and no one had seen him since.

Probably he got restless and flitted off to spend what I've given him in the wineshops and cathouses. Too bad. In spite of his scapegrace style, I thought he was basically reliable, and meant to do something or other that'd give him a chance at a better life.

Never mind. I've Patrol business on hand.

Everard excused himself from further activities and went alone into the city. As a hireling admitted him to the house of Zakarbaal, Yael Zorach appeared. Phoenician dress and hairdo became her charmingly well, but he was too preoccupied to appreciate it. The same strain showed on her features. "This way," she said, unwontedly curt, and led him to the inner chambers.

Her husband sat in conference with a craggy-faced, bushy-bearded man whose costume varied in numerous ways from local male dress. "Oh, Manse," Chaim exclaimed. "What a relief. I wondered if we'd have to send for you, or what." He switched to Temporal: "Agent Manson Everard, Unattached, let me present Epsilon Korten, director of Jerusalem Base."

The other man rose in a future-military fashion and snapped a salute. "An honor, sir," he said. Nonetheless, his rank was not much below Everard's. He was responsible for temporal activities throughout the Hebrew lands, between the birth of David and the fall of Judah. Tyre might be more important in secular history, but it would never draw a tenth of the visitors from uptime that Jerusalem and its environs did. The position he held told Everard immediately that he was both a man of action and a scholar of profundity.

"I'll have Hanai bring in refreshments, and then tell the household to stay out of here and not let anybody in," Yael proposed.

Everard and Korten spent those minutes getting an acquaintance started. The latter was born in twenty-ninth century New Edom on Mars. While he didn't brag, Everard gathered that his com-

puter analyses of early Semitic texts had joined
his exploits as a spaceman in the Second Aster-
oid War to attract Patrol recruiters. They sounded
him out, got him to take tests which proved him
trustworthy, revealed the existence of the organization, accepted his enlistment, trained him—the
usual procedure. What was less usual was his
level of competence. In many ways, his job was
more demanding than Everard's.

"You'll understand that this situation is especially alarming to my office," he said when the
foursome had settled down by themselves. "If
Tyre is destroyed, Europe may take decades to
show any major effects, the rest of the world
centuries—millennia, in the Americas or Austral-
asia. But it will be an immediate catastrophe for
Solomon's kingdom. Lacking Hiram's support and
the prestige it confers, he probably can't hold his
tribes together long; and without Tyre at their
backs, the Philistines won't be slow to seek revenge.
Judaism, Yahwistic monotheism, is new and frail,
still half pagan. My extrapolation is that it won't
survive either. Yahweh will sink to being one
more character in a crude and mutable pantheon."

"And there goes a good deal of Classical civilization," Everard added. "Judaism influenced philosophy as well as events among both the Alexan-
drine Greeks and the Romans. Obviously, no
Christianity, therefore no Western civilization, or
Byzantine, or any of their successors. No telling
what will arise instead." He thought of another
altered world, which he had helped abort, and a
wound twinged that he would bear throughout
his life.

"Yes, of course," said Korten impatiently. "The

point is, granted that the resources of the Patrol are finite—and, yes, spread terribly thin over a continuum that has many nexuses as critical as this one—I don't believe it should concentrate all available effort on rescuing Tyre. If that happens, and we fail, everything is lost; the chances of our being able to restore the original world become vanishingly small. No, let us establish a strong standby—personnel, organization, plans—in Jerusalem, ready to minimize the effects there. The less that Solomon's kingdom suffers, the less powerful the change vortex will be. That should give us more likelihood of damping it out altogether."

"Do you mean to, to write Tyre off?" Yael asked, dismayed.

"No, certainly not. But I do want us to have some insurance against its loss."

"That in itself is playing fast and loose with history." Chaim's tone trembled.

"I know. But extreme situations call for extreme measures. I came here first to discuss it with you, but please be advised that I intend to press for this policy in the highest echelons." Korten turned to Everard. "Sir, I regret the need to reduce further the slender resources you have at your command, but my judgment is that we must."

"They aren't slender," the American grumbled, "they're downright emaciated." *Following the preliminary legwork, what has the Patrol got here other than me?*

Does that mean the Danellians know I'll succeed? Or does it mean they'll agree with Korten—even, that Tyre is "already" doomed? If I fail—if I die—

He straightened, reached into his pouch for pipe and tobacco, and said: "My lady and gentlemen, this could too easily turn into a shouting match. Let's talk it over like reasonable people. The beginning of that is to assemble what hard facts we have, and look at them. Not that I've collected many so far."

The debate went on for hours.

It was afternoon before Yael suggested they break for food. "Thanks," Everard said, "but I think I'd better get back to the palace. Otherwise Hiram might suspect I'm loafing, at his expense. I'll check in again tomorrow, okay?"

The truth was that he had no appetite for the usual heavy meal of the day, roast lamb or whatever else it would be. He'd rather get a slab of bread and a hunk of goat cheese at some foodstall, while he tried to sort out this new problem. (Thank technology again. Without the gene-tailored protective microbes the Patrol medics had implanted in him, he'd never have dared touch local stuff that wasn't cooked dead. And vaccinations against every sort of disease that came and went through the ages would long since have overloaded his immune system.)

Twentieth-century style, he shook hands all around. Korten might be wrong, or he might not be, but he was pleasant, able, and well-intentioned. Everard went forth into a street that brooded and simmered beneath the sun.

Pum waited. He rose less exuberantly than before. An odd gravity was on the thin young face. "Master," he breathed, "can we talk unheard?"

They found themselves a tavern where they were the only customers. In actuality, it was a lean-to roof shading a small area on which cushions lay; you sat cross-legged, and the landlord fetched clay goblets of wine from inside his home. Everard paid him in beads, after desultory haggling. Foot traffic swarmed and babbled up and down the street on which the shop intruded, but at this hour men were generally busied. They'd relax here, those who could afford to, when cooling shadows had fallen between the walls.

Everard sipped the thin, sour drink and grimaced. In his opinion, nobody understood wine before about the seventeenth century A.D. Beer was worse. No matter. "Speak, son," he said. "And you needn't waste breath or time calling me the radiance of the universe and offering to lie down for me to wipe my feet on. What have you been doing?"

Pum gulped, shivered, leaned forward. "O lord of mine," he began, and his voice broke in an adolescent squeak, "your underling has dared take much upon his head. Upbraid me, beat me, have me whipped, whatever your will may be, if I have transgressed. But never, I beg, never think I have sought anything but your welfare. My sole wish is to serve you as far as my poor abilities allow."

A brief grin flashed. "You see, you pay so well!"

Soberness returned: "You are a strong man, a man of great powers, in whose service I may hope to flourish. Now for that, I must prove myself worthy. Any lout can carry your baggage or lead you to a pleasure house. What can Pummairam do, over and above this, that my lord will

wish to keep him as a retainer? Well, what does
my lord require? What does he need?

"Master, it pleases you to pose as a rude
tribesman, but from the very first I had a feeling
there was far more to you. Of course you would
not confide in a chance-met guttersnipe. So, without knowledge of you, how could I tell what use I
might be?"

Yeah, Everard thought, *in his kind of hand-to-
mouth existence, he had to develop a pretty keen
intuition, or else go under.* He kept his tone mild:
"I am not angry. But tell me what you did."

Pum's big, russet-hued eyes met his and stayed,
almost as equal to equal. "I made bold to query
others about my master. Always carefully, never
letting out what my purpose was or, in sooth,
letting the person suspect what he or she revealed.
As proof of this, has anyone seemed to doubt my
lord?"

"M-m . . . no . . . not any more than I could
expect. Who did you talk with?"

"Well, the lovely Pleshti—Bo-ron-u-wen, for a
start." Pum lifted a palm. "Master! She said never
a word you would not have approved. I read her
face, her movements, while I asked certain questions. No more. She refused me answers, now
and then, herself, and those refusals told me
something too. And her body does not know how
to keep secrets. Is that her fault?"

"No." *Also, I wouldn't be surprised but what
you reopened your door a crack that night and
eavesdropped. Never mind. I don't want to know.*

"Thus I learned you are not of the . . . the Geyil
folk, is that their name? It was no surprise. I had
already guessed as much. You see, although I am

sure my master is terrible in battle, he is as forbearing with women as a mother with her child. Would a half-savage wanderer be?"

Everard laughed ruefully. *Touché!* On previous missions, he'd sometimes heard remarks about his lack of normal callousness, but nobody else had drawn conclusions from it.

Encouraged, Pum hurried on: "I shan't weary my lord with details. Menials are always watching the mighty, and love to gossip about them. I may have deceived Sarai the housekeeper a tiny bit. Since I was your footman, she saw no reason to bid me begone. Not that I asked her very much directly. That would have been both foolish and unnecessary. I was content to get myself steered toward the dwelling of Jantin-hamu, where they were agog over their visitor yesterday eventide. Thus did I get a hint of what it is my lord seeks."

He puffed himself up. "That, resplendent master, was what his servant required. I hied myself down to the docks and started gadding about. Lo!"

A billow passed through Everard. "What did you find?" he nearly yelled.

"What," Pum declaimed, "but a man who lived through the shipwreck and onslaught of demons?"

Gisgo appeared to be in his mid-forties, short but wiry, his weathered nutcracker face full of life. Over the years, he had risen from deckhand to coxswain, a skilled and well-rewarded post. Over the years, too, his cronies had tired of hearing about his remarkable experience. They took it for just another tall tale, anyway.

Everard appreciated what a fantastic piece of detective work Pum had done, tracing the man down by getting sailors in wineshops to talk about who told what kind of yarns. He himself could never have managed it; they'd have been too leery of such an outsider, who moreover was a royal guest. Like sensible people throughout history, the average Phoenician wanted as little to do with his government as possible.

It had been a lucky break that Gisgo was home in voyaging season. However, he had attained enough seniority and saved enough wealth that he need no more join long expeditions, hazardous and uncomfortable. His ship was on the Egypt run, and took layovers between passages.

In his neat fifth-floor apartment, his two wives brought refreshments while he lolled back and spouted at his guests. A window gave on a court between tenements. The view was of clay walls and laundry strung on lines between. Yet sunlight came in alongside an eddy of breeze, to touch souvenirs of many a trip—a miniature Babylonian cherub, a syrinx from Greece, a faience hippopotamus from the Nile, an Iberian juju, a leaf-shaped bronze dagger from the North. . . . Everard had made a substantial golden gift, and the mariner waxed expansive.

"Aye," Gisgo said, "that was an eldritch journey, 'twas. Bad time of year, equinox drawing nigh, and those there Sinim from who knows where, carrying misfortune in their bones for aught we knew. But we were young, the whole crew of us, from the captain on down; we reckoned on wintering in Cyprus, where the wines are strong and

the girls are sweet; those Sinim, they'd pay well,
they would. For that kind of metal, we were ready
to give the fig to death and hell. I've since grown
wiser, but won't claim I'm gladder, no, no. I'm
still spry, but I feel the teeth gnawing, and believe
me, my friends, it was better to be young."

He signed himself. "The poor lads who went
down, may their shades rest peaceful." With a
glance at Pum: "One of them looked like you,
younker. Gave me a start, you did, when first we
met. Adiyaton, was that his name? Aye, I think
so. Maybe he was your grandsire?"

The boy gestured ignorance. He had no way of
knowing.

"I've made my offerings for the lot of them, I
have," Gisgo went on, "as well as in thanks for
my own deliverance. Always stand by your friends
and pay your debts, then the gods will help you
in your need. They surely helped me.

"The Cyprus run is tricky at best. Can't make
camp; it's overnight on the open sea, sometimes
for days on end if the wind's foul. This time—ah,
this time! Scarce were we beyond sight of land
when the gale struck, and little did it avail us to
spread oil on those waters. Out oars and keep her
head to the waves, it was, till breath failed and
sinews cracked but we must row regardless. Black
as a pig's bowels, it was, and howling and lash-
ing and rolling and pitching while the salt crusted
my eyes and stung the cracks in my lips—and
how to keep stroke when we couldn't hear the
cox's drum through the wind?

"But on the midships catwalk I saw the chief
of the Sinim, cloak flapping about him, faced
straight into the blast, and laughing, laughing!

"I don't know whether he was bold, or land-lubber-ignorant of the danger, or wiser than I then was in the ways of the sea. Afterward I've harked back, in the light of much hard-won knowledge, and decided that with any luck we could have ridden out the storm. That was a well-found ship, and her officers knew their trade. However, the gods, or the demons, would have it otherwise.

"For suddenly, crack and blaze! The brightness blinded me. I lost hold of my oar, like most of us did. Somehow I fumbled out and got a grip on it again before it slid away between the tholes. That may have saved my sight, because I wasn't looking up when the second bolt smote.

"Aye, we'd been hit by lightning. Twice. I'd heard no thunder, but maybe the roar of the waves and shriek of the wind covered that. When the dazzle began to clear from my eyes, I saw the mast aflame like a torch. The hull was slashed and weakened. I felt the sea shiver my skull, and my arse, too, as it broke the ship apart under me.

"That scarce seemed to matter right away. For by that fitful, ragged light I glimpsed things in heaven, like yonder winged bull but huge as real oxen and ashine as if cast in iron. Men were astride them. They swooped downward—

"Then everything went to pieces. I found myself in the water, clutching my oar. A couple other men in my sight had got hold of flotsam also. But the fury wasn't done with us. A lightning bolt struck down, straight into poor Hurum-abi, my drinking friend since I was a kid. He must've been killed right off. Me, I ducked below and held my breath as long's I could.

"When I must needs bring my nose up for air, I seemed to be alone in the sea. But overhead was a swarm of those dragons or chariots or whatever they were, a-dart through the wind. Flame raged between them. I went under again.

"I think they were soon gone to wherever in the Beyond they'd come from, but I was too busy staying alive to pay any more heed. Finally I made it to land. What had happened seemed unreal, like a mad dream. Maybe it was. I don't know. What I do know is that I'm the single man on that ship who ever came back. Praise Tanith, eh, girls?" Undaunted by memory, Gisgo pinched the bottom of his nearest wife.

More reminiscence followed, which took a couple of hours to disentangle. Finally Everard could ask, his tongue dry despite the wine: "Do you remember just when this was? How many years ago?"

"Why, sure I do, sure I do," Gisgo answered. "An even one score and six years, come fifteen days before the fall equinox, or pretty near to that."

He waved a hand. "How do I know, you wonder? Well, it's like the Egyptian priests, that keep such a close calendar because their river floods and falls every year. A seaman who doesn't take care, he's not likely to get old. Did you know that beyond the Pillars of Melqart the sea rises and falls like the Nile, but twice a day? You'd better watch those times sharp, if you'd fare in those parts.

"But the Sinim, they were what really drove the idea home in this head. There I was, attendant on my captain while they bargained with

him for passage, and they kept talking about
exactly which day we'd depart—talking him into
it, you understand. I listened, and I thought what
gains might lie in that kind of remembering, and
told myself I'd make a point of it. Back then, I
couldn't read or write, but what I could do was
mark whatever special things happened each year,
and keep those happenings in order and count
back over them when I needed to. So this was the
year in between a venture to the Red Cliff Shores
and the year when I caught the Babylonian
disease—"

Everard and Pum emerged and began walking
from the Sidonian Harbor quarter, down a Street
of the Ropemakers now filling with dusk and
quietness, toward the palace.

"My lord gathers his forces, I see," murmured
the boy after a while.

The Patrolman nodded absently. His mind was
in a storm of its own.

Varagan's procedure seemed clear to him. (Everard felt well-nigh certain it was Merau Varagan,
perpetrating a fresh enormity.) From wherever in
space-time his hideout was, he and half a dozen
of his confederates had sought the Usu area,
twenty-six years ago. Others must have carried
them on hoppers, which let them off and immediately returned. The Patrol couldn't hope to catch
the vehicles in that brief an interlude, when the
exact place and moment were unknown. Varagan's
band had gone afoot into town and ingratiated
themselves with King Abibaal.

They must have done this *after* bombing the temple, leaving the ransom note, and probably making the attempt on Everard—after, that is, in terms of their world lines, their continuity of experience. It would not have been hard to pick such a target, or even plant such an assassin. Scientists studying Tyre had written books which were readily available. The preliminary mischief would give Varagan an idea as to the feasibility of his entire scheme. Having decided that it would be worth a substantial investment of lifespan and effort, he thereupon sought the detailed knowledge, the kind that seldom gets into books, which he would need in order to do a really thorough job of wrecking this society.

When they had learned as much at the court of Abibaal as they felt was called for, Varagan and his followers left town in conventional wise, so as not to engender stories among the people that would spread and persist and eventually give the Patrol a lead. For the same reason, the dying out of public interest in them, they wanted it thought that they had perished.

Hence their departure date, on which they had insisted; a scouting flight had revealed that a storm would suddenly rise within hours. Those of the gang who were to pick them up had fired energy beams to destroy the ship and kill the witnesses. Had they not chanced to miss Gisgo, they would have covered their tracks almost completely. In fact, without Sarai's assistance, Everard would most likely never have heard of those Sinim who were unfortunately lost at sea.

From his base, Varagan had "already" dispatched agents to keep an eye on Patrol HQ in

Tyre, as the time of his demonstration attack drew near. If such a gunman succeeded in recognizing and killing one or more of the scarce, valued Unattached officers, excellent! It would increase the probability of the Exaltationists getting what they wanted—whether that be the matter transmuter or the destruction of the Danellian future. Everard didn't think Varagan cared which. Either would gratify his power hunger and *Schadenfreude*.

Well, but Everard had found the spoor. He could loose the hounds of the Patrol—

Can I?

He gnawed his Celtic mustache and thought irrelevantly how glad he'd be to mow the damned fungus off, once this operation was finished.

Will it be?

Outnumbered, outgunned, Varagan was not necessarily outsmarted. His scheme had a built-in fail-safe that might be impossible to break.

The trouble was, the Phoenicians possessed neither clocks nor accurate navigation instruments. Gisgo didn't know, any closer than a week or two, when his ship suffered disaster; nor did he know, any closer than fifty miles or so, where it had been at the time. Therefore Everard didn't.

Of course, the Patrol could easily ascertain the date, and the course for Cyprus was known. But anything more precise required keeping watch from the air nearby, didn't it? And the enemy must have detectors which would warn him of that. The pilots who were to scuttle the ship and take away Varagan's group could arrive prepared for a dogfight. They wouldn't need but a few minutes to carry out their mission, then they'd be untraceably gone.

Worse, they might cancel the mission altogether. They could wait for a more favorable instant to recover their associates—or, worse yet, do it at an earlier time, before the ship ever sailed. In either case, Gisgo would not have (had) the experience which Everard had just heard him relate. The trail that the Patrolman had so painfully uncovered would never have existed. *Probably* the long-range consequences to history would be trivial, but there was no guarantee of that, once you started monkeying around with events.

For the same reasons, certain nullification of clues and possible upheaval in the continuum, the Patrol could not anticipate Varagan's plan. It dared not, for instance, swoop down on the ship and arrest the passengers before the gale and the Exaltationists struck.

Looks like the only way we can proceed is to appear exactly where they are, within that time-slot of five minutes or less when the riders carry out their dirty work. But how are we to pinpoint it without alerting them?

"I think," said Pum, "my lord intends to do battle, in a strange realm where wizards are his foes."

Am I that transparent to him? "Yes, it may be," Everard replied. "I'll first recompense you well, for you've been a right-hand man to me."

The youth plucked his sleeve. "Lord," he implored, "let your servant follow you."

Astounded, Everard stopped in mid-stride. "Huh?"

"I would not be parted from my master!" cried Pum. Tears gleamed in his eyes and down his cheekbones. "Better death at his side—aye, better the demons cast me down to hell—than return to that cockroach life you raised me from. Teach me what I should do. You know I learn fast. I shall not be afraid. You have made me into a man!"

By God, I do believe that for once his passion is perfectly genuine.

It's out of the question, of course.

IS it? Everard stood thunderstruck.

Pum danced before him, laughing and weeping. "My lord will do it, my lord will take me!"

And maybe, maybe, after this is all over, if he's survived—maybe we'll have gained something very precious.

"The danger will be great," Everard said slowly. "Moreover, I await things and happenings from which hardy warriors would flee, screaming. And earlier, you'll have to acquire knowledge which most of the wise men in this world could not even understand, were it told them."

"Try me, my lord," answered Pum. A sudden calm had come upon him.

"I will! Let's go!" Everard strode so fast that the youth must trot to keep up.

Basic indoctrination would take days, assuming Pum could handle it. That was okay, though. It would take a while anyway to collect the necessary intelligence and organize a task force. Besides, meanwhile there would be Bronwen. Everard couldn't tell if he himself would live through the conflict. Let him first receive whatever joy came his way, and try to give it back.

Captain Baalram was reluctant. "Why should I enroll your son?" he demanded. "I've a full crew already, including two apprentices. This one is a landlubber born, small, and scrawny."

"He's stronger than he seems," replied the man who called himself Adiyaton's father. (A quarter century hence, he would call himself Zakarbaal.) "You'll find him clever and willing. As for experience, everybody begins with none, true? See here, sir. I'm anxious for him to get into a trading career. For the sake of that, I'll be happy to . . . make it worth your while personally."

"Well, now." Baalram smiled and stroked his beard. "That's different. What amount of tuition had you in mind?"

Adiyaton (who, a quarter century hence, would have no precautionary need not to call himself Pummairam) looked gleeful. Inwardly, he shivered, for he gazed upon a man who must soon die.

From where the Patrol squadron waited, high in heaven, the storm was a blue-black mountain range crouched on the northern horizon. Elsewhere the sea reached argent and sapphire across the curve of the planet, save where islands broke the sheen and, eastward, the Syrian coast made a darkling line. Low in the west, the sun shone as cold as the blue around it. Wind whittered in Everard's ears.

On the front saddle of his time hopper, he huddled into a parka. The rear seat was empty, like those of about half the two-score vehicles that shared the sky with him. Their pilots hoped to transport prisoners. The rest were guncraft, eggs of armor wherein fire waited to hatch. Light clanged off metal.

Damn! Everard thought. *I'm freezing. How much longer? Has something gone wrong? Did Pum betray himself to the enemy, or has his equipment failed, or what?*

A receiver dial secured to the steering bar beeped and winked red. Breath exploded out of him, white vapor that the wind strewed and swallowed. Despite his years as a hunter of men, he must gulp before he could snap into his throat mike: "Signal received by commander. Triangulation stations, report."

Down ahead, in wrack and spindrift, the enemy band had appeared. They had commenced their evil labors. But Pum had reached inside his garb and pressed the button on a miniature radio transmitter.

Radio. The Exaltationists wouldn't anticipate something that primitive. Everard hoped.

Now, Pum, boy, are you able to find shelter, protect yourself, the way you were told to? Fear laid fingers around the Patrolman's gullet. He'd doubtless begotten sons, here and there through the ages, but this was the closest he had ever come to having one.

Words crackled in his earphones. Numbers followed. Instruments a hundred miles apart had precisely found the beleaguered ship. Clocks had already recorded the first split second of reception.

"Okay," Everard said. "Compute spatial coordinates for each vehicle according to our strategy. Troopers, stand by for instructions."

That required several minutes. He felt a chilly

peace welling up within him. His unit was committed. At this exact moment, it was in battle yonder. Let that happen which the Norns willed.

The data came crisply. "Everybody set?" he called. "Advance!"

He himself verniered controls and flipped the main drive toggle. His machine sprang forward through space, backward through time, to the moment when Pum had hailed it.

Wind raved. The hopper rocked and yawed in its antigrav field. Fifty yards below, black in this gloom, waves roared. The spume blown off them was sleet-colored. Everard saw by the light of a great torch some ways off. A resinous mast, fanned by the storm, burned fiercely. Tarry, flaming pieces of the ship were quenched in steam as it broke apart.

Everard tugged down his optical amplifiers. Vision became stark. It showed him that his command had arrived correctly, so as to englobe the half-dozen enemy vehicles everywhere above the billows.

It had not come soon enough to prevent them from starting their butchery. They had done that on the instant of their own appearance. Not knowing where any one of them would be, but knowing that each was lethally well-armed, Everard had perforce caused his group to show up at a distance where it could assess the situation before the killers noticed it.

They would, in a heartbeat or two. "Attack!" Everard roared needlessly. His steed hurtled forward.

A blue-white hell-beam speared through murk. Zigzagging as he flew, he felt it miss him by inches: heat, sting of ozone, crack of air. He didn't see it, for his goggles had automatically stopped down a glare that would have blinded.

Nor did he shoot back, though he drew his blaster. That wasn't his business. Heaven was already lurid with such lightnings. The waters reflected them as if also afire.

There was no good way to seize any enemy pilots. Everard's gunners had orders to kill, at once, before the reavers realized how outnumbered they were and skipped off into space-time. The job of the single-riding Patrolmen was to capture those spies who had been aboard the ship.

He didn't expect he'd find them clinging to the sections of hull that swung to and fro in the swells and disintegrated. Men would check those, of course, just in case. But likeliest the travelers were afloat by themselves. They'd surely taken the precaution of wearing cartridge-inflatable life jackets under their contemporary kaftans.

Pum could not risk doing so. As a crewboy, he'd have looked wrong in much more than a loincloth. It served to conceal his transmitter, but nothing else. Everard had made certain he learned to swim.

Few Punic sailors could. Everard glimpsed one who gripped a plank. Almost, he went to the rescue. But no, he mustn't. Baalram and his mariners had gone under—except for Gisgo, whose survival revealed itself to be no accident. The Patrol had pounced in time to save him from being hunted down as he drifted; and he had the strength to keep hold of his heavy sweep till it washed ashore. The rest, his shipmates, his friends—they died and their kin mourned them, as would be the fate of seafarers for the next several thousand years . . . and afterward spacefarers, timefarers. . . . At least these men perished so that their people, and untold billions of people in the future, might live.

It was a bleak consolation.

Everard's reheightened vision brought him sight of another head, unmistakable, yes, a man who bobbed about free as a cork—an enemy to take. He swung low. The man looked up out of froth and turmoil. Malignancy wrenched at his mouth. A hand rose from the water. It carried an energy pistol.

Everard was quicker to shoot. A thin beam stabbed. The man's scream was lost in the gale. Likewise was his weapon. He gaped at seared flesh and naked bone on that wrist.

Here Everard felt no pity. But he had not wanted to slay, in this encounter. Live captives, under painless, harmless, absolute psychointerrogation, could direct the Patrol to the lairs of all sorts of interesting villainies.

Everard lowered his vehicle. Its motor throbbed, holding it in place against the waves that crashed over it, the wind that tore and hooted and chilled. His legs clenched tight on the frame. He leaned from his saddle, got a hold on the semiconscious man, lifted him and laid him across the bow. *Okay, let's get some altitude!*

It was sheer chance, but not the less satisfying, that he, Manse Everard, turned out to be the Patrol agent who clapped hands on Merau Varagan.

The squadron sought a quiet place, to make

assessment before it went uptime. Its choice was an uninhabited Aegean islet. White cliffs rose out of cerulean waters, whose calm was stirred only by glitter of sunlight and foam. Gulls flew equally lucent, and mewed through the lulling of the breeze. Shrubs thrust forth among boulders. Warmth baked pungencies out of their leaves. Far and far away, a sail passed by. It could have been driving the ship of Odysseus.

The constables held conference. They had suffered no harm apart from a few wounds. For those, analgesics and antishock medications were directly available, and later hospital treatment would restore whatever had been lost. They had shot down four Exaltationist vehicles; three got away, but would be hunted, would be hunted. They had taken a full complement of captives.

One of the Patrolmen, homing on the transmitter, had plucked Pummairam from the sea.

"Good show!" Everard bawled, and hugged the boy to him.

They sat on a bench at the Egyptian Harbor. It was as private a spot as any, since everyone roundabout was too busy to eavesdrop; and soon the pulse of Tyre would beat no more for either of them. They did draw stares. In honor of the occasion, which had included various recreations around town, Everard had bought them both kaftans of the finest linen and most beautiful dye, fit for the kings they felt themselves to be. He didn't care about the clothing, except that it would make duly impressive his farewell at Hiram's court, but Pum was ecstatic.

The quay resounded—slap of feet, thud of hoofs, creak of wheels, rumble of rolled barrels. A cargo was in from Ophir, by way of Sinai, and stevedores were unloading its costly bales. Sweat beneath the sun made their muscled bodies shine. Sailors lounged in a nearby lean-to tavern, where a girl danced to music of flute and tabor; they drank, gambled, laughed, boasted, swapped yarns of countries beyond and beyond. A vendor sang the praises of the sweetmeats on his tray. A donkey cart passed laden. A priest of Melqart, in gorgeous robes, talked with an austere foreigner who served Osiris. A couple of red-haired Achaeans swaggered piratically by. A long-bearded warrior from Jerusalem and a bodyguard for a visiting Philistine dignitary exchanged glares, but the peace of Hiram stayed their swords. A black man in leopard skin and ostrich plumes drew a swarm of Phoenician urchins. An Assyrian walked weightily, holding his staff like a spear. An Anatolian and a blond man from the North of Europe reeled arm in arm, beerful and cheerful. . . . The air smelled of dyeworks, dung, smoke, tar, but also of sandalwood, myrrh, spice, and salt spray.

It would die at last, all of this, centuries hence, as everything must die; but first, how mightily would it have lived! How rich would be its heritage!

"Yes," Everard said, "I don't want you to get above yourself—" He chuckled. "—though are you ever below yourself? Still, Pum, you're a remarkable find. We didn't simply rescue Tyre, we won you."

A trifle more hesitant than usual, the youngster stared before him. "You explained that, lord, when teaching me. That hardly anybody in this age of the world is able to imagine travel through time and the marvels of tomorrow. It is no use to tell them, they merely get bewildered and frightened." He cradled his downy chin. "Maybe I am different because I was always on my own, never cast into a mold and let harden." Happily: "Then I praise the gods, or whatever they were, that kicked me into such a life. It prepared me for a new life with my master."

"Well, no, not really that," Everard replied. "We won't see each other often again, you and I."

"What?" exclaimed Pum, stricken. "Why? Has your servant offended you, O my lord?"

"Not in any way." Everard patted the thin shoulder beside him. "On the contrary. But mine is a roving commission. What we want you for is an agent in place, here in your home country, which you know in and out as a foreigner like me—or Chaim and Yael Zorach—never can. Don't worry. It will be a colorful task, and require as much of you as you can give."

Pum gusted a sigh. His smile flashed white. "Well, that will do, master! In truth, I was a little daunted at the thought of faring always among aliens." His tone dropped. "Will you ever come visit me?"

"Sure, once in a while. Or if you like, you can join me in assorted interesting future locales when you take your furloughs. We Patrollers work hard, and sometimes dangerously, but we have our fun."

Everard paused, then went on: "Of course, first you need training, education, every kind of knowledge and skill you lack. You'll go to the Academy, elsewhere in space and time. There

you'll spend years, and they won't be easy years —
though I believe on the whole you'll revel in them.
At last you'll return to this same year in Tyre, aye,
this same month, and take up your duties."

"I will be full-grown?"

"Right. In fact, they'll put quite a bit of height
and weight on you, as well as information into
you. You'll need a new identity, but that won't be
hard to arrange. The same name will serve; it's
common enough. You'll be Pummairam the sailor,
who shipped out years before as a youthful deckhand, won a fortune in trade goods, and is ready
to buy a ship and organize his own ventures. You
won't be especially conspicuous, that would defeat our purpose, but you'll be a prosperous and
well-regarded subject of King Hiram."

The boy clasped hands together. "Lord, your
benevolence overwhelms his servant."

"It isn't done with doing that," Everard answered. "I have discretionary authority in a case
like this, you know, and I am going to make
certain arrangements on your behalf. You can't
pass for a respectable man when you settle down
unless you get married. Very well, you'll marry
Sarai."

Pum squeaked. His gaze upon the Patrolman
was dismayed.

Everard laughed. "Oh, come!" he said. "She
may not be any beauty, but she's not hideous
either; we owe her much; and she's loyal, intelligent, versed in the ways of the palace, lots of
useful stuff. True, she'll never know who you
really are. She'll just be the wife of Captain
Pummairam and mother of his children. If any
questions arise in her mind, I think she'll be too

wise to ask them." Sternly: "You will be good to her. Do you hear?"

"Well—ah, well—" Pum's attention strayed to the dancing girl. Phoenician males lived by the double standard, and Tyre held more than its share of joyhouses. "Yes, sir."

Everard slapped the other's knee. "I read your mind, son. However, you may find you're not so interested in roaming. For a second wife, what would you say to Bronwen?"

It was a pleasure to watch Pum being flabbergasted.

Everard grew serious. "Before leaving," he explained, "I mean to give Hiram a gift, not the sort of present that's customary but something spectacular, like a gold ingot. The Patrol has unlimited wealth and a relaxed attitude toward requisitions. For the sake of his honor, Hiram can refuse me nothing in his turn. I'll ask for his slave Bronwen and her children. When they are mine, I'll formally manumit them and furnish her a dowry.

"I've sounded her out. If she can have freedom in Tyre, she doesn't really want to go back to her homeland and share a wattle-and-daub hut with ten or fifteen fellow tribesfolk. But to stay here, she must have a husband for herself, a stepfather for her kids. How about you?"

"I—would I—might she—" The blood came and went through Pum's face.

Everard nodded. "I promised I'd find her a decent man."

She was wistful. Still, practicality takes precedence over romance in this era, as it does in most.

It may be hard on him later, seeing his family

grow old while he only fakes it. But what with his missions through time, he'll have them for many decades of his life; and he's not brought up to the American kind of sensitivity, after all. It should go reasonably well. No doubt the women will become friends, and league to quietly rule Captain Pummairam's roost for him.

"Then . . . oh, my lord!" The youth leaped to his feet and pranced.

"Easy, easy." Everard grinned. "On your calendar, remember, you've years to go before you're established. Why delay? Seek the house of Zakarbaal and report to the Zorachs. They'll get you started."

For my part . . . well, it'll take me a few days yet to wind up my stay at the palace in graceful and plausible fashion. Meanwhile, Bronwen and I—Everard sighed, with a wistfulness of his own.

Pum was gone. Feet flying, kaftan flapping, the purple wharf rat sped to the destiny he would make for himself.

THE SORROW OF ODIN THE GOTH

"Then I heard a voice in the world: 'O woe
    for the broken troth,
And the heavy Need of the Niblungs, and
    the Sorrow of Odin the Goth!'"
      —William Morris, *Sigurd the Volsung*

372

Wind gusted out of twilight as the door opened.
Fires burning down the length of the hall flared
in their trenches; flames wavered and streamed
from stone lamps; smoke roiled bitter back from
the roof-holes that should have let it out. The
sudden brightness gleamed off spearheads, ax-
heads, swordguards, shield bosses, where weapons
rested near the entry. Men, crowding the great
room, grew still and watchful, as did the women

who had been bringing them horns of ale. It was
the gods carved on the pillars that seemed to move
amidst unrestful shadows, one-handed Father
Tiwaz, Donar of the Ax, the Twin Horsemen—
they, and the beasts and heroes and entwining
branches graven into the wainscot. *Whoo-oo* said
the wind, a noise as cold as itself.

Hathawulf and Solbern trod through. Their
mother Ulrica strode between them, and the look
upon her face was no less terrible than the look
on theirs. The three of them halted for a heartbeat or two, a long time for those who awaited
their word. Then Solbern shut the door while
Hathawulf stepped forward and raised his right
arm. Silence clamped down on the hall, save for
the crackling of fires and seething of breath.

Yet it was Alawin who spoke first. Rising from
his bench, his slim frame aquiver, he cried, "So
we'll take revenge!" His voice cracked; he had but
fifteen winters.

The warrior beside him hauled at his sleeve
and growled, "Sit. It is for the lord to tell us."
Alawin gulped, glared, obeyed.

A smile of sorts brought forth teeth in Hathawulf's yellow beard. He had been in the world nine
years longer than yon half-brother, four years more
than his full brother Solbern, but he seemed older,
and not only because of height, wide shoulders,
wildcat gait; leadership had been his for the last
five of those years, after his father Tharasmund's
death, and hastened the growth of his soul. There
were those who whispered that Ulrica kept too
strong a grip on him, but any who questioned his
manhood would have had to meet him in a fight
and been unlikely to walk away from it.

"Yes," he said, without loudness, nevertheless heard from end to end of the building. "Bring forth the wine, wenches; drink well, all my men, make love to your wives, break out your war-gear; friends who have come hither offering help, take my deepest thanks: for tomorrow dawn we ride to slay my sister's murderer."

"Ermanaric," uttered Solbern. He was shorter and darker than Hathawulf, more given to tending his farm and to shaping things with his hands than to war or the chase; but he spat forth the name as if it had been a foulness in his mouth.

A sigh, rather than a gasp, ran around the throng, though some of the women shrank back, or moved closer to husbands, brothers, fathers, youths whom they might have married someday. A few thanes growled, almost gladly, deep in their throats. Grimness came upon others.

Among the latter was Liuderis, who had quelled Alawin. He stood up on his bench, so as to be seen above heads. A stout, grizzled, scarred fellow, formerly Tharasmund's trustiest man, he asked heavily: "You would fare against the king, to whom you gave your oath?"

"That oath became worthless when he had Swanhild trodden beneath the hoofs of horses," answered Hathawulf.

"Yet he says Randwar plotted his death."

"He says!" Ulrica shouted. She stalked forth until what light there was flickered more fully across her: a big woman, her coiled braids half gray and half still ruddy around a face whose lines had frozen into the sternness of Weard herself. Costly furs trimmed Ulrica's cloak; the gown beneath was of Eastland silk; amber from the Northlands glowed around her neck: for she was the daughter of a king, who had married into the god-descended house of Tharasmund.

She halted, fists clenched, and flung at Liuderis and the rest: "Well might Randwar the Red have sought to overthrow Ermanaric. Too long have the Goths suffered from that hound. Yes, I call him hound, Ermanaric, unfit to live. Tell me not how he made us mighty and his sway reaches from the Baltic Sea to the Black. It is *his* sway, not ours, and it will not outlast him. Tell yourselves, rather, of scot well-nigh ruinous to pay, of wives and maidens dishonored, of lands unrightfully seized and folk driven from their homes, of men hewn down or burned in their surrounded dwellings merely because they dared speak against his deeds. Remember how he slew his nephews and their families when he did not get their treasure. Think how he had Randwar hanged, on nothing more than the word of Sibicho Mannfrithsson—Sibicho, that viper forever hissing in the king's ear. And ask yourselves this. Even if Randwar had indeed become Ermanaric's foe, betrayed before he could strike to avenge outrage upon his kin—even if this be so, why should Swanhild die too? She was only his wife." Ulrica drew breath. "She was also the daughter of Tharasmund and myself, the sister of your chief Hathawulf and of Solbern his brother. They, who sprang from Wodan, shall send Ermanaric below to be her slave."

"You talked to your sons alone for half a day, my lady," said Liuderis. "How much of this is your will, not theirs?"

Hathawulf brought hand to sword. "You over-speak yourself," he snapped.

"I meant no ill—" the warrior began.

"The earth is tearful with the blood of Swanhild the fair," said Ulrica. "Will it bear for us ever again, if we do not wash it with the blood of her murderer?"

Solbern stayed more calm: "You Teurings know well how trouble has been waxing for years between the king and our tribe. Why else did you rally to us when you heard what happened? Do you not all think that belike this deed of his was done to test our mettle? If we sit quietly at our hearths—if Heorot takes whatever weregild he might deign to offer—he will know he is free to crush us altogether."

Liuderis nodded, folded arms across breast, and answered steadily, "Well, you shall not fare to battle without my sons and me, while this old head remains above ground. I did but wonder if you and Hathawulf are being rash. Ermanaric is strong indeed. Would it not be better if we bide our time, make quite ready, gather men of neighbor tribes, before we strike?"

Hathawulf smiled afresh, a little more warmly than erstwhile. "We thought about that," he said in a level tone. "If we give ourselves time, we give the king time, too. Nor do I believe we can raise very many spears against him. Not while the Huns prowl the marches, vassal folk are sullen about paying tribute, and the Romans might see, in a war of Goth upon Goth, a chance to enter and lay all beneath them. Besides, Ermanaric will not sit idle long before he moves to humble the Teurings. No, we must attack now, before he awaits us—catch him unawares, overwhelm his

guardsmen—they do not much outnumber you
who are here—slay Ermanaric in one quick, clean
blow, and afterward call a folkmoot to pick a new
king who shall be righteous."

Liuderis nodded again. "I have spoken my mind,
you have spoken yours. Now let us have an end of
speaking. Tomorrow we ride." He sat down.

"It is a risk," Ulrica said. "These are my last
living sons, and maybe they fare to their deaths.
That is as Weard wills, who sets the doom of
gods and men alike. But rather would I have my
sons die boldly than kneel to their sister's murderer.
No luck would come of that."

Young Alawin leaped anew to his feet on the
bench. His knife flashed forth. "We won't die!" he
shouted. "Ermanaric will, and Hathawulf will be
king of the Ostrogoths!"

A slow roar, like an incoming tide, lifted from
the men.

Solbern the sober walked down the hall. The
crowd made way for him. Strewn rushes rustled
and the clay floor thudded beneath his boots.
"Did I hear you say 'we'?" he asked through the
rumbling. "No, you're a boy. You stay home."

The downy cheeks reddened. "I am man enough
to fight for my house!" Alawin shrilled.

Ulrica stiffened where she stood. Cruelty lashed
from her: " 'Your' house, by-blow?"

The growing din died away. Men traded uneasy
stares. It did not bode well, such an unleashing
of olden hatred at such an hour as this. Alawin's
mother Erelieva had not merely been a leman of
Tharasmund's, she had become the one woman
for whom he really cared, and Ulrica had gloated
almost openly when every child that Erelieva

bore him, save for this firstborn, died small. After
the chieftain himself went down hell-road, friends
of hers had gotten her hastily married off to a
yeoman who lived far from the hall. Alawin stayed,
the seemly thing for a lord's son to do, but Ulrica
was always stinging him.

Eyes clashed through smoke and shadow-
haunted firelight. "Yes, my house," Alawin called,
"and Swanhild m-m-my sister too." His stammer
made him bite his lip for shame.

"Easy, easy." Hathawulf raised his arm again.
"You have the right, lad, and do well to claim it.
Yes, ride with us, come dawn." His glance defied
Ulrica. She twisted her mouth but said naught.
Everybody guessed she was hoping the stripling
would be killed.

Hathawulf strode toward the high seat at the
middle of the hall. His words rang: "No more
bickering! We'll be merry this eventide. But first,
Anslaug—" this to his wife—"come sit beside
me, and together we'll drink the beaker of Wodan."

Feet stamped, fists pounded wood, knives lifted
like torches. The women themselves began to yell
with the men: "Hail, hail, hail!"

The door flew open.

Dusk had deepened fast, when autumn was on
hand, so that the newcomer stood in the middle
of blackness. Wind flapped the edges of his blue
cloak, flung a few dead leaves in past him, whistled and chilled along the room. Folk turned to
see who had come, drew a sharp breath, and
those who had been seated now scrambled to
stand. It was the Wanderer.

Tallest he stood among them, holding his spear
more like a staff than a weapon, as if he had no

need of iron. A broad-brimmed hat shaded his
face, but not the wolf-gray hair and beard, nor
the gleam of his gaze. Few of them here had ever
seen him before, most had never happened to be
nigh when he made his seldom showings; but
none failed to know the forefather of the Teuring
headmen.

Ulrica was first to muster hardihood. "Greeting,
Wanderer, and welcome," she said. "You honor
our roof. Come, take the high seat, and I will
bring you a horn of wine."

"No, a goblet, a Roman goblet, the best we
have," said Solbern.

Hathawulf came back to the door, squared his
shoulders, and stood before the Elder. "You know
what is afoot," he said. "What word have you for
us?"

"This," answered the Wanderer. His voice was
deep, and did not sound like the southern Goths',
or like any's whom they had met. Men supposed
his mother tongue was the tongue of the gods.
Tonight it fell heavily, as if grief weighted it. "You
are bound upon vengeance, Hathawulf and Solbern, and that stands not to be altered; it is the
will of Weard. But Alawin shall not go with you."

The youth shrank back, whitening. A near sob
broke harsh from his throat.

The Wanderer's look ranged down the hall to
lay hold upon him. "This is needful," he went on,
word by slow word. "I lay no slur on you when I
say that you are only half-grown, and would die
bravely but uselessly. All who are men have first
been boys. No, I tell you instead that yours shall
be another task, more hard and strange than
vengeance, for the welfare of that kindred which

sprang from your father's father's mother Jorith—"
did his tone waver the least bit?—"and myself.
Abide, Alawin. Your time will come soon enough."

"It . . . shall be done . . . as you will, lord," said
Hathawulf out of a stiffened gullet. "But what
does this mean . . . for those of us who ride forth?"

The Wanderer regarded for him for a while
that grew very still before answering: "You do not
wish to know. Be the word good or ill, you do not
wish to know."

Alawin sank to his bench, laid head in hands,
and shuddered.

"Farewell," said the Wanderer. His cloak swirled,
his spear swung about, the door shut, he was
gone.

1935

I didn't change clothes till my vehicle had brought
me across space-time. Then, in a Patrol base
which masqueraded as a warehouse, I shed the
garb of the Dnieper basin, late fourth century,
and donned that of the United States, middle
twentieth century.

The basic patterns, shirts and trousers for men,
gowns for women, were the same. Differences of
detail were countless. Despite its coarse fabrics,
the Gothic outfit was more comfortable than a tie
and jacket. I stowed it in the baggage box of my
hopper, along with such special items as the little
gadget I'd used to listen in, from outside, on the
proceedings in the hall of the Teuring sachem.
Since my spear wouldn't fit, I left it strapped to

the side of the machine. I wouldn't be going anyplace on that except back to the milieu where such weapons belonged.

The officer on duty today was in his early twenties—young by current standards; in most eras he'd long since have been an established family man—and somewhat in awe of me. True, my status as a member of the Time Patrol was almost as much a technicality as his. I had no part in policing the spatiotemporal lanes, rescuing travelers in distress, or anything glamorous like that. I was merely a scientist of sorts; "scholar" was probably more accurate. However, I did make trips on my own, which he was not qualified to do.

He peered at me as I emerged from the hangar to the nondescript office, allegedly of a construction company, which was our front in this town during these years. "Welcome home, Mr. Farness," he said. "Uh, you had a pretty rough go-around, didn't you?"

"What makes you think so?" I replied automatically.

"Your expression, sir. The way you walk."

"I was in no danger," I rapped. Not caring to talk about it, except to Laurie and maybe not her either for a while, I brushed past him and stepped out onto the street.

Here also it was fall, the kind of crisp and brilliant day New York often enjoyed until it became uninhabitable; this year chanced to be the one before I was born. Masonry and glass gleamed higher than high, up into a blueness where a few bits of cloud scudded along on the breeze that gave me its cool kiss. Cars were not so many that they put more than a tang into it, less than the aroma of the roast chestnut carts that were beginning to come out of estivation. I went over to Fifth Avenue and walked uptown past glamorous shops, among some of the most beautiful women in the world, as well as people from all the rich diversity of our planet.

My hope was that by going afoot to my place, I'd work out part of the tension and misery in me. The city could not only stimulate, it could heal, right? This was where Laurie and I had chosen to dwell, we who could have settled practically anywhere in the past or the future.

No, of course that isn't quite correct. Like most couples, we wanted a nest in reasonably familiar surroundings, where we didn't have to learn everything from scratch and stay always on guard. The '30's were a marvelous milieu if you were a white American, in good health and with money. What amenities were lacking, such as air conditioning, could be unobtrusively installed, not to be used when you had visitors who would never know that time travelers exist. Granted, the Roosevelt gang was in charge, but the conversion of the Republic to the Corporate State was not very far along as yet and didn't affect Laurie's and my private lives; the outright disintegration of this society wouldn't become a fast and obvious process till (my opinion) after the 1964 election.

In the Middle West, where my mother was now carrying me, we'd have had to be annoyingly circumspect. But most New Yorkers were tolerant, or at least incurious. A beard down to my chest, and shoulder-length hair which I'd pulled into a queue while at the base, didn't draw many stares,

nor more than a few cries of "Beaver!" from little
boys. To our landlord, our neighbors, and other
contemporaries, we were a retired professor of
Germanic philology and his wife, our oddities to
be expected. It was no lie, either, as far as it went.

Therefore my walk should have eased me somewhat, restored that perspective which Patrol agents
must have, lest certain of the things they witness
drive them mad. We must understand that what
Pascal said is true of every human being in the
whole of space-time, ourselves included: "The
last act is tragic, however pleasant all the comedy
of the other acts. A little earth on our heads, and
all is done with forever."—understand it in our
bones, so that we can live with it calmly if not
serenely. Why, those Goths of mine were getting
off lightly compared to, say, millions of European
Jews and Gypsies, less than ten years futureward,
or millions of Russians at this very moment.

It was no good. They *were* my Goths. Their
ghosts crowded around me till street, buildings,
flesh and blood became the unreal, the half-
remembered dream.

Blindly, I hastened my steps, toward whatever
sanctuary Laurie could give.

We occupied a huge flat overlooking Central
Park, where we liked to stroll on mild nights. The
doorman at the apartment need not double as an
armed guard. I hurt him today by the curtness
with which I returned his greeting, and realized it
when in the elevator, but then my regret was too
late. To jump back through time and change the
incident would have violated the Prime Directive
of the Patrol. Not that something that trivial
would have threatened the continuum; it's flex-

ible within limits, and the effects of alterations usually damp out fast. Indeed, there's an interesting metaphysical question about the extent to which time travelers discover the past, versus the extent to which they create it. Schrödinger's cat lurks in history as well as in its box. Yet the Patrol exists in order to assure that temporal traffic does not abort that scheme of events which will at last bring forth the Danellian superhumans who founded the Patrol when, in their own remote past, ordinary men learned how to travel temporally.

My thoughts had fled into this familiar territory while I stood caged in the elevator. It made the ghosts more distant, less clamorous. Nevertheless, when I let myself into our home, they followed.

A smell of turpentine drifted amidst the books which lined the living room. Laurie was winning somewhat of a name as a painter, here in the 1930's when she was no longer the preoccupied faculty wife she had been later in our century. Offered a job in the Patrol, she had declined; she lacked the physical strength that a field agent — male or, especially, female — was bound to need upon occasion, while routine clerical or reference work didn't interest her. To be sure, we'd shared vacations in mighty exotic milieus.

She heard me enter and ran from her studio to meet me. The sight lifted my spirits a tiny bit. In spattered smock, red hair tucked under a kerchief, she was still slender, supple, and handsome. The lines around her green eyes were too fine to notice until she got near enough to embrace me.

Our local acquaintances tended to envy me a

wife who, besides being delightful, was far younger than myself. In fact, the difference in birthdates is a mere six years. I was in my mid-forties, and prematurely gray, when the Patrol recruited me, whereas she had kept most of her youthful looks. The antithanatic treatment that our organization provides will arrest the aging process but not reverse its effects.

Besides, she spent most of her life in ordinary time, sixty seconds to the minute. As a field agent, I'd go through days, weeks, or months between saying goodbye to her in the morning and returning for dinner—an interlude during which she could pursue her career without me underfoot. My cumulative age was approaching a hundred years.

Sometimes it felt like a thousand. That showed.

"Hi, there, Carl, darling!" Her lips pulsed against mine. I drew her close. If a dab of paint got onto my suit, what the hell? Then she stepped back, took both my hands, and sent her gaze across me and into me.

Her voice dropped low: "It's hurt you, this trip."

"I knew it would," I answered out of my weariness.

"But you didn't know how much. . . . Were you gone long?"

"No. Tell you about it in a while, the details. I was lucky, though. Hit a key point, did what I needed to do, and got out again. A few hours of observation from concealment, a few minutes of action, and *fini*."

"I suppose you might call it luck. Must you return soon?"

"In that era, yes, quite soon. But I want a while here to—to rest, get over what I saw was about to happen. . . . Can you stand me around, brooding at you, for a week or two?"

"Sweetheart." She came back to me.

"I have to work up my notes anyway," I said into her ear, "but evenings we can go out to dinner, the theater, have fun together."

"Oh, I hope you'll be able to have fun. Don't pretend for my sake."

"Later, things will be easier," I assured us. "I'll simply be carrying out my original mission, recording the stories and songs they'll make about this. It's just . . . I've got to get through the reality first."

"Must you?"

"Yes. Not for scholarly purposes, no, I guess not. But those are my people. They are."

She hugged me tighter. She knew.

What she did not know, I thought in an uprush of pain—what I hoped to God she did not know—was why I cared so greatly about yonder descendants of mine. Laurie wasn't jealous. She'd never begrudged the while that Jorith and I had had. Laughing, she'd said it deprived her of nothing, while it gave me a position in the community I was studying which might well be unique in the annals of my profession. Afterward she'd done her best to console me.

What I could not bring myself to tell her was that Jorith was not simply a close friend who happened to be a woman. I could not say to her that I had loved one who lay dust these sixteen hundred years as much as I loved her, and still did, and maybe always would.

300

The home of Winnithar the Wisentslayer stood on
a bluff above the River Vistula. It was a thorp,
half a dozen houses clustered around a hall, with
barns, sheds, cookhouse, smithy, brewery, and
other workplaces nearby: for his family had long
dwelt here, and waxed great among the Teurings.
Westward reached meadows and croplands. Eastward, across the water, wilderness remained,
though settlement was encroaching heavily upon
it as the tribe grew in numbers.

They might have logged off the woods altogether,
save that more and more of them were moving
away. This was a time of unrest. Not only were
plundering warbands on the trail; whole folk
were pulling up stakes, and clashing when they
met. Word drifted from afar that the Romans were
often at each other's throats too, while the mighti-
ness which their forefathers had built crumbled.
As yet, few Northerners had done anything bolder
than to raid along the Imperial borders. But the
southlands just outside those borders, warm, rich,
scantily defended by their dwellers, beckoned many
a Goth to come carve out a new home for himself.

Winnithar stayed where he was. However, that
forced him to pass almost as much of each year
in fighting—especially against Vandals, though
sometimes against Gothic tribes, Greutungs or
Taifals—as he passed in farming. As his sons
neared manhood, they began to yearn elsewhere.

Thus matters stood when Carl arrived.

He came in winter, when hardly anybody traveled. On that account, men made strangers doubly
welcome, who broke the sameness of their lives.

At first, spying him at a mile's reach, they took him for a mere gangrel, since he fared alone and afoot. Nonetheless they knew their chief would want to see him.

He drew nigh, striding easily over the frozen ruts of the road, making a staff of his spear. His blue cloak was the only color in that landscape of snow-decked fields, stark trees, dull sky. Hounds bayed and growled at him; he showed no fear, and afterward the men came to understand that he could have stricken those dead that attacked him. Today they called the beasts to heel and met the newcomer with sudden respect—for it became plain that his garments were of the finest, and not the least way-stained, while he himself was awesome. Taller than the tallest here he loomed, lean but sinewy, a graybeard as lithe as a youth. What had those pale eyes of his beheld?

A warrior went ahead to greet him. "I hight Carl," he said when asked: nothing further. "Fain would I guest you a while." The Gothic words came readily from him, but their sound, and sometimes their order or endings, were not of any dialect known to the Teurings.

Winnithar had stayed in his hall. It would have been unseemly for him to gape like an underling. When Carl entered, Winnithar said from his high seat, "Be welcome if you come in peace and honesty. May Father Tiwaz ward you and Mother Frija bless you."—as was the ancient custom of his house.

"My thanks," Carl answered. "That was kindly spoken to a fellow you may well think is a beggar. I am not, and hope this gift will be found worthy." He reached in the pouch at his belt and drew

forth an arm-ring which he handed over to Winnithar. Gasps arose from those who had jostled
close to watch, for the ring was heavy, of pure
gold, cunningly wrought and set with gems.

The host kept his calmness, barely. "That is a
gift a king might have given. Share my seat,
Carl." It was the place of honor. "Abide for as
long as you wish." He clapped his hands. "Ho,"
he shouted, "bring mead for our guest, and for
me that I may drink his health!" To the swains,
wenches, and children milling about: "Back to
your work, you. We can all hear whatever he
chooses to tell us after the evening meal. Now
he's doubtless weary."

Grumblingly, they heeded. "Why say you that?"
Carl asked him.

"The nearest dwelling where you might have
spent last night is a goodly walk from this,"
Winnithar replied.

"I was at none," Carl said.

"What?"

"You would be bound to find that out. I would
not have you believe I lied to you."

"But—" Winnithar peered at him, tugged his
mustache, and said slowly: "You are not of these
parts; aye, you must have fared far. Yet your garb
is clean, though you carry no change of clothes,
nor food or aught else that a traveler should. Who
are you, whence have you come, and . . . how?"

Carl's tone was mild, but those who listened
heard what steel underlay it. "There are things I
may not talk about. I do give you my oath—may
Donar's lightning smite me if it is false—that I am
no outlaw, nor foe to your kindred, nor a sort whom
it would shame you to have beneath your roof."

"If honor demands that you keep certain secrets, none shall pry," said Winnithar. "But you understand that we cannot help wondering—" Clear to see was the relief with which he broke off and exclaimed: "Ah, here comes the mead. That's my wife Salvalindis who bears your horn to you, as befits a guest of rank."

Carl hailed her courteously, though his gaze kept straying to the maiden at her side, who brought Winnithar his draught. She was sweetly formed and moved like a deer; unbound hair streamed golden past a face with fine bones, shyly smiling lips, eyes big and the hue of summer heaven.

Salvalindis noticed. "You meet our oldest child," she told Carl, "our daughter Jorith."

1980

After basic training at the Patrol Academy, I returned to Laurie on the same day as I'd left her. I'd need a spell to rest and readapt; it was rather a shock transferring from the Oligocene period to a Pennsylvania college town. We must also set our mundane affairs in order. For my part, I should finish out the academic year before resigning "to take a better-paying job abroad." Laurie saw to the sale of our house and the disposal of goods we didn't want to keep—wherever and whenever else we were going to establish residence.

It wrenched us, bidding goodbye to the friends of years. We promised to make occasional visits, but knew that those would be few and far between, until they ceased entirely. The required lies were too great a strain. As was, we left an impression that my vaguely described new position was a cover for a post in the CIA.

Well, I had been warned at the beginning that a Time Patrol agent's life becomes a series of farewells. I had yet to learn what that really meant.

We were still in the course of uprooting ourselves when I got a phone call. "Professor Farness? This is Manse Everard, Unattached operative. I wonder if we could meet for a talk, like maybe this weekend."

My heart bounded. Unattached is about as high as you can get in the organization; throughout the million or more years that it guards, such personnel are rare. Normally a member, even if a police officer, works within a single milieu, so that he or she can get to know it inside out, and as part of a closely coordinated team. The Unattached may go anyplace they choose and do virtually anything they see fit, responsible only to their consciences, their peers, and the Danellians.

"Uh, sure, certainly, sir," I blurted. "Saturday would be fine. Do you want to come here? I guarantee you a good dinner."

"Thanks, but I'd prefer it was my digs—the first time, anyway. Got my files and computer terminal and things like that handy. Just the two of us, please. Don't worry about airline schedules. Find a spot, as it might be your basement, where nobody will see. You've been issued a locator, haven't you? . . . Okay, read off the coordinates and call me back. I'll pick you up on my hopper."

I found out later that that was characteristic of him. Large, tough-looking, wielding more power than Caesar or Genghis ever dreamed of, he was as comfortable as an old shoe.

Me on the saddle behind his, we skipped through space, rather than time, to the current Patrol base in New York City. From there we walked to the apartment he maintained. He didn't like dirt, disorder, and danger any better than I did. However, he felt he needed a *pied-à-terre* in the twentieth century, and had grown used to these lodgings before decay had advanced overly far.

"I was born in your state in 1924," he explained. "Entered the Patrol at age thirty. That's why I decided I should be the guy who interviewed you. We have pretty much the same background; we ought to understand each other."

I took a steadying gulp of the whisky and soda he'd poured for us and said cautiously, "I'm not too sure, sir. Heard something about you at the school. Seems you led quite an adventurous life even before you joined. And afterward—Me, I've been a quiet, stick-in-the-mud type."

"Not really." Everard glanced at a sheet of notes he held. His left hand curled around a battered briar pipe. Once in a while he'd take a puff or a sip. "Let's refresh my memory, shall we? You didn't see combat during your Army hitch, but that was because you served your two years in what we laughingly call peacetime. You did, though, make top scores on the target range. You've always been an outdoorsman, mountaineering, skiing, sailing, swimming. In college, you played football and won your letter in spite of that lanky build. In grad school your hobbies included fenc-

ing and archery. You've traveled a fair amount,
not always to the safe and standard places. Yes,
I'd call you adventurous enough for our purposes.
Possibly a tad too adventurous. That's one thing
I'm trying to sound you out about."

Feeling awkward, I glanced again around the
room. On a high floor, it was an oasis of quiet
and cleanliness. Bookshelves lined the walls, save
for three excellent pictures and a pair of Bronze
Age spears. Else the only obvious souvenir was a
polar bear rug that he had remarked was from
tenth-century Greenland.

"You've been married twenty-three years, to the
same lady," Everard remarked. "These days, that
indicates a stable character."

There was no sign of femininity here. To be
sure, he might well keep a wife, or wives, elsewhen.

"No children," Everard went on. "Hm, none of
my business, but you do know, don't you, that if
you want, our medics can repair every cause of
infertility this side of menopause? They can compensate for a late start on pregnancies, too."

"Thanks," I said. "Fallopian tubes—Yes, Laurie
and I have discussed it. We may well take advantage someday. But we don't think we'd be wise to
begin parenthood and my new career simultane-
ously." I formed a chuckle. "If simultaneity means
anything to a Patroller."

"A responsible attitude. I like that." Everard
nodded.

"Why this review, sir?" I ventured. "I wasn't
invited to enlist merely on the strength of Herbert
Ganz's recommendation. Your people put me
through a whole battery of far-future psych tests
before they told me what it meant."

They'd called it a set of scientific experiments. I'd cooperated because Ganz had asked me to, as a favor to a friend of his. It wasn't his field; he was in Germanic languages and literature, the same as me. We'd met at a professional gathering, become drinking buddies, and corresponded quite a bit. He'd admired my papers on *Deor* and *Widsith*, I'd admired his on the Gothic Bible.

Naturally, I did not know then that it was his. It was published in Berlin in 1853. Later he was recruited into the Patrol, and eventually he came uptime under an alias, in search of fresh talent for his undertaking.

Everard leaned back. Across the pipe, his gaze probed at me. "Well," he said, "the machines told us you and your wife are trustworthy, and would both be delighted by the truth. What they could not measure was how competent you'd be in the job for which you were proposed. Excuse me, no insult intended. Nobody is good at everything, and these missions will be tough, lonesome, delicate." He paused. "Yes, delicate. The Goths may be barbarians, but that doesn't mean they are stupid, or that they can't be hurt as badly as you or me."

"I understand," I said. "But look, all you need do is read the reports I'll have filed in my own personal future. If the early accounts show me bungling, why, just tell me to stay home and become a book researcher. The outfit needs those too, doesn't it?"

Everard sighed. "I have inquired, and been told you performed — will perform — will have performed — satisfactorily. That isn't enough. You don't realize, because you haven't experienced it, how overburdened the Patrol is, how ghastly thin we're spread across history. We can't examine every detail of what a field agent does. That's especially true when he or she isn't a cop like me, but a scientist like you, exploring a milieu poorly chronicled or not chronicled at all." He treated himself to a swallow of his drink. "That's why the Patrol does have a scientific branch. So it can get a slightly better idea of what the hell the events *are* that it is supposed to keep careless time travelers from changing."

"Would it make a significant difference, in a situation as obscure as that?"

"It might. In due course, the Goths play an important role, don't they? Who knows what a happening early on—a victory or a defeat, a rescue or a death, a certain individual getting born or not getting born—who knows what effect that could have, as its results propagate through the generations?"

"But I'm not even concerned with real events, except indirectly," I argued. "My objective is to help recover various lost stories and poems, and unravel how they evolved and how they influenced later works."

Everard grinned ruefully. "Yeah, I know. Ganz's big deal. The Patrol has bought it because it is an opening wedge, the single such wedge we've found, to getting the history of that milieu recorded."

He knocked back his drink and rose. "How about another?" he proposed. "And then we'll have lunch. Meanwhile, I wish you'd tell me exactly what your project is."

"Why, you must have talked to Herbert—to Professor Ganz," I said, astonished. "Uh, thanks,

I would like a refill."

"Sure," Everard said, pouring. "Retrieve Germanic literature of the Dark Ages. If 'literature' is the right word for stuff that was originally word of mouth, in illiterate societies. Mere chunks of it have survived on paper, and scholars don't agree on how badly garbled those copies are. Ganz's working on the, um-m, the Nibelung epic. What I'm vague about is where you fit in. That's a story from the Rhineland. You want to go gallivanting solo away off in eastern Europe, in the fourth century."

His manner did more than his whisky to put me at ease. "I hope to track down the Ermanaric part," I told him. "It isn't properly integral, but a connection did develop, and besides, it's interesting in its own right."

"Ermanaric? Who dat?" Everard gave me my glass and settled himself to listen.

"Maybe I better backtrack a little," I said. "How familiar are you with the Nibelung-Volsung cycle?"

"Well, I've seen Wagner's *Ring* operas. And when I had a mission once in Scandinavia, toward the close of the Viking period, I heard a yarn about Sigurd, who killed the dragon and woke the Valkyrie and afterward mucked everything up."

"That's a fraction of the whole story, sir."

" 'Manse' will do, Carl."

"Oh, uh, thanks. I feel honored." Not to grow fulsome, I hurried on in my best classroom style: "The Icelandic *Volsungasaga* was written down later than the German *Nibelungenlied*, but contains an older, more primitive, and lengthier version of the story. The *Elder* and the *Younger*

Edda have some of it too. Those are the sources that Wagner mainly borrowed from.

"You may recall that Sigurd the Volsung got tricked into marrying Gudrun the Gjuking instead of Brynhild the Valkyrie, and this led to jealousy between the women and at last to his getting killed. In German, those persons are called Siegfried, Kriemhild of Burgundy, Brunhild of Isenstein; and the pagan gods don't appear; but no matter now. According to both stories, Gudrun, or Kriemhild, later married a king called Atli, or Etzel, who is none other than Attila the Hun.

"Then the versions really diverge. In the *Nibelungenlied*, Kriemhild lures her brothers to Etzel's court and has them set on and destroyed, as her revenge for their murder of Siegfried. Theodoric the Great, the Ostrogoth who took over Italy, gets into that episode under the name of Dietrich of Bern, though in historical fact he flourished a generation later than Attila. A follower of his, Hildebrand, is so horrified at Kriemhild's treachery and cruelty that he slays her. Hildebrand, by the way, has a legend of his own, in a ballad whose entirety Herb Ganz wants to find, as well as in derivative works. You see what a cat's cradle of anachronisms this is."

"Attila the Hun, eh?" Everard murmured. "Not a very nice man. But he operated in the middle fifth century, when those bully boys were already riding high in Europe. You're going to the fourth."

"Correct. Let me give you the Icelandic tale. Atli enticed Gudrun's brothers to him because he wanted the Rhinegold. She tried to warn them, but they came anyway under pledge of safe conduct. When they wouldn't surrender the hoard or tell Atli where it was, he had them put to death. Gudrun got even for that. She butchered the sons she'd borne him and served them to him as ordinary food. Later she stabbed him as he slept, set his hall afire, and left Hunland. With her she took Svanhild, her daughter by Sigurd."

Everard frowned, concentrating. It couldn't be easy to keep track of these characters.

"Gudrun came to the country of the Goths," I said. "There she married again and had two sons, Hamther and Sorli. The king of the Goths is called Jormunrek in the saga and in the Eddic poems, but there is no doubt that he was Ermanaric, who is a real if shadowy figure around the middle and late fourth century. Accounts differ whether he married Svanhild and she was falsely accused of infidelity, or she married somebody else whom the king caught plotting against him and hanged. In either case, he had poor Svanhild trampled to death by horses.

"By this time, Gudrun's boys, Hamther and Sorli, were young men. She egged them on to kill Jormunrek in vengeance for Svanhild. Along the way they met their half-brother Erp, who offered to accompany them. They cut him down. The manuscripts are vague as to the reason why. My guess is he was their father's child by a concubine and there was bad blood between them and him.

"They proceeded to Jormunrek's headquarters and the attack. They were two alone, but invulnerable to steel, so they slew men right and left, reached the king, and wounded him severely. Before they could finish the job, though, Hamther let slip that stones could hurt them. Or, according to the saga, Odin suddenly appeared, in the guise of an old man with one eye, and betrayed this information. Jormunrek called to his remaining warriors to stone the brothers, and that is how they died. There the tale ends."

"Grim, hey?" said Everard. He pondered for a minute. "But it seems to me that whole last episode— Gudrun in Gothland—must've been tacked on at a much later date. The anachronisms have gotten completely out of hand."

"Of course," I agreed. "That very commonly happens in folklore. An important story will attract lesser ones to it. Even in trifling ways. For instance, it wasn't W. C. Fields who said that a man who hates children and dogs can't be all bad. It was somebody else, I forget who, introducing Fields at a banquet."

Everard laughed. "Don't tell me the Patrol should monitor Hollywood history!" He grew serious again. "If that sanguinary little yarn doesn't really belong in the Nibelung canon, why do you want to trace it? Why does Ganz want you to?"

"Well, it did reach Scandinavia, where it did inspire a couple of pretty good poems—if those weren't just redactions of something earlier—and did hook up to the Volsung saga. The connections, the whole evolution, interest us. Also, Ermanaric gets mention elsewhere—in certain Old English lays, for instance. So he must have figured in a lot of legend and bardic work that was since forgotten. He *was* powerful in his day, though apparently not a very nice man himself. The lost Ermanaric cycle might well be as important and brilliant as anything that has come down to us from the West and the North. It may have influenced Germanic literature in scores of unsuspected ways."

"Do you intend to go straight to his court? I wouldn't recommend that, Carl. Too many field agents get killed because they got careless."

"Oh, no. Something horrible happened, from which stories sprang and traveled far, even reaching into historical chronicles. I think I can bracket when it happened, too, within about ten years. But I mean to familiarize myself thoroughly with the whole milieu before I venture into that episode."

"Good. What is your plan?"

"I'll take an electronic cram in the Gothic language. I can read it already, but want to speak it fluently, though doubtless my accent will be odd. I'll also want a cram on what little is known about customs, beliefs, *et cetera*. That'll be very little. The Ostrogoths, if not the Visigoths, were still on the bare fringes of Roman awareness. Surely they changed considerably before they moved west.

"So I'll begin well downtime of my target dates; somewhat arbitrarily, I'm thinking of 300 AD. I'll get acquainted with people. Next I'll reappear at intervals and learn what's been going on in my absence. In short, I'll keep track of events as they march toward *the* event. When it finally comes, I shouldn't be caught by surprise. Afterward I'll drop in here and there, from time to time, and listen to the poets and storytellers, and get their words on a concealed recorder."

Everard scowled. "Um-m, that kind of procedure — Well, we can discuss the possible complications. You'll move around a fair amount geographically too, won't you?"

"Yes. According to what traditions of theirs got

written down in the Roman Empire, the Goths originated in what's now central Sweden. I don't believe that numerous a breed could have come from that limited an area, even allowing for natural increase, but it may have furnished leaders and organization, the way the Scandinavians did for the nascent Russian state in the ninth century.

"I'd say the bulk of the Goths started as dwellers along the southern Baltic littoral. They were the easternmost of the Germanic peoples. Not that they were ever a single nation. By the time they reached western Europe, they were separated into the Ostrogoths, who took over Italy, and the Visigoths, who took over Iberia. Gave those regions fairly good government, by the way, the best government they'd had for a long while. Eventually the invaders were overrun in their turn, and vanished into the general populations."

"But earlier?"

"Historians make unclear mention of tribes. By 300 AD, Goths were firmly established along the Vistula, in the middle of what's currently Poland. Before the end of that century, the Ostrogoths were in the Ukraine and the Visigoths just north of the Danube, the Roman frontier. A great folk migration, apparently, over the course of generations, because they seem at last to have abandoned the North entirely; there, Slavic tribes moved in. Ermanaric was an Ostrogoth, so that's the branch I mean to follow."

"Ambitious," Everard said doubtfully. "And you a new chum."

"I'll gain experience as I go along, uh, Manse. You admitted yourself, the Patrol is shorthanded. Moreover, I'll be acquiring a lot of that history which you want."

He smiled. "You should, at that." Rising: "Come on, finish your drink and let's go eat. We'll need a change of clothes, but it'll be worth the trouble. I know a local saloon, back in the 1890's, that sets out a magnificent free lunch."

300–302

Winter descended and then slowly, in surges of wind, snow, icy rain, drew back. For those who dwelt in the thorp by the river, and soon for their neighbors, the dreariness of the season was lightened that year. Carl abode among them.

At first the mystery surrounding him roused fear in many; but they came to see that he bore neither ill will nor bad luck. The awe of him did not dwindle. Rather, it grew. From the beginning, Winnithar said that for such a guest to sleep on a bench, like a common thane, was unfitting, and turned a shut-bed over to him. He offered Carl the pick of the thrall women to warm it, but the stranger made refusal, in mannerly wise. He did accept food and drink, and he did bathe and seek the outhouse. However, the whisper went about that maybe these things were not needful for him, save as a show of being mortal.

Carl was soft-spoken and friendly, in a somewhat lofty way. He could laugh, crack a joke, tell a funny tale. He went forth afoot or ahorse, in company, to hunt or call on the nearer yeomen or join in offerings to the Anses and in the feasting that followed. He took part in contests such as shooting or wrestling, until it had become clear that no man could best him. When he played at knucklebones or board games, he did not always win, though the idea arose that this was because he chose not to make folk afraid of witchcraft. He would talk to anybody, from Winnithar to the lowliest thrall or littlest toddler, and listen with care; indeed, he drew them out, and was kindly toward underlings and animals.

But as for his own inward self, that remained hidden.

This did not mean that he sat sullen. No, he made words and music come forth asparkle as none had ever done before. Eager to hear songs, lays, stories, saws, everything that went about, he gave overflowing measure in return. For he seemed to know all the world, as if he had wandered it himself for longer than a lifetime.

He told of Rome, the mighty and troubled, of its lord Diocletian, his wars and his stern laws. He answered questions about the new god, him of the Cross, of whom the Goths had heard a bit from traders or from slaves sold this far north. He told of the Romans' great foes, the Persians, and what wonders they had wrought. Onward his words ranged, evening after evening—on southward to lands where it was always hot, and people had black skins, and beasts prowled that were akin to lynxes but the size of bears. Other beasts did he show them, drawing pictures in charcoal on slabs of wood, and they cried aloud in their astonishment; set beside an elephant, an aurochs or even a troll-steed was nothing! Near the ends of the East, he said, lay a realm larger, older, more marvelous than Rome or Persia. Its dwellers were of a hue like wan amber, and had eyes that appeared to be aslant. Plagued by wild tribes north of them, they had built a wall as long as a mountain range, and had since then been striking back out of that redoubt. This was why the Huns had come west. They, who had broken the Alans and were vexing the Goths, were only a rabble in the slanting gaze of Khitai. And all this vastness was not all there was. If you traveled westward till you had crossed the Roman holding called Gaul, you would come to the World Sea of which you had heard fables, and if there you took ship— but craft such as plied the rivers were not big enough—and sailed on and on, you would find the home of the wise and wealthy Mayas. . . .

Tales Carl also had of men, women, and their deeds—Samson the strong, Deirdre the fair and unhappy, Crockett the hunter. . . .

Jorith, daughter of Winnithar, forgot she was of age to be wedded. She would sit among the children on the floor, at Carl's feet, and hearken while her eyes caught firelight and became suns.

He was not steadily on hand. Often he would say he must be by himself, and stride off out of sight. Once a lad, brash but skilled at stalking, followed him unseen, unless it was that Carl deigned not to heed him. The boy came back white and ashudder, to stammer forth that the graybeard had gone into Tiwaz's Shaw. None went under those darkling pines save on Midwinter Eve, when three blood offerings—horse, hound, and slave—were made so that the Binder of the Wolf would bid darkness and cold begone. The boy's father flogged him, and thereafter nobody spoke openly of it. If the gods allowed it to happen, best not ask into their reasons.

Carl would return in a few days, freshly clothed and bearing gifts. Those were small things, but beyond price, be it a knife whose steel held an edge uncommonly long, a scarf of lustrous foreign fabric, a mirror outdoing buffed brass or a still pond — the treasures arrived and arrived, until everybody of any standing, man or woman, had gotten at least one. About this he said merely, "I know the makers."

Spring stole northward, snow melted, buds burst into leaf and flower, the river brawled in spate. Homebound birds filled heaven with wings and clamor. Lambs, calves, foals tottered across paddocks. Folk came forth, blinking in sudden brightness; they aired out their houses, garments, and souls. The Spring Queen drove Frija's image from farm to farm to bless the plowing and sowing, while garlanded youths and maidens danced around her oxcart. Longings quickened.

Carl went away still, but now he would be back on the same evening. More and more were he and Jorith together. They would even stroll into woods, down blossoming lanes, over meadows, out of everybody else's ken. She walked as though lost in dreams. Salvalindis her mother scolded her about unseemliness — did she care naught for her good name? — until Winnithar quelled his wife. The chieftain was a shrewd reckoner. As for Jorith's brothers, they glowed.

At length Salvalindis took her daughter aside. They sought an outbuilding where the household's women met to weave and sew when there was no other work for them. There was now, so that these two were alone in its dimness. Salvalindis put Jorith between herself and the broad, stone-weighted loom, as if to trap her, and asked bluntly, "Have you been less idle with that man Carl than you've become at home? Has he had you?"

The maiden flushed, twisted fingers together, stared downward. "No," she breathed. "He can, whenever he wants. How I wish he would. But we've only held hands, kissed a little, and—and—"

"And what?"

"Talked. Sung songs. Laughed. Been grave. Oh, mother, he's not aloof. With me, he's kinder and, and sweeter than . . . than I knew a man could be. He talks to me as he would to somebody who can think, not just be a wife—"

Salvalindis' lips pinched. "*I* never stopped thinking when I married. Your father may see a powerful ally in Carl. But I see in him a man without land or kin, belike a warlock but rootless, rootless. What gain can our house have of linking with him? Goods, aye; knowledge; but what use are those when foemen threaten? What would he leave to his sons? What would bind him to you after the freshness is gone? Girl, you're being a fool."

Jorith clenched her fists, stamped her foot, and yelled through tears that were more of rage than woe: "Hold your tongue, old crone!" At once she shrank back, as aghast as Salvalindis.

"You speak thus to your mother?" the latter said. "Aye, a warlock he is, who's cast a spell on you. Throw that brooch he gave you into the river, do you hear?" She turned and left the room. Her skirts made an angry rustling.

Jorith wept, but did not obey.

And soon everything changed.

On a day when rain blew like spears, while Donar's wagon boomed aloft and the flash of his ax blinded heaven, a man galloped into the thorp. He sagged in the saddle, and his horse was near falling from weariness. Nevertheless he shook an arrow on high and shrilled to those who had come out through the mud to meet him: "War! The Vandals draw nigh!"

Brought into the hall, he said before Winnithar: "My word is from my father, Aefli of Staghorn Dale. He had it from a man of Dagalaif Nevittasson, who fled the slaughter at Elkford so as to carry warning. But already we at Aefli's had marked a ruddiness on the skyline, where surely farmsteads were afire."

"Two bands of them, then," Winnithar muttered. "At least. Belike more. They're out early this year, and in strength."

"How could they leave their grounds untended in seeding time?" asked a son of his.

Winnithar gusted a sigh. "They've bred more hands than they need for work. Besides, I hear of a King Hildaric, who's brought their clans beneath him. Thus they can field greater hosts than erstwhile, which move faster and under a better plan than we're able. Aye, could be Hildaric means to rid these lands of us, for the good of his own overflowing realm."

"What shall we do?" an iron-steady old warrior wanted to know.

"Gather the neighborhood men and go to meet as many others as time allows, like Aefli's, if he hasn't already been overrun. At the Rock of the Twin Horsemen as aforetime, eh? It may be that, together, we'll not hit a Vandal troop too big for us."

Carl stirred where he sat. "But what of your homes?" he asked. "Raiders could outflank you, unbeknownst, and fall on steadings like yours." He left the rest unspoken: plunder, burning, women in their best years borne off, everybody else cut down.

"We must risk that. Else we'll be whipped piecemeal." Winnithar grew silent. The longfires leaped and flickered. Outside, wind hooted and rain dashed against walls. His gaze sought Carl's. "We have no helmet or mail that would fit you. Maybe you can fetch gear for yourself from wherever you get things."

The outsider sat stiff. Lines deepened in his face.

Winnithar's shoulders slumped. "Well, this is no fight of yours, is it?" he sighed. "You're no Teuring."

"Carl, oh, Carl!" Jorith came out from among the women.

For a while that reached onward, she and the gray man looked at each other. Then he shook himself, turned to Winnithar, and said: "Fear not. I'll abide by my friends. But it must be in my own way, and you must follow my redes, whether or not you understand them. Are you willing to that?"

Nobody cheered. A sound like the wind passed down the shadowy length of the hall.

Winnithar mustered heart. "Yes," he said. "Now let riders of ours take war-arrows around. But the rest of us shall feast."

—What happened in the next few weeks was never really known. Men fared, pitched camp, fought, came home afterward or did not. Those who did, which was most of them, often had wild tales to tell. They spoke of a blue-cloaked spearman who rode through the sky on a mount that was not a horse. They spoke of dreadful monsters charging at Vandal ranks, and eerie lights in the dark, and blind fear coming upon the foe, until he cast his weapons from him and fled screaming. They spoke of somehow always finding a Vandal gang before it had quite reached a Gothic thorp, and putting it to flight, making sheer lack of loot cause clan after clan to give up and trek off. They spoke of victory.

Their chiefs could say slightly more. It was the Wanderer who had told them where to go, what to await, how best to form array for battle. It was he who outsped the gale as he brought warning and summons, he who got Greutung and Taifal and Amaling help, he who overawed the haughty till they worked side by side as he ordered.

These stories faded away in the course of the following lifetime or two. They were so strange. Rather, they sank back among the older stories of their kind. Anses, Wanes, trolls, wizards, ghosts, had not such beings again and again joined the quarrels of men? What mattered was that for a half-score years, the Goths along the upper Vistula knew peace. Let us get on with the harvest, said they: or whatever else they wanted to do with their lives.

But Carl came back to Jorith as the rescuer.

— He could not really wed her. He *had* no acknowledged kin. Yet men who could afford it had always taken lemans; the Goths held that to be no shame, if the man provided well for woman and children. Besides, Carl was no mere swain, thane, or king. Salvalindis herself brought Jorith to him, where he waited in a flower-decked loft-room, after a feast at which splendid gifts passed to and fro.

Winnithar had timber cut and ferried across the river, and a goodly house raised for the two. Carl wanted some odd things in the building, such as a bedroom by itself. There was also another room, kept locked save when he went in alone. He was never there long, and no more did he go off to Tiwaz's Shaw.

Men said between themselves that he made far too much of Jorith. They were apt to swap looks, or walk away from others, like some fuzz-cheeked boy and a thrall girl. However . . . she ran her home well enough, and anyway, who dared mock at him?

He himself left most of a husband's tasks to a steward. He did bring in the goods that the household needed, or the wherewithal to trade for them. And he became a great trader. These years of peace were not years of listlessness. No, they brought more chapmen than ever before, carrying amber, furs, honey, tallow from the North, wine, glass, metalwork, cloth, fine pottery from the South and West. Ever eager to meet somebody new, Carl guested passersby lavishly, and went to the fairs as well as the folkmoots.

In those moots he, who was not a tribesman, only watched; but after the day's talk, things would get lively around his booth.

Nonetheless, men wondered, and women too. Word trickled back that a man, gray but hale, whom nobody formerly knew, was often seen among other Gothic tribes. . . .

It may be that those absences of his were the reason why Jorith was not at once with child; or it may be that she was rather young, just sixteen winters, when she came to his bed. A year had gone by before the signs were unmistakable.

Although her sicknesses grew harsh, joy shone from her. Again his behavior was strange, for he seemed to care less about his get that she bore than about her own well-being. He even oversaw what she ate, providing her with things like outland fruits regardless of season though forbidding her as much salt as she was wont to. She obeyed gladly, saying this showed he loved her.

Meanwhile life went on in the neighborhood, and death. At the burials and grave-ales, nobody made bold to speak freely with Carl; he was too close to the unknown. On the other hand, the heads of household who had chosen him were taken aback when he refused the honor of being the man hereabouts who would swive the next Spring Queen.

Remembering what else he had done and was doing on their behalf, they got over that.

Warmth; harvest; bleakness; rebirth; summer again; and Jorith was brought to her childbed.

Long was her toil. She suffered the pains bravely, but the women who attended her became very glum. The elves would not have liked it had a man seen her during that time. Bad enough how Carl had demanded unheard-of cleanliness. They could only hope that he knew what he was about.

He waited it out in the main room of his house. When callers came, he had mead and drink set forth as was right, but stayed curt in his speech.

When they left at nightfall, he did not sleep but sat alone in the dark until sunrise. Now and then the midwife or a helper would shuffle out to tell him how the birth was going. By the light of the lamp she bore, she saw how his glance sought the door he kept locked.

Late in the second day, the midwife found him among his friends. Silence fell upon them. Then that which she bore in her arms let out a wail — and Winnithar a shout. Carl rose, his nostrils white.

The woman knelt before him, unfolded the blanket, and on the earthen floor, at the father's feet, laid a man-child, still bloody but lustily sprattling and crying. If Carl did not take the babe up onto his knee, she would carry it into the woods and leave it for the wolves. He never stopped to see if aught might be wrong with it. He snatched the wee form to him while he croaked, "Jorith, how fares Jorith?"

"Weak," said the midwife. "Go to her now if you will."

Carl gave her back his son and hastened to the bedroom. The women who were there stood aside. He bent over Jorith. She lay white, sweat-clammy, hollowed out. But when she saw her man, she reached feebly upward and smiled the ghost of a smile. "Dagobert," she whispered. That was the name, old in her family, that she had wished for, were this a boy.

"Dagobert, yes," Carl said low. Unseemly though it was in sight of the rest, he bent to kiss her.

She lowered her lids and sank back onto the straw. "Thank you," came from her throat, barely to be heard. "The son of a god."

"No—"

Suddenly Jorith shuddered. For a moment she clutched at her brow. Her eyes opened again. The pupils were fixed and wide. She grew bonelessly limp. Breath rattled in and out.

Carl straightened, whirled, and sped from the room. At the locked door, he took forth his key and went inside. It banged behind him.

Salvalindis moved to her daughter's side. "She is dying," she said flatly. "Can his witchcraft save her? Should it?"

The forbidden door swung back. Carl came out, and another. He forgot to close it. Men glimpsed a thing of metal. Some remembered what he had ridden who flew above the battle-fields. They huddled close, gripped amulets or drew signs in the air.

Carl's companion was a woman, though clad in rainbow-shimmery breeks and tunic. Her countenance was of a kind never seen before—broad and high in the cheekbones like a Hun's, but short of nose, coppery-golden of hue, beneath straight blue-black hair. She held a box by its handle.

The two dashed to the bedroom. "Out, out!" Carl roared, and chased the Gothic women before him like leaves before a storm.

He followed them, and now remembered to shut the door on his steed. Turning around, he saw how everybody stared at him, while they shrank away. "Be not afraid," he said thickly. "No harm is here. I have but fetched a wise-woman to help Jorith."

For a while they all stood in stillness and gathering murk.

The stranger trod forth and beckoned to Carl. There was that about her which drew a groan from him. He stumbled to her, and she led him by the elbow into the bedroom. Silence welled out of it.

After another while folk heard voices, his full of fury and anguish, hers calm and ruthless. Nobody understood that tongue.

They returned. Carl's face looked aged. "She is sped," he told the others. "I have closed her eyes. Make ready her burial and feast, Winnithar. I will be back for that."

He and the wise-woman entered the secret room. From the midwife's arms, Dagobert howled.

2319

I'd flitted uptime to 1930's New York, because I knew that base and its personnel. The young fellow on duty tried to make a fuss about regulations, but him I could browbeat. He put through an emergency call for a top-flight medic. It happened to be Kwei-fei Mendoza who had the opportunity to respond, though we'd never met. She asked no more questions than were needful before she joined me on my hopper and we were off to Gothland. Later, however, she wanted us both at her hospital, on the moon in the twenty-fourth century. I was in no shape to protest.

She had me take a kettle-hot bath and sent me to bed. An electronic skullcap gave me many hours of sleep.

Eventually I received clean clothes, something

to eat (I didn't notice what), and guidance to her office. Seated behind an enormous desk, she waved me to take a chair. Neither of us spoke for a minute or three.

Evading hers, my gaze shifted around. The artificial gravity that kept my weight as usual did nothing to make the place homelike for me. Not that it wasn't quite beautiful, in its fashion. The air bore a tinge of roses and new-mown hay. The carpet was a deep violet in which star-points twinkled. Subtle colors swirled over the walls. A big window, if window it was, showed the grandeur of mountains, a craterscape in the distance, heaven black but reigned over by an Earth nearly full. I lost myself in the sight of that glorious white-swirled blueness. Jorith had lost herself there, two thousand years ago.

"Well, Agent Farness," Mendoza said at length in Temporal, the Patrol language, "how do you feel?"

"Dazed but clear-headed," I muttered. "No. Like a murderer."

"You should certainly have left that child alone."

I forced my attention toward her and replied, "She wasn't a child. Not in her society, or in most throughout history. The relationship helped me a lot in getting the trust of the community, therefore in furthering my mission. Not that I was cold-blooded about it, please believe me. We were in love."

"What has your wife to say on that subject? Or did you never tell her?"

My defense had left me too exhausted to resent what might else have seemed nosiness. "Yes, I did. I . . . asked her if she'd mind. She thought it over and decided not. We'd spent our younger days in the 1960's and '70's, remember. . . . No, you'd scarcely have heard, but that was a period of revolution in sexual mores."

Mendoza smiled rather grimly. "Fashions come and go."

"We'd stayed monogamous, my wife and I, but more out of preference than principle. And look, I always kept visiting her. I love her, I really do."

"And she doubtless reckoned it best to let you have your middle-aged fling," Mendoza snapped.

That stung. "It wasn't! I tell you, I loved Jorith, the Gothic girl, I loved her too." Grief took me by the throat. "Was there absolutely nothing you could do?"

Mendoza shook her head. Her hands rested quietly on the desk. Her tone softened. "I told you already. I'll tell you in detail if you wish. The instruments—no matter how they work, but they showed an aneurysm of the anterior cerebral artery. It hadn't been bad enough to produce symptoms, but the stress of a long and difficult primiparous labor caused it to rupture. No kindness to revive her, after such extensive brain damage."

"You couldn't repair that?"

"Well, we could have brought the body uptime, restarted the heart and lungs, and used neuron cloning techniques to produce a person that resembled her, but who would have had to learn almost everything over from the beginning. My corps does not do that sort of operation, Agent Farness. It isn't that we lack compassion, it's simply that we have too many calls on us already, to help Patrol personnel and their . . . proper families. If ever we started making exceptions, we'd be swamped. Nor would you have gotten your sweetheart back, you realize. She would not have gotten herself back."

I rallied what force of will was left me. "Suppose we went downtime of her pregnancy," I said. "We could bring her here, fix that artery, blank her memories of the whole trip, and return her to— live out a healthy life."

"That's your wishfulness speaking. The Patrol does not change what has been. It preserves it."

I sank deeper into my chair. Variable contours sought in vain to comfort me.

Mendoza relented. "But don't feel too much guilt, you," she said. "You couldn't have known. If the girl had married somebody else, as she surely would have, the end would have been the same. I get the impression you made her happier than most females of her era."

Her tone gathered strength: "You, though, you've given yourself a wound that will take long to scar over. It never will, unless you resist the supreme temptation—to keep going back to her lifetime, seeing her, being with her. That is forbidden, under severe penalties, and not only because of the risks it might pose to the time-stream. You'd wreck your spirit, even your mind. And we need you. Your wife needs you."

"Yes," I achieved saying.

"Hard enough will be watching your descendants and hers endure what they must. I wonder if you should not transfer entirely from your project."

"No. Please."

"Why not?" she flung at me.

"Because I—I can't just abandon them—as if Jorith had lived and died for nothing."

"That will be for your superiors to decide. You'll get a stiff reprimand at the very least, as close to the black hole as you've orbited. Never again may you interfere to the degree you did." Mendoza paused, glanced from me, stroked her chin, and murmured, "Unless certain actions prove necessary to restore equilibrium. . . . But that is not my province."

Her look returned to my misery. Abruptly she leaned forward over the desk, made a reaching gesture, and said:

"Listen, Carl Farness. I'm going to be asked for my opinion of your case. That's why I brought you here, and why I want to keep you a week or two—to get a better idea. But already—you're not unique, my friend, in a million years of Patrol operations!—already I've begun to see you as a decent sort, who may have blundered but largely through inexperience.

"It happens, has happened, will happen, over and over. Isolation, in spite of furloughs at home and liaisons with prosaic fellow members like me. Bewilderment, in spite of advance preparation; culture shock; human shock. You witnessed what to you were wretchedness, poverty, squalor, ignorance, needless tragedy—worse, callousness, brutality, injustice, wanton manslaughter—You couldn't encounter that without it hurting you. You had to assure yourself that your Goths were no worse than you are, merely different; and you had to seek past that difference to the underlying identity; and then you had to try to help, and if along the way you suddenly found a door open on something dear and wonderful—

"Yes, inevitably, time travelers, including Patrollers—many of them form ties. They perform actions, and sometimes those are intimate. It doesn't normally pose a threat. What matters the precise, the obscure and remote, ancestry of even a key figure? The continuum yields but rebounds. If its stress limits aren't exceeded, why, the question becomes unanswerable, meaningless, whether such minor doings change the past, or have 'always' been a part of it.

"Do not feel too guilty, Farness," she ended, most quietly. "I would also like to start you recovering from that, and from your grief. You are a field agent of the Time Patrol; this is not the last mourning you will ever have reason to do."

302–330

Carl kept his word. Stone-silent, he leaned on his spear and watched while her kinfolk laid Jorith in the earth and heaped a barrow above her. Afterward he and her father honored her by an arval to which they bade the whole neighborhood come, and which lasted three days. There he spoke only when spoken to, though at those times polite enough in his lordly way. While he did not seek to dampen anybody's merriment, that feast was quieter than most.

When guests had departed, and Carl sat alone by his hearth save for Winnithar, he told the chieftain: "Tomorrow I go too. You will not see me often again."

"Have you then done whatever you came for?"

"No, not yet."

Winnithar did not ask what it was. Carl sighed and added: "As far as Weard allows, I mean to watch over your house. But that may not be so far."

At dawn he bade farewell and strode off. Mists lay heavy and chill, soon hiding him from the sight of men.

In years that followed, tales grew. Some thought they had glimpsed his tall form by twilight, entering the grave-mound as if by a door. Others said no; he had led her away by the hand. Their memories of him slowly lost humanness.

Dagobert's grandparents took the babe in, found a wet nurse, and raised him like their own. Despite his uncanny begetting, he was not shunned nor let run wild. Instead, folk reckoned his friendship well worth having, for he must be destined to mighty deeds—on which account, he should learn honor and seemly ways, as well as the skills of a warrior, hunter, and husbandman. Children of gods were not unheard of. They became heroes, or women passing wise and fair, but were nonetheless mortal.

After three years, Carl came briefly calling. As he watched his son, he murmured, "How he does look like his mother."

"Aye, in the face," Winnithar agreed, "but he'll not lack manliness; that's already plain to see, Carl."

None else made bold any more to bespeak the Wanderer by that name—nor by the name they supposed was right. At drinking time they did as he wished, saying forth what tales and verses they had lately heard. He asked whence those sprang, and they could tell him of a bard or two,

whom he said he would visit. He did, later, and
the makers reckoned themselves lucky to have *his*
notice. For his part, he told spellbinding things
as of yore. However, now he was shortly gone
again, not to return for years.

Meanwhile Dagobert grew apace, a lad brisk,
merry, handsome, and well-liked. He was but
twelve when he accompanied his half-brothers,
Winnithar's two oldest sons, on a trip south with
a crew of traders. They wintered there, and came
back in spring brimful of wonders. Yes, yonder
were lands for the taking, rich, wide, watered by
a Dnieper River that made this Vistula seem a
brook. The northern valleys there were thickly
wooded but farther south the countryside lay
open, pastureland for herds and flocks, bride-like
awaiting the farmer's plow. Whoever held it would
also sit astride a flow of goods through the Black
Sea ports.

As yet, not many Goths had moved thither. It
was the westerly tribes that had made the really
great trek, into the lands north of the Danube.
There they were at the Roman frontier, which
meant a spate of barter. On the bad side, should
it come to war, the Romans remained formidable—
especially if they could put an end to their civil
strife.

The Dnieper flowed safely far from the Empire.
True, Heruls had come from the North and settled along the Azov shore: wild men, who would
doubtless give trouble. Yet because they were
such wolfish beings, who scorned to wear mail or
fight in ranks, they were less fearsome than the
Vandals. Likewise true, north and east of them
laired the Huns, horsemen, stockbreeders, akin to

trolls in their ugliness, filth, and bloodlust. They were said to be the direst warriors in the world. But the more glory in beating them if they attacked; and a Gothic league could beat them, for they were split into clans and tribes, likelier to fight each other than to raid farms and towns.

Dagobert was ablaze to be off, and his brothers eager. Winnithar urged caution. Let them learn more ere making a move that could not be unmade. Besides, come the time, they should go not as a few families, prey to reavers, but in force. It looked as though that would soon be possible.

For these were the days when Geberic of the Greutung tribe was drawing the eastern Goths together. Some he fought and broke to his will, others he won over by talk, whether threat or promise. Among the latter were the Teurings, who in Dagobert's fifteenth year hailed Geberic their king.

This meant that they paid scot to him, which was not heavy; sent men to fight for him when he wanted, unless it was the season of sowing or harvest; and heeded such laws as the Great Moot made for the whole realm. In return, they need no longer beware of fellow Goths who had joined him, but rather had the help of these against common foes; trade bloomed; and they themselves had men at each year's Great Moot, to speak and to vote.

Dagobert did well in the king's wars. In between, he would fare south, as a captain of guards for the chapmen's bands. There he went around and learned much.

Somehow, the rare visits of his father always took place when he was at home. The Wanderer gave him fine gifts and sage counsel, but talk between them was awkward, for what can a young fellow say to one like that?

Dagobert did lead in making sacrifice at a shrine which Winnithar had built where the house formerly stood in which the boy was born. That house Winnithar had burned, for her to have whose howe stood behind it. Strangely, at this halidom the Wanderer forbade bloodshed. Only first fruits of the earth might be offered. The story arose that apples cast in the fire before the stone became the Apples of Life.

When Dagobert was full grown, Winnithar sought a good wife for him. This became Waluburg, a maiden strong and comely, daughter of Optaris at Staghorn Dale, who was the second most powerful man among the Teurings. The Wanderer blessed the wedding by his presence.

He was also there when Waluburg bore her first child, a boy whom they named Tharasmund. In the same year was born the first son of King Geberic that lived to manhood, Ermanaric.

Waluburg throve, giving her man healthy children. Dagobert stayed unrestful, though; folk said that was the blood of his father in him, and that he heard the wind at the edge of the world forever calling. When he came back from his next trip south, he brought news that a Roman lord hight Constantine had finally put down his rivals and become master of the whole Empire.

It may be that this fired Geberic, however forcefully the king had already gone forth. He spent a few more years rallying the East Goths; then he summoned them to follow him and make an end of the Vandal pest.

Dagobert had by now decided he would indeed move south. The Wanderer had told him that that would not be unwise; it was the fate of the Goths, and he might as well be early and get a better pick of holdings. He went about talking this over with yeomen great and small, for he knew his grandfather was right about going in strength. Yet when the war arrow came, in honor he could not but heed. He rode off at the head of better than a hundred men.

That was a grim struggle, ending in a battle which fattened wolves and ravens. There fell the Vandal King Visimar. There too died the older sons of Winnithar, who had hoped to be off with Dagobert. He himself lived, not even badly wounded, and won ringing fame by his doughtiness. Some said that the Wanderer had warded him on the field, spearing foemen, but this he denied. "My father was there, yes, to be with me on the night before the last clash—naught else. We spoke of many and strange things. I asked him not to demean me by doing my fighting for me, and he said that was not the will of Weard."

The upshot was that the Vandals were routed, overrun, and forced to depart their lands. After scouring to and fro for several years beyond the River Danube, dangerous but wretched, they besought the Emperor Constantine for leave to settle in his realm. Not loth to have fresh warriors guarding his marches, he let them cross into Pannonia.

Meanwhile Dagobert found himself the leader of the Teurings, through his marriage, his inheritance, and the name he had won. He spent a time making them ready, and thereupon took them south.

Few stayed behind, so glittering was the hope. Among those who did were old Winnithar and Salvalindis. When the wagons had creaked away, the Wanderer sought those two out, one last time, and was kind to them, for the sake of what had been and of her who slept by the River Vistula.

1980

Manse Everard was not the officer who raked me over the coals for my recklessness, and barely agreed to let me continue in the mission — largely, he grumbled, at Herbert Ganz's urging, because there was nobody to replace me. Everard had his reasons for holding back. Those eventually became evident, as did the fact he'd been studying my reports.

Between the fourth century and the twentieth, I'd passed about two years of personal lifespan since losing Jorith. My grief had dwindled to wistfulness — if only she could have had more of the life she loved and made lovely! — except once in a while when it rose in full force and struck again. In her quiet way, Laurie had helped me toward acceptance. Never before had I understood in full what a wonderful person she was.

I was at home on furlough, New York, 1932, when Everard called and asked for another conference. "Just a few questions, a couple hours' bullshooting," he said, "and afterward we can go out on the town. Your wife too, of course. Ever see Lola Montez in her heyday? I've got tickets, Paris, 1843."

Winter had fallen uptime. Snow tumbled past the windows of his apartment, making a cave of white stillness for us. He gave me a toddy and inquired what I particularly liked in the way of music. We agreed on a koto performance, by a player in medieval Japan whose name the chronicles have forgotten but who was the finest that ever lived. Time travel has its rewards as well as its pains.

Everard made a production of stuffing and lighting his pipe. "You never filed an account of your relationship to Jorith," he said in a tone almost casual. "It only came out in the course of the inquiry, after you'd sent for Mendoza. Why?"

"It was . . . personal," I answered. "Didn't see that it was anybody else's business. Oh, they cautioned us about that sort of thing at the Academy, but regs don't actually forbid it."

Looking at his dark, bowed head, I had the eerie knowledge that he must have read everything I would write. He knew my personal future as I did not—as I would not until I had been through it. The rule is very seldom waived that keeps an agent from learning his or her destiny; a causal loop is the least undesirable thing that could all too easily result.

"Well, I don't aim to repeat a scolding you've already had," Everard said. "In fact, between the two of us, I feel that Coordinator Abdullah got needlessly stuffy. Operatives must have discretion, or they'd never get their jobs done, and plenty of them have sailed closer to the wind than you did."

He spent a minute kindling his tobacco before

he went on, through the blue haze: "However, I would like to ask you about a couple of details. More to get your reaction than on any deep philosophical grounds — though I admit to being curious, too. You see, on that basis, maybe I can give you a few useful procedural suggestions. I'm not a scientist myself, but I have kicked around history, prehistory, and even posthistory, quite a lot."

"You have that," I agreed with enormous respect.

"Well, okay, for openers, the most obvious. Early on, you intervened in a war between Goths and Vandals. How do you justify that?"

"I answered that question at the inquiry, sir . . . Manse. I knew better than to kill anybody, since my own life was never in jeopardy. I helped organize, I collected intelligence, I inspired fear in the enemy — flying around on antigrav, throwing illusions, projecting subsonic beams. If anything, by making them panic, I saved lives on both sides. But my essential reason was that I'd spent a lot of effort — Patrol effort — establishing a base in the society I was supposed to study, and the Vandals threatened to destroy that base."

"You weren't afraid of touching off a change in uptime events?"

"No. Oh, perhaps I should have thought it over more carefully, and gotten expert opinions, before acting. But it did look like almost a textbook case. That was merely a large-scale raid the Vandals were mounting. Nowhere did history record it. The outcome either way was insignificant . . . except to individuals, certain of whom were important to my mission as well as me. And as for the lives of those individuals — and the line of descent that I started myself, back yonder — why, those are minor statistical fluctuations in the gene pool. They soon average out."

Everard scowled. "You're giving me the standard arguments, Carl, same as you did the board of inquiry. They got you off the hook there. But don't bother today. What I'm trying to make you know, not in your forebrain but in your marrow, is that reality never conforms very well to the textbooks, and sometimes it doesn't conform at all."

"I believe I am beginning to see that." My humility was genuine. "In the lives I've been following downtime. We have no *right* to take people over, do we?"

Everard smiled, and I felt free to savor a long draught from my glass. "Good. Let's drop generalities and get into the details of what you're actually after. For instance, you gave your Goths things they'd never have had without you. The physical presents are not to worry about; those'll rust or rot or be lost quickly enough. But accounts of the world and stories from foreign cultures."

"I had to make myself interesting, didn't I? Why else should they recite old, familiar stuff for me?"

"M-m, yeah, sure. But look, wouldn't whatever you told them get into their folklore, alter the very matter you went to study?"

I allowed myself a chuckle. "No. There I did have a psychosocial calculation run in advance, and used it for a guide. Turns out that societies of this kind have highly selective collective memories. Remember, they're illiterate, and they live in a mental world where marvels are commonplace.

What I said about, say, the Romans merely added detail to information they already had from travelers; and those details would shortly be garbled down to the general noise level of their concepts of Rome. As for more exotic material, well, what was somebody like Cuchulainn but one more foredoomed hero, such as they'd heard scores of yarns about? What was the Han Empire but one more fabulous country beyond the horizon? My immediate listeners were impressed; but afterward they passed it on to others, who merged everything into their existing sagas."

Everard nodded. "M-m-m-hm." He smoked for a bit. Abruptly: "What about yourself? You're not a clutch of words; you're a concrete and enigmatic person who keeps appearing among them. You propose to do it for generations. Are you setting up in business as a god?"

That was the hard question, for which I'd spent considerable time preparing. I let another swallow of my drink glow down my throat and warm my stomach before I replied, slowly: "Yes, I'm afraid so. Not that I intended it or want it, but it does seem to have happened."

Everard scarcely stirred. Lazily as a lion, he drawled, "And you maintain that doesn't make a historical difference?"

"I do. Please listen. I've never claimed to be a god, or demanded divine prerogatives, or anything like that. Nor do I propose to. It's just come about. In the nature of the case, I arrived alone, dressed like a wayfarer but not like a bum. I carried a spear because that's the normal weapon for a man on foot. Being of the twentieth century, I'm taller than the average for the fourth, even among Nordic types. My hair and beard are gray. I told stories, described distant places, and, yes, I did fly through the air and strike terror into enemies — It couldn't be helped. But I did not, repeat not establish a new god. I merely fitted an image they'd long worshipped, and in the course of time, a generation or so, they came to assume I must be him."

"What's his name?"

"Wodan, among the Goths. Cognate to western German Wotan, English Woden, Frisian Wons, *et cetera*. The late Scandinavian version is best known: Odin."

I was surprised to see Everard surprised. Well, of course the reports I filed with the guardian branch of the Patrol were much less detailed than the notes I was compiling for Ganz. "Hm? Odin? But he was one-eyed, and the boss god, which I gather you are not. . . . Or are you?"

"No." How soothing it was to get back into lecture gear. "You're thinking of the Eddic, the Viking Odin. But he belongs to a different era, centuries later and hundreds of miles northwestward.

"For my Goths, the boss god, as you put it, is Tiwaz. He goes straight back to the old Indo-European pantheon, along with the other Anses, as opposed to aboriginal chthonic deities like the Wanes. The Romans identified Tiwaz with Mars, because he was the war god, but he was much else as well.

"The Romans thought Donar, whom the Scandinavians called Thor, must be the same as Jupiter, because he ruled over weather; but to the Goths, he was a son of Tiwaz. Likewise for Wodan, whom the Romans identified with Mercury."

"So mythology evolved as time passed, eh?" Everard prompted.

"Right," I said. "Tiwaz dwindled to the Tyr of Asgard. Little memory of him was left, except that it was he who'd lost a hand in binding the Wolf that shall destroy the world. However, 'tyr' as a common noun is a synonym in Old Norse for 'god.'

"Meanwhile Wodan, or Odin, gained importance, till he became the father of the rest. I think—though this is something we have to investigate someday—I think that was because the Scandinavians grew extremely warlike. A psychopomp, who'd also acquired shamanistic traits through Finnish influence, was a natural for a cult among aristocratic warriors; he brought them to Valhalla. At that, Odin was most popular in Denmark and maybe Sweden. In Norway and its Icelandic colony, Thor loomed larger."

"Fascinating." Everard gusted a sigh. "So much more to know than any of us will ever live to learn. . . . Well, but tell me about your Wodan figure in fourth-century eastern Europe."

"He still has two eyes," I explained, "but he already has the hat, the cloak, and the spear, which is really a staff. You see, he's the Wanderer. That's why the Romans thought he must be Mercury under a different name, same as they thought the Greek god Hermes must be. It all goes back to the earliest Indo-European traditions. You can find hints of it in India, Persia, the Celtic and Slavic myths—but those last are even more poorly chronicled. Eventually, my service will—

"Anyhow. Wodan-Mercury-Hermes is the Wanderer because he's the god of the wind. This leads to his becoming the patron of travelers and traders. Faring as widely as he does, he must have learned a great deal, so he likewise becomes associated with wisdom, poetry . . . and magic. Those attributes join with the idea of the dead riding on the night wind—they join to make him the Psychopomp, the conductor of the dead down to the Afterworld."

Everard blew a smoke ring. His gaze followed it, as if some symbol were in its twistings. "You've gotten latched onto a pretty strong figure, seems," he said low.

"Yes," I agreed. "Repeat, it was none of my intention. If anything, it complicates my mission without end. And I'll certainly be careful. But . . . it is a myth which already existed. There were countless stories about Wodan's appearances among men. That most were fable, while a few reflected events that really happened—what difference does it make?"

Everard drew hard on his pipe. "I dunno. In spite of my study of this episode, as far as it's gone, I don't know. Maybe nothing, no difference. And yet I've learned to be wary of archetypes. They have more power than any science in history has measured. That's why I've been quizzing you like this, about stuff that should be obvious to me. It isn't, down underneath."

He did not so much shrug as shake his shoulders. "Well," he growled, "never mind the metaphysics. Let's settle a couple of practical matters, and then get hold of your wife and my date and go have fun."

337

Throughout that day, battle had raged. Again and again had the Huns dashed themselves over the Gothic ranks, like storm-waves that break on a cliff. Their arrows darkened the sky ere lances lowered, banners streamed, earth shook to the thunder of hoofs, and the horsemen charged. Fighters on foot, the Goths stood fast in their arrays. Pikes slanted forward, swords and axes and bills gleamed at the ready, bows twanged and slingstones flew, horns brayed. When the shock came, deep-throated shouts made answer to the yelping Hunnish war-cries.

Thereafter it was hew, stab, pant, sweat, kill, die. When men fell, feet as well as hoofs crushed rib cages and trampled flesh to red ruin. Iron dinned on helmets, rattled on ringmail, banged the wood of shields and the hardened leather of breastplates. Horses wallowed and shrieked, throats pierced or hocks hamstrung. Wounded men snarled and sought to thrust or grapple. Seldom was anybody sure whom he had struck or who had smitten him. Madness filled him, took him unto itself, whirled black through his world.

Once had the Huns broken an enemy line. They yelled their glee as they reined mounts around to butcher from behind. But as if out of nowhere, a fresh Gothic troop rolled upon them, and now it was they who were trapped. Few escaped. Otherwise, Hunnish captains who saw a charge fail would sound the retreat. Those riders were well drilled; they pulled out of bowshot, and for a while the hosts breathed hard, slaked thirst, cared for their hurt, glared across the ground between.

The sun sank westward, blood-red in a greenish heaven. Its light glimmered on the river and on the wings of carrion fowl awheel overhead. Shadows ran long down slopes of silvery grass, welled upward in dales, turned clumps of trees black and shapeless. A breeze flitted cold across gore-muddied earth, ruffled the hair of the corpses that lay in windrows, whistled as if to call them hence.

Drums thuttered. The Huns drew into squadrons. A last trumpet shrilled, and they made their last onslaught.

Bone-weary though they were, the Goths cast it back, and reaped men by the hundreds. Well and truly had Dagobert sprung his trap. When first he heard of an invader army—slaying, raping, looting, burning—he called for his folk to gather beneath a single standard. Not only the Teurings, but kindred settlers heeded. He lured the Huns into this hollow that led down to the Dnieper, where cavalry was cramped, before his main body poured over the ridges on either side and barred retreat.

His small round shield lay gnawed to splinters. His helmet was battered, his mail ragged, sword blunt, body a single bruise. Yet he stood in the forefront of the Gothic center, and his banner flew above him. When the attack came, he moved like a wildcat.

A horse reared huge. He glimpsed the man in the saddle: short but broad, clad in stenchful skins beneath what armor he had, head shaven save for a pigtail, thin beard braided in twain, big-nosed face made hideous by patterned scars.

The Hun wielded a singlehand ax. Dagobert
stepped aside while the hoofs crashed down. He
struck, and met the other weapon on its way.
Steel rang. Sparks showered athwart dusk. Dagobert slewed his blade around and raked it over
the rider's thigh. That would have been a deadly
slash had the edge still been sharp. As was,
blood runneled forth. The Hun yammered and
smote anew. He hit the Gothic helmet full on.
Dagobert staggered. He regained his feet — and
his enemy was gone, swept off in the whirlwind
of struggle.

From another horse, suddenly there, a lance
struck forward. Dagobert, half dazed, took it between neck and shoulder. The Hun saw him sink,
and pressed ahead at the hole opened in the
Gothic line. From the ground, Dagobert threw his
sword. It hit the Hun's arm and shook loose the
spear. Dagobert's nearest fellow hacked with a
bill. The Hun toppled. His body dragged from a
stirrup.

All at once, there was no fight. Broken, snatched
by terror, those of the foe that lived fled. Not as a
host, but each for himself, they stampeded.

"After them," Dagobert gasped where he lay.
"Let none go free — avenge our dead, make safety
for our land —" Weakly, he slapped the ankle of
his standard bearer. The man bore the banner
forward, and the Goths followed, slaying and
slaying. Few indeed were the Huns that returned
home.

Dagobert pawed at his neck. The point had
gone in on the right. Blood pumped forth. The
racket of war moved off. Nearer were the cries of
the crippled, man and horse, and of the ravens

that circled low. Those also grew dim in his hearing. His eyes sought the last glimpse of sun.

Air shimmered and stirred. The Wanderer had arrived.

He dismounted from his eldritch steed, knelt in the muck, sent hands across the wound in his son. "Father," Dagobert whispered, a gurgle through the blood that filled his mouth.

Anguish went over the face that he remembered as stern and aloof. "I cannot save — I may not — they would not —" the Wanderer mumbled.

"Have . . . we . . . won?"

"Yes. We'll be rid of the Huns for many a year. Your doing."

The Goth smiled. "Good. Now take me away, father —"

Carl held Dagobert in his arms till death had come, and for a long while afterward.

1933

"Oh, Laurie!"

"Hush, darling. It was to be."

"My son, my son!"

"Come close. Don't be afraid to cry."

"But he was so young, Laurie."

"A man grown, just the same. You won't forsake *his* children, your grandchildren. Will you?"

"No, never. Though what can I do? Tell me what I can do for them. They're doomed, Jorith's d-d-descendants will die, I may not change that, how can I help them?"

"We'll think about it later, dear. First, please

rest, be quiet, sleep."

337–344

Tharasmund was in his thirteenth winter when his father Dagobert fell. Nonetheless, after they had buried their leader in a hill-high barrow, the Teurings hailed the lad their chieftain. A stripling he was, but full of promise, and they would have no other house than his over them.

Besides, after the battle on the Dnieper, they awaited no danger in the morrow. That had been an alliance of several Hunnish tribes which they smashed. The rest would not be hasty to move on Goths, nor would the Heruls. Whatever warfare got waged would likeliest be afar, and not in defense but on behalf of King Geberic. Tharasmund should have time in which to grow and learn. Moreover, would he not have the favor and counsel of Wodan?

Waluburg his mother married again, a man named Ansgar. He was of lesser station than she, but well-to-do, able, not greedy for power. He and she ruled well over their holdings and gave good leadership to their folk until Tharasmund came of age. If they stayed on thus somewhat beyond that year, before withdrawing to live quietly, it was at his wish. The restlessness of his line was in him too, and he wanted freedom to travel.

This was well, for in those days many changes passed through the world. A chieftain must know them before he could hope to deal with them.

Rome lay once more at peace with itself, though

before he died Constantine had divided rule of
the Empire between East and West. For the Eastern seat of lordship he had chosen the city
Byzantium, renaming it after himself. It waxed
swiftly in size and wealth. After clashes in which
they took a drubbing, the Visigoths made treaty
with Rome, and traffic became brisk across the
River Danube.

Constantine had declared Christ the single god
of the state. Spokesmen for that faith went far
and wide. More and more of the West Goths
hearkened. Those who stayed by Tiwaz and Frija
misliked that greatly. Not only might the old gods
grow angry and bring woe to a thankless people;
to take the new one opened a way for Constantinople to win mastery, slowly but without ever a
sword being drawn. The Christians said this
counted for less than salvation; besides, from a
worldly standpoint, it was better to be in the
Empire than out. Year by year, embitterment crept
between the factions.

At their distance, the Ostrogoths were slow to
become much aware of these matters. Christians
among them were mostly slaves brought from
western parts. There was a church at Olbia, but
it was for the use of Roman traders—wooden,
small and shabby when set against the ancient
marble temples, emptily though those now echoed.
However, as the trade grew, dwellers inland also
began to meet Christians, some of them priests.
Here and there, free women took baptism, and a
few men.

The Teurings would have none of this. Their
gods were doing well by them, as by all the East
Goths. Broad acres yielded riches; likewise did

barter north and south, and their share of tribute
paid by folk whom the king had overcome.

Waluburg and Ansgar built a new hall that
would be worthy of Dagobert's son. On the right
bank of the Dnieper it rose, upon a height overlooking the river's gleam, ripple of wind through
grass and croplands, stands of timber where birds
nested in flocks to becloud heaven. Carven dragons
reared over its gables; horns of elk and aurochs
above the doors were gilded; pillars within bore
the images of gods — save for Wodan, who had a
richly bedecked halidom nearby. Outbuildings
sprang up around it, and lesser homes, until the
thorp could almost be called a village. Life boomed
about, men, women, children, horses, hounds,
wagons, weapons, sounds of talk, laughter, song,
footfalls on cobblestones, hammer, saw, wheels,
fire, oaths, or now and then somebody weeping.
A shed down by the water held a ship, when it
was not faring abroad, and the wharf often
welcomed vessels that plied the stream with their
wonderful cargoes.

Heorot, they named the hall, because the Wanderer, wryly smiling, had said that was the name
of a famous dwelling in the North. He came by
every few years, for a few days at a time, to hear
what there was to hear.

Tharasmund grew up darker than his father,
brown-haired, heavier of bone and features and
soul. That was not bad, thought the Teurings. Let
him burn off his lust for adventure early, and
gain knowledge as he did; then he ought to settle
down and steer them soberly. They felt they were
going to need a steadfast man at their head.
Stories had reached them of a king who was

hauling the Huns together as Geberic had done the Ostrogoths. Word from the northern mother country was that Geberic's son and likely heir, Ermanaric, was a cruel and overbearing sort. Moreover, the odds were that erelong the royal house would move south, out of the swamps and damps, down to these sunny lands where the bulk of the nation was now found. The Teurings wanted a leader who could stand up for their rights.

The last journey that Tharasmund made began when he was of seventeen winters, and lasted for three years. It took him through the Black Sea to Constantinople itself. Thence his ship returned; that was the only news his kin had of him. Yet they did not fear—because the Wanderer had offered to accompany his grandson throughout.

Afterward Tharasmund and his men had stories to brighten evenings for as long as they lived. Following their stay in New Rome—marvel upon marvel, happening upon happening—they went overland, across the province of Moesia and thus to the Danube. On its far side they settled down among the Visigoths for a year. The Wanderer had insisted on that, saying that Tharasmund must form friendships with them.

And indeed it came to pass that the youth met Ulrica, a daughter of King Athanaric. That mighty man still offered to the old gods; and the Wanderer had sometimes appeared in his realm too. He was glad to make an alliance with a chieftainly house in the East. As for the young ones, they got along. Already Ulrica was haughty and hard, but she bade fare to run her household well, bear sound children, and uphold her man in his doings.

Agreement was reached: Tharasmund would proceed home, gifts and pledges would go back and forth, in a year or so his bride would come to him.

The Wanderer stayed but a single night at Heorot before he said farewell. Of him, Tharasmund and the rest related little other than that he had led them wisely, albeit he often disappeared for a while. He was too strange for them to chatter about.

Once, though, years later, when Erelieva lay at his side, Tharasmund told her: "I opened my heart to him. He wanted that, and heard me out, and somehow it was as if love and pain dwelt together behind his eyes."

1858

Unlike most Patrol agents above the rank of routineer, Herbert Ganz had not abandoned his former surroundings. Middle-aged when recruited, and a confirmed bachelor, he liked being Herr Professor at the Friedrich Wilhelm University in Berlin. As a rule, he would come back from his time trips within five minutes of departure to resume an orderly, slightly pompous academic existence. For that matter, his jaunts were seldom to anywhere but a superbly equipped office centuries uptime, and scarcely ever to the early Germanic milieus which were his field of research.

"They are unsuitable for a peaceful old scholar," he had said when I asked why. "And *vice versa*. I would make a fool of myself, earn contempt, arouse suspicion, perhaps get killed. No, my usefulness is in study, organization, analysis, hypothesis. Let me enjoy my life in these decades that suit me. Too soon will they end. Yes, of course, before Western civilization begins self-destruction in earnest, I must needs have aged my appearance, until I simulate my death. . . . What next? Who knows? I will inquire. Perhaps I should simply start over elsewhere: *exempli gratia,* post-Napoleonic Bonn or Heidelberg."

He felt it incumbent on him to give hospitality to field operatives when they reported in person. For the fifth time in my lifespan thus far, he and I followed a gargantuan midday meal by a nap and a stroll along Unter den Linden. We came back to his house through a summer twilight. Trees breathed fragrance, horsedrawn vehicles clop-clopped past, gentlemen raised their tall hats to ladies of their acquaintance whom they met, a nightingale sang in a rose garden. Occasionally a uniformed Prussian officer strode by, but his shoulders did not obviously carry the future.

The house was spacious, though books and bric-a-brac tended to disguise that fact. Ganz led me to the library and rang for a maid, who entered arustle in black dress, white cap and apron. "We shall have coffee and cakes," he directed. "And, yes, put on the tray a bottle of cognac, with glasses. Thereafter we are not to be disturbed."

When she had left on her errand, he lowered his portly form onto a sofa. "Emma is a good girl," he remarked while he polished his pince-nez. Patrol medics could easily have corrected his eyeballs, but he'd have had trouble explaining why he no longer required lenses, and declared it

made no particular difference. "Of a poor peas-
ant family—*ach*, they breed fast, but the nature
of life is that it overflows, not true? I take an
interest in her. Avuncular only, I assure you. She
is to leave my service in three years because she
marries a fine young man. I will provide a modest dowry in the guise of a wedding present, and
stand godfather to their firstborn." Trouble crossed
the ruddy, jowly visage. "She dies of tuberculosis
at the age of forty-one." He ran a hand over his
bare scalp. "I am allowed to do nothing about
that except provide some medicines that make
her comfortable. We dare not mourn, we of the
Patrol: certainly not beforehand. I should save
pity, sense of guilt, for my poor unwitting friends
and colleagues, the brothers Grimm. Emma's life
is better than most of mankind will ever have
known."

I made no reply. Our privacy being assured, I
got more intent than necessary on setting up the
apparatus I'd brought in my luggage. (Here I
passed for a visiting British scholar. I'd practiced
my accent. An American would have been pestered
with too many questions about Red Indians and
slavery.) While Tharasmund and I were among
the Visigoths, we'd met Ulfilas. I'd recorded that
event, as I did all of special interest. Surely Ganz
would want a look at Constantinople's chief missionary, the Apostle to the Goths, whose transla-
tion of the Bible was virtually the sole source of
information about their language which survived
until time travel came along.

The hologram sprang into being. Suddenly the
room—chandelier, bookshelves, up-to-date furniture which I knew as Empire, busts, framed etch-

ings and oils, crockery, Chinese-motif wallpaper, maroon drapes — became the mystery, darkness around a campfire. Yet I was not there, in my own skull: for it was myself on whom I looked, and he was the Wanderer.

(The recorders are tiny, operating on the molecular level, self-directing as they collect full sensory input. Mine, one of several I took along, was hidden in the spear that I had leaned against a tree. Wanting to encounter Ulfilas informally, I'd laid out the route of my party to intercept that of his as we both traveled through what the Romans had known as Dacia before they withdrew from it, and I in my day knew as Rumania. After mutual avowals of peaceful intentions, my Ostrogoths and his Byzantines pitched tents and shared a meal.)

Trees walled the forest meadow in gloom. Flame-lit smoke rose to hide stars. An owl hooted, over and over. The night was still mild, but dew had begun chilling the grass. Men sat cross-legged near the coals, save for Ulfilas and me. He had stood up in his zeal, and I could not let myself be dominated before the others. They stared, listened, furtively drew signs of Ax or Cross.

Despite his name — Wulfila, originally — he was short, thick-set, fleshy-nosed; for he took after Cappadocian grandparents, carried off in the Gothic raid of 264. In accordance with the treaty of 332, he had gone to Constantinople as both hostage and envoy. Eventually he returned to the Visigoths as missionary. The creed he preached was not that of the Nicean Council, but the austere doctrine of Arius, which it had rejected as heresy. Nonetheless he moved in the vanguard of

Christendom, the morrow.

"—No, we should not merely trade stories of our farings," he said. "How can those be sundered from our faiths?" His tone was soft and reasonable, but keen was the gaze he leveled at me. "You are no ordinary man, Carl. That I see plain upon you, and in the eyes of your followers. Let none take offense if I wonder whether you are entirely human."

"I am no evil demon," I said.

Was it truly me looming over him, lean, gray, cloaked, doomed and resigned to foreknowledge— yon figure out of darkness and the wind? On this night, one and a half thousand years after that night, I felt as if it were somebody else, Wodan indeed, the forever homeless.

Ulfilas' fervor burned at him: "Then you will not fear to debate."

"What use, priest? You know well that the Goths are not a people of the Book. They would offer to Christ in his lands; they often do. But you never offer to Tiwaz in his."

"No, for God has forbidden that we bow down to any save him. It is only God the Father who may be worshipped. To the Son, let men give due reverence, yes; but the nature of Christ—" And Ulfilas was off on a sermon.

It was not a rant. He knew better. He spoke calmly, sensibly, even good-humoredly. He did not hesitate to employ pagan imagery, nor did he try to lay more than a groundwork of ideas before he let conversation go elsewhere. I saw men of mine nodding thoughtfully. Arianism better fitted their traditions and temperament than did a Catholicism of which they had no knowledge anyway. It would be the form of Christianity that all Goths finally took; and from this would spring centuries of trouble.

I had not made a particularly good showing. But then, how could I in honesty have argued for a heathenism in which I had no belief and which I knew was going under? For that matter, how could I in honesty have argued for Christ?

My eyes, 1858, sought Tharasmund. Much lingered in his young countenance of Jorith's dear features. . . .

—"And how goes the literary research?" Ganz asked when my scene was done.

"Quite well." I escaped into facts. "New poems; lines in them that definitely look ancestral to lines in *Widsith* and *Walthere*. To be specific, since the battle at Dnieper side—" That hurt, but I brought forth my notes and recordings, and plowed ahead.

344–347

In the same year that Tharasmund returned to Heorot and took up chieftainship over the Teurings, Geberic died in the hall of his fathers, on a peak of the High Tatra. His son Ermanaric became king of the Ostrogoths.

Late in the next year Ulrica, daughter of Visigothic Athanaric, came to her betrothed Tharasmund, at the head of a great and rich retinue. Their marriage was a feast long remembered, a week where food, drink, gifts, games, merriment, and brags went unstinted for hundreds of guests.

Because his grandson had asked him to, the Wanderer himself hallowed the pair, and by torchlight led the bride to the loft where the groom awaited her.

There were those, not of the Teuring tribe, who muttered that Tharasmund seemed overweening, as though he would fain be more than his king's handfast man.

Shortly after the wedding he must hasten off. The Heruls were out and the marches aflame. To beat them back and lay waste some of their own country became a winter's work. No sooner was it done but Ermanaric sent word that he wanted all heads of tribes to meet with him in the motherland.

This proved worthwhile. Plans got hammered out for conquests and other things that needed doing. Ermanaric shifted his court south to where the bulk of his people were. Besides many of his Greutungs, the tribal chiefs and their warriors went along. It was a splendid trek, on which bards lavished words that the Wanderer soon heard chanted.

Therefore Ulrica was late in becoming fruitful. However, after Tharasmund met her again, he soon filled her belly for her, and mightily well. She said to her women that of course it would be a man-child, and live to become as renowned as his forebears.

She gave him birth one winter night—some said easily, some said scornful of any pains. Heorot rejoiced. The father sent word around that he would hold a naming feast.

This was a welcome break in the season's murk, added to the Yuletide gatherings. People flocked thither. Among them were men who thought it might be a chance to draw Tharasmund aside for a word or two. They bore grudges against King Ermanaric.

The hall was bedight with evergreen boughs, weavings, burnished metal, Roman glass. Though day reigned yet over snowfields outside, lamps brightened the long room. Clad in their best, the leading yeomen and wives among the Teurings ringed the high seat, where rested crib and babe. Lesser folk, children, hounds crowded along the walls. Sweetness of pine and mead filled air and heads.

Tharasmund stepped forth. In his hand was a holy ax, to hold above his son while he called down Donar's blessing. From her side Ulrica bore water out of Frija's well. None there had witnessed anything like this erenow, save for the firstborn of a royal house.

"We are met—" Tharasmund broke off. All eyes swung doorward, and breath went like a wave. "Oh, I hoped! Be welcome!"

Spear slowly thumping floor, the Wanderer neared. He bent his grayness over the child.

"Will you, lord, bestow his name?" Tharasmund asked.

"What shall it be?"

"From his mother's kin, to bind us closer to the West Goths, Hathawulf."

The Wanderer stood altogether still for a while that went on and on. At last he lifted his head. The hatbrim shadowed his face. "Hathawulf," he said low, as if to himself. "Oh, yes. I understand now." A little louder: "Weard will have it so. Well, then, so be it. I will give him his name."

1934

I came out of the New York base into the cold and early darkness of December, and went uptown afoot. Lights and window displays threw Christmas at me, but shoppers were not many. On street corners in the wind, Salvation Army musicians blatted or Santa Clauses rang bells at their kettles for charity, while sad vendors offered this or that. They didn't have a Depression among the Goths, I thought. But the Goths had less to lose. Materially, anyway. Spiritually—who could tell? Not I, no matter how much history I had seen or would ever see.

Laurie heard my tread on the landing and flung our apartment door wide. We had set the date beforehand for my latest return, after she'd be back from Chicago, where she had a show. She embraced me hard.

As we went on inside, her joy dimmed. We stopped in the middle of the living room. She took both my hands in hers, regarded me for a mute spell, and asked low, "What stabbed you . . . this trip?"

"Nothing I shouldn't have foreseen," I answered, hearing my voice as dull as my soul. "Uh, how'd the exhibition go?"

"Fine," she replied efficiently. "In fact, two pictures have already sold for a nice sum." Concern welled forth: "With that out of the way, sit down. Let me bring you a drink. God, you look blackjacked."

"I'm all right. No need to wait on me."

"Maybe I feel a need to. Ever think of that?" Laurie hustled me into my usual armchair. I slumped down in it and stared out the window. Lights afar made a hectic glimmer along the sill, at the feet of night. The radio was tuned to a program of carols. *"O little town of Bethlehem—"*

"Kick off your shoes," Laurie advised from the kitchen. I did, and it was as if that were the real act of homecoming, like a Goth unbuckling his sword belt.

She brought in a pair of stiff Scotch-and-lemons, and brushed lips across my brow before settling herself in the chair opposite. "Welcome," she said. "Welcome always." We raised glasses and drank.

She waited quietly for me to be ready.

I got it out in a rush: "Hamther has been born."

"Who?"

"Hamther. He and his brother Sorli died trying to avenge their sister."

"I know," she whispered. "Oh, Carl, darling."

"First child of Tharasmund and Ulrica. The name is actually Hathawulf, but it's easy to see how that got elided to Hamther as the story flowed north over centuries. And they want to call their next son Solbern. The timing is right, too. Those will be young men—will have been—when—" I couldn't go on.

She leaned forward just long enough that a touch of her hand reached my awareness.

Afterward, her tone stark, she said: "You don't have to go through with this. Do you, Carl?"

"What?" Astonishment made me stop hurting for an instant. "Of course I do. My job, my duty."

"Your job is to trace out whatever people put into verses and stories. Not what they actually did. Skip forward, dear. Let . . . Hathawulf be safely dead when next you return there."

"No!"

I realized I'd shouted, took a deep and warming draught, made myself confront her and state levelly: "I've thought about that. Believe me, I have. And I can't. Can't abandon them."

"Can't help them, either. It's predestined, everything."

"We don't know just what will . . . did happen. Or how I might be able to—No, Laurie, please don't say any more about that."

She sighed. "Well, I can understand. You've been with generations of them, as they grew and lived and suffered and died; but to you it hasn't been so long." To you, she did not say, Jorith is a very near memory. "Yes, do what you must, Carl, while you must."

I had no words, because I could feel her own pain.

She smiled shakily. "You've got a furlough now, though," she said. "Put your work aside. I went out today and brought back a small Christmas tree. How'd you like if we trimmed it this evening, after I've fixed a gourmet dinner?"

" 'Peace on the earth, good will to men,
From Heav'n's all-gracious King—' "

348–366

Athanaric, king of the West Goths, hated Christ. Besides holding fast to the gods of his fathers, he feared the Church as a sly agent of the Empire. Let it gnaw away long enough, he said, and folk would find themselves bending the knee to Roman overlords. Therefore he egged men on against it, thwarted the kin of murdered Christians when they sought weregild, at last rammed laws through his Great Moot that left them open to wholesale slaughter as soon as some happening made tempers flare. Or so he thought. For their part, the baptized Goths, who by now were not few, drew together and spoke of letting the Lord God of Hosts decide the outcome.

Bishop Ulfilas called them unwise. Martyrs became saints, he agreed, but it was the body of the faithful that kept the Word alive on earth. He sought and obtained permission from Emperor Constantius for his flock to move into Moesia. Leading them across the Danube, he saw them settled under the Haemus Mountains. There they became a peaceable lot of herdsmen and farmers.

When this news reached Heorot, Ulrica laughed aloud. "Then my father is rid of them!"

She cried that too soon. For the next thirty years and more, Ulfilas worked on in his vineyard. Not every Christian Visigoth had followed him south. Some remained, among them chieftains strong enough to protect themselves and their underlings. These received missionaries, whose labors bore fruit. Athanaric's persecutions caused the Christians to seek a leader of their own. They found one in Frithigern, also of the royal house. While it never came to open war between the factions, there were clashes aplenty. Younger, soon wealthier than his rival because of being favored by traders from the Empire, Frithigern brought many West Goths to join the Church as the years wore on, merely because that seemed a promising thing to do.

It touched the Ostrogoths little. The number of Christians among them did swell, but slowly and without rousing undue trouble. King Ermanaric cared naught about gods of any sort or about the next world. He was too busy seizing as much as he could of this one.

Up and down eastern Europe his wars raged. In several seasons' fierce campaigning he broke the Heruls. Those who did not submit moved off to join westerly tribes bearing the same name. Aestii and Vendi were easier prey for Ermanaric. Unsated, he took his armies north, beyond the lands that his father had made tributary. In the end, a sweep of earth from the Elbe River to the Dnieper mouth acknowledged him overlord.

In these farings Tharasmund gained renown and booty. Yet he liked not the king's harshness. Often in the moots he stood up not only for his own tribe but for others, on behalf of their ancient rights. Then Ermanaric must needs back down, however sullenly. The Teurings were as yet too powerful, or he not powerful enough, for him to make foemen of. This was the more true since many Goths would have feared to draw blade against a house whose strange forebear still guested it from time to time.

The Wanderer was there when they gave name to the third child of Tharasmund and Ulrica, Solbern. The second had died in its crib, but Solbern, like his brother, grew up strong and handsome. The fourth child was a girl, whom they called Swanhild. For her, too, the Wanderer appeared, but fleetingly, and thereafter he was not seen for years. Swanhild became very fair to look upon, and of a sweet and merry nature.

Ulrica bore three more children. They were far apart and none lived long. Tharasmund was mostly away from home, fighting, trading, taking counsel with men of worth, leading his Teurings in their common business. Upon his returns he was apt to sleep with Erelieva, the leman he had taken soon after Swanhild's birth.

She was neither slave nor base-born, but the daughter of a well-to-do yeoman. Indeed, on the distaff side she too descended from Winnithar and Salvalindis. Tharasmund met her while he rode about among the tribesfolk, as was his yearly wont when he was abroad, to hear whatever they had on their minds. He lengthened his stay at that home, and they two were much in each other's company. Later he sent messengers to ask if she would come to him. They brought rich gifts for her parents, as well as promises of honor for her and bonds between the families. This was no offer to refuse lightly, and the lass was eager, so erelong she went off with Tharasmund's men.

He kept his word and cherished her. When she bore him a son, Alawin, he gave as lavish a feast as he had done for Haþawulf and Solbern. She had few further children, and sickness took them away early on, but he did not care for her the less.

Ulrica grew bitter. It was not that Tharasmund kept another woman. Most men who could afford it did that, and he had gone through more than his share. What galled Ulrica was the standing he gave Erelieva—second only to her own in the household, and above it in his heart. She was too proud to start a fight she would be bound to lose, but her feelings were plain. Toward Tharasmund she became cold, even when he sought her bed. This made him do so seldom, and merely in hopes of more offspring.

During his lengthy absences, Ulrica went out of her way to scorn Erelieva and say barbed words about her. The younger woman flushed but bore it quietly. She had won her friends. It was Ulrica the overbearing who grew lonely. Therefore she gave much heed to her sons; they grew closely bound to her.

Withal, they were mettlesome lads, quick to learn everything that beseemed a man, well-liked wherever they fared. They were unlike, Hathawulf the hotter, Solbern the more thoughtful, but fondness linked them. As for their sister Swanhild, all the Teurings—Erelieva and Alawin among them—loved her.

Throughout that time, years passed between visits by the Wanderer, and then they were short. This brought folk still more into awe of him. When his craggy form came striding over the hills, men blew a call on horns, and from Heorot riders galloped forth to greet and escort him. He was even quieter than of yore. It was as if some secret grief weighed upon him, though none dared ask what. This showed most sharply whenever Swanhild passed by in her budding loveliness, or came prideful and atremble if her mother had allowed her to bring the guest his wine, or sat among the other youngsters at his feet while he told tales and uttered wise sayings. Once he sighed to her father, "She is like her great-grandmother."

The hardy warrior shivered a little in his coat. How long had that woman lain dead?

At an earlier guesting the Wanderer showed surprise. Since his last appearance, Erelieva had come to Heorot and had borne her son. Shyly, she brought the babe to show the Elder. He sat unspeaking for many heartbeats before he asked, "What is his name?"

"Alawin, lord," she answered.

"Alawin!" The Wanderer laid hand over brow. "Alawin?" After another while, almost in a whisper: "But you are Erelieva. Erelieva—Erp—yes, maybe that's how you'll be remembered, my dear." Nobody understood what he meant.

—The years blew by. Throughout, the might of King Ermanaric waxed. Likewise did his greed and cruelty.

When he and Tharasmund were in their fortieth winter, the Wanderer called again. Those who met him were grim of face and curt of speech. Heorot was aswarm with armed men. Tharasmund greeted the guest in a bleak gladness. "Forefather and lord, have you come to our help—you who once drove the Vandals from olden Gothland?"

The Wanderer stood as if graven in stone. "Best you tell me from the beginning what this is about," he said at last.

"So that we may make it clear in our own heads? But it is. Well . . . your will be done." Tharasmund pondered. "Let me send for two more."

Those proved an odd pair. Liuderis, stout and grizzled, was the chieftain's trustiest man. He served as steward of Tharasmund's lands and as captain of fighters when Tharasmund was not there himself. The second was a red-haired youth of fifteen, beardless but strong, with a wrath

beyond his years in the green eyes. Tharasmund
named him as Randwar, son of Guthric, not a
Teuring but a Greutung.

The four withdrew to a loftroom where they
could talk unheard. A short winter day was drawing to its close. Lamps gave light to see by and a
brazier some warmth, though men sat wrapped
in furs and their breath smoked white through
gloominess. It was a room richly furnished, with
Roman chairs and a table where mother-of-pearl
was inlaid. Tapestries hung on walls and carvings were on the shutters across the windows.
Servants had brought a flagon of wine and glass
goblets from which to drink it. Sounds of the life
everywhere around boomed up through an oak
floor. Well had the son and the grandson of the
Wanderer done for themselves.

Yet Tharasmund scowled, shifted about in his
seat, ran fingers through unkempt brown locks
and over close-cropped beard, before he could
turn to his visitor and rasp: "We ride to the king,
five hundred strong. His latest outrage is more
than anyone may bear. We will have justice for
the slain, or else the red cock shall crow on his
roof."

He meant fire—uprising, war of Goth upon
Goth, overthrow and death.

None could tell whether the Wanderer's face
stirred. Shadows did, across the furrows therein,
as lamps flickered and murk prowled. "Tell me
what he has done," he said.

Tharasmund nodded stiffly at Randwar. "You
tell, lad, as you told us."

The youth gulped. Fury rose through the bash-
fulness he had felt in this presence. Fist smote

knee, over and over, while he related roughly:

"Know, lord—though I think you already know —that King Ermanaric had two nephews, Embrica and Fritla. They were sons of a brother of his, Aiulf, who fell in war upon the Angles in the North. Ever did Embrica and Fritla fight well themselves. Here in the South, two years ago, they led a troop eastward against the Alanic allies of the Huns. They bore home a mighty booty, for they had sacked a place where the Huns kept tribute wrung from many a region. Ermanaric heard of it and declared it was his, as king. His nephews said no, for they had carried out that raid on their own. He asked them to come talk the matter over. They did, but first they hid the treasure away. Although he had plighted their safety, Ermanaric had them seized. When they would not tell him where the hoard was, he first had them tortured, then put to death. Thereafter he sent men to scour their lands for it. Those failed; but they ravaged widely about, burned the homes of Aiulf's sons, cut down their families—to teach obedience, he said. My lord," Randwar screamed, "was that rightful?"

"It is apt to be the way of kings." The Wanderer's tone was like iron given a voice. "What is your part in the business?"

"My . . . my father was also a son of Aiulf, who died young. My uncle Embrica and his wife raised me. I'd been on a long hunting trip. When I came back, the steading was an ash heap. Folk told me how Ermanaric's men had had their way with my foster mother before they slit her throat. She . . . was kin to this house. I sought hither."

He sank back in his chair, struggled not to sob,

tossed off his beaker of wine.

"Aye," Tharasmund said heavily, "she, Matha-swentha was my cousin. You know that high families often marry across tribal lines. Randwar here is more distant kin to me; nonetheless, we share some of that blood which has been spilt. Also, he knows where the treasure is, sunken beneath the Dnieper. It is well that Weard sent him off just then and so spared him from capture. That gold would buy the king too much might."

Liuderis shook his head. "I don't understand," he muttered. "After everything I've heard, I still don't. Why does Ermanaric behave thus? Has a fiend possessed him? Or is he only mad?"

"I think he is neither," Tharasmund said. "I think in some measure his counselor Sibicho— not even a Goth, but a Vandal in his service— Sibicho has hissed evil into his ear. But Ermanaric was always ready to listen, oh, yes." To the Wanderer: "For years has he been raising the scot we must pay, and calling free-born women to his bed whether they will or no, and otherwise riding roughshod over the folk. I think he means to break the will of those chieftains who have with-stood him. If we yield to this latest thing, we will be the readier to yield to the next."

The Wanderer nodded. "Yes, you're doubtless right. I would say, besides, that Ermanaric en-vies the power of the Roman Emperor, and wants the same for himself over the Ostrogoths. Moreover, he hears of Frithigern rising to oppose Athanaric among the Visigoths, and means to scotch any such rival in his kingdom."

"We ride to demand justice," Tharasmund said. "He must pay double weregild, and at the Great

Moot vow upon the Stone of Tiwaz to abide henceforward by olden law and right. Else I will raise the whole country against him."

"He has many on his side," the Wanderer warned: "some for troth given him, some for greed or fear, some who feel you must have a strong king to keep your borders, now when the Huns are gathering themselves together like a snake coiling to strike."

"Yes, but that king need not be Ermanaric!" blazed from Randwar.

Hope kindled in Tharasmund. "Lord," he said to the Wanderer, "you who smote the Vandals, will you stand by your kindred again?"

Trouble freighted the answer. "I . . . cannot fight in your battles. Weard will not have it so."

Tharasmund was mute for a space. At last he asked, "Will you at least come with us? Surely the king will heed *you*."

The Wanderer was wordless longer, until there dragged from him: "Yes, I will see what I can do. But I make no promises. Do you hear me? I make no promises."

And thus he fared off beside the others, at the head of the band.

Ermanaric kept dwellings throughout the realm. He and his guards, wisemen, servants traveled between them. News was that soon after the killings he had boldly moved to within three days' ride of Heorot.

Those were three days of scant cheer. Snow lay in a crust over the lands. It creaked beneath hoofs. The sky was low and flat gray, the air still and raw. Houses huddled under thatch. Trees stood bare, save where firs made a gloom. No-

body said much or sang at all, not even around
the campfire before crawling into sleeping bags.

But when they saw their goal, Tharasmund
winded his horn and they arrived at a full gallop.

Cobblestones rang, horses neighed as the Teurings drew rein in the royal courtyard. Guards to
about the same number stood ranked before the
hall, spearheads agleam though pennons adroop.
"We will have speech with your master!" Tharasmund roared.

That was a chosen insult, a word used as if
yonder men were not free but kept to heel like
hounds or Romans. The captain flushed before
he snapped, "A few of you may get leave to enter,
but the rest must first pull back."

"Yes, do," Tharasmund murmured to Liuderis.
The elder warrior growled aloud, "Oh, we will,
since we make you troopers uneasy—but not far,
nor idle for long before we get knowledge that our
leaders are safe from treachery."

"We have come to talk," said the Wanderer in
haste.

He, Tharasmund, and Randwar dismounted.
Doorkeepers stood aside for them and they passed
through. More guardsmen filled the benches
within. Against common usage, they were armed.
At the middle of the east wall, flanked by his
courtiers, Ermanaric sat waiting.

He was a big man who bore himself unbend-
ingly. Black locks and spade beard ringed a stern,
lined face. In splendor was he attired, golden
bands heavy over brow and wrists; flamelight
shimmered across the metal. His clothes were of
foreign dyed stuffs, trimmed with marten and
ermine. In his hand was a wine goblet, not glass

but cut crystal; and rubies sparkled on his fingers.

Silent he abided until the three wayworn, mud-splashed newcomers reached his high seat. A time longer did he glower at them before he said, "Well, Tharasmund, you go in unusual company."

"You know who these are," answered the Teuring chief, "and what our errand must be."

A scrawny, ash-pale man on the king's right, Sibicho the Vandal, whispered in his ear. Erman-aric nodded. "Sit down, then," he said. "We will drink and eat."

"No," Tharasmund told him. "We will take no salt or stoup of you before you have made peace with us."

"You talk over-boldly, you."

The Wanderer lifted his spear on high. A hush fell, which made the longfires seem to crackle the louder. "If you are wise, king, you will hear this man out," he said. "Your land lies bleeding. Wash that wound and bind on herbs ere it swells and sickens."

Ermanaric met his gaze and replied, "I do not brook mockery, old one. I will listen if he keeps watch on his tongue. Tell me in few words what you want, Tharasmund."

That was like a slap on the cheek. The Teuring must swallow thrice before he could bark out his demands.

"I thought you would want some such," Erman-aric said. "Know that Embrica and Fritla fell on their own deeds. They withheld from their king what was rightly his. Thieves and foresworn men are outlaw. However, I am forgiving. I am willing to pay weregild for their families and holdings . . . after that hoard has been turned over to me."

"What?" yelled Randwar. "You dare speak thus, you murderer?"

The guardsmen rumbled. Tharasmund laid a warning hand on the boy's arm. To Ermanaric he said: "We call for double weregild as an acknowledgment of the wrong you did. No less can we take and still keep our honor. But as for the ownership of the treasure, let the Great Moot decide; and whatever it decides, let all of us handsel peace."

"I do not haggle," Ermanaric answered in a frosty voice. "Take my offer and begone—or refuse it and begone, lest I make you sorry for your insolence."

The Wanderer trod forth. Again he raised his spear to bring silence. The hat shadowed his face, making him twice uncanny to behold; the blue cloak fell from his shoulders like wings. "Hear me," he said. "The gods are righteous. Whoso flouts the law and grinds down the helpless, him will they bring to doom. Ermanaric, hearken before it is too late. Hearken before your kingdom is rent asunder."

A mumble and rustle went along the hall. Men stirred, made signs, gripped hafts as though for comfort. Eyeballs rolled white amidst smoke and dimness. This was the Wanderer who spoke.

Sibicho tugged the king's sleeve and muttered something. Ermanaric nodded. He leaned forward, his forefinger stabbed like a knife, and he said so that it rang back from the rafters:

"You have guested houses of mine erenow, old one. Ill does it become you to threaten me. And unwise you are, whatever children and crones and doddering gaffers may babble of you—unwise you are, if you think I fear you. Yes, they tell that you're Wodan himself. What care I? I trust in no wispy gods, but in the strength that is mine."

He sprang to his feet. His sword whirred forth and gleamed aloft. "Do you care to meet me in fight, old gangrel?" he cried. "We can go stake out a ground this very hour. Meet me there, man to man, and I'll cleave that spear of yours in twain and drive you howling hence!"

The Wanderer did not stir; his weapon shuddered a bit. "Weard will not have that," he wellnigh whispered. "But I warn you most gravely, for the sake of every Goth, make peace with these men you have aggrieved."

"I will make peace if they will," Ermanaric said, grinning. "You have heard my offer, Tharasmund. Do you take it?"

The Teuring braced himself, while Randwar snarled like a wolf at bay, the Wanderer stood as if he were only an idol, and Sibicho leered from the bench. "No," he croaked. "I cannot."

"Then go, the lot of you, before I have you whipped back to your kennels."

At that, Randwar drew blade. Tharasmund and Liuderis snatched for theirs; iron flashed everywhere. The Wanderer said aloud: "We will go, but only for the sake of the Goths. Bethink you again, king, while yet you are a king."

He urged his companions away. Ermanaric began to laugh. His laughter hounded them down the length of the hall.

1935

Laurie and I went walking in Central Park. March gusted boisterous around us. A few patches of snow lingered, otherwise grass had started to green. Shrubs and trees were in bud. Beyond those boughs, the city towers gleamed newly washed by weather, on into a blueness where some clouds held a regatta. The chill was just enough to make blood tingle.

Lost in my private winter, I scarcely noticed.

She gripped my hand. "You shouldn't have, Carl." I felt how she shared the pain, as far as she was able.

"What else could I do?" I replied out of the dark. "Tharasmund asked me to come along, I told you. How could I refuse, and ever sleep easy again?"

"Do you now?" She dropped that question fast. "Okay, maybe it was all right, allowable, to lend whatever consolation there might be in your presence. But you spoke up. You tried to head off the conflict."

"Blessed are the peacemakers, they taught me in Sunday school."

"That clash is inescapable. Isn't it? In the self-same tales and poems you went back to study."

I shrugged. "Tales. Poems. How much fact is in them? Oh, yes, history knows what became of Ermanaric at the end. But *did* Swanhild, Hathawulf, Solbern die as the saga says? If anything of the kind ever happened—if it isn't just a romantic imagining, centuries later, that a chronicler chanced to take seriously—did it necessarily happen to *them*?" I cleared my stiffened throat. "My job in the Patrol is to help discover what the events really were that it exists to preserve."

"Dearest, dearest," she sighed, "you're hurting so much. It's twisting your judgment. Think. I've thought — oh, but I've thought — and of course I haven't been there myself, but maybe that's given me a perspective you . . . you've chosen not to have. Everything you've reported, throughout this whole affair, everything shows events driving toward a single goal. If you, as a god, could have bluffed the king into reconciliation, you would have, surely. But no, that isn't the shape of the continuum."

"It flexes, though! What difference can a few barbarians' lives make?"

"You're raving, Carl, and you know it. I . . . lie awake a lot myself, afraid of what you might blunder into. You're too close again to what is forbidden. Maybe you've already crossed the threshold."

"The time lines would adjust. They always do."

"If that were true, we wouldn't need a Patrol. You must understand the risk you've been running."

I did. I made myself confront it. Nexus points do occur, where it matters how the dice fell. They aren't oftenest the obvious ones, either.

An example bobbed into my memory, like a drowned corpse rising to the surface. An instructor at the Academy had given it as being suitable for cadets out of my milieu.

Enormous consequences flowed from the Second World War. Foremost was that it left the Soviets in control of half Europe. (Nuclear weapons were indirect; they would have come into being at approximately that time regardless, since the principles were known.) Ultimately, that military-political situation led to happenings which affected the destiny of humankind for hundreds of years afterward—therefore forever, because those centuries had their own nexuses.

And yet Winston Churchill was right when he called the struggle of 1939–1945 "the Unnecessary War." The weakness of the democracies was important in bringing it on, true. Nonetheless, there would not have been a threat to make them quail, had Nazism not taken control of Germany. And that movement, originally small and scoffed at, later chastised (though far too mildly) by the Weimar authorities—that movement would not, could not have come to power in the country of Bach and Goethe, except through the unique genius of Adolf Hitler. And Hitler's father had been born as Alois Schicklgruber, illegitimate, result of a chance affair between an Austrian bourgeois and a housemaid of his. . . .

But if you headed off that liaison, which you could easily have done without harming anybody, then you aborted all history that followed. By 1935, say, the world would already be different. Maybe it would become better than the original (in some respects; for a while) or maybe it would become worse. I could imagine, for example, that humans never got into space. Surely they would not have done it anywhere near as soon; it might well have occurred too late to rescue a gutted Earth. I could *not* imagine that any peaceful utopia would have resulted.

No matter. If things back in Roman times changed significantly because of me, I'd still be there; but when I returned to this year, my whole civilization would never have existed. Laurie would never have.

"I . . . don't agree I was taking risks," I argued. "My superiors read my reports, honest reports they are. They'll let me know if I'm going off the track."

Honest? I wondered. Well, yes, they related what I observed and did, without any lies or concealment, though in spare style. But the Patrol didn't want emotional breastbeating, did it? And I wasn't expected to render every last trivial detail, was I? Impossible to do, anyway.

I drew breath. "Look," I said, "I know my place. I'm simply a literary and linguistic scholar. But wherever I can help—wherever I safely can—I've got to. Don't I?"

"You're you, Carl."

We walked on. Presently she exclaimed, "Hey, man, you're on furlough, vacation, remember? We're supposed to relax and enjoy life. I've been making plans for us. Just listen."

I saw tears in her eyes, and did my best to return the cheerfulness she laid over them.

366–372

Tharasmund led his men back to Heorot. There they disbanded and sought their own homes. The Wanderer bade farewell. "Do not rush into action," was his counsel. "Bide your time. Who knows what may happen?"

"I think you do," said Tharasmund.

"I am no god."

"You have told me that more than once, but naught else. What are you, then?"

"I may not unhood it. But if this house owes me anything for what I have done over the years, I claim the debt now, and lay upon you that you gang slowly and warily."

Tharasmund nodded. "I would in any case. It will take time and skill to bring enough men into a brotherhood that Ermanaric cannot stand against. After all, most would rather sit on their farms and hope trouble passes them by, whoever else it may strike. Meanwhile, the king will likeliest not risk an open breach before he feels he is ready. I must keep ahead of him, but I know full well that a man can walk farther than he can run."

The Wanderer took his hand, made as if to speak, but blinked hard, wheeled, strode off. The last sight Tharasmund had of him was his hat, cloak, and spear, away down the winter road.

Randwar settled into Heorot, a living remembrance of wrongs. Yet he was too young and full of life to brood very long. Soon he, Hathawulf, and Solbern were fast friends, together in hunt, sports, games, every kind of merriment. He likewise saw much of their sister Swanhild.

Equinox brought melting ice, bud, blossom, and leaf. During the cold season Tharasmund had gone widely around among the Teurings and beyond, to speak in private with leading men. In spring he stayed home and busied himself with work upon his lands; and every night he and Erelieva had joy of each other.

The day came when he cried cheerily: "We've plowed and sown, cleaned and rebuilt, midwifed our kine and sent them to pasture. Let's be free for a while! Tomorrow we hunt."

On that dawn he kissed Erelieva in front of all the men who were going with him, before he sprang to the saddle and led them off. Hounds bayed, horses whinnied, hoofs thudded, horns lowed. At the edge of sight, where the road swung around a shaw, he turned about to wave at her.

She saw him again that eventide, but then he was a reddened lich.

The men who bore him indoors, on a litter made of a cloak lashed to two spearshafts, told in dulled voices what had happened. Entering the forest that began several miles hence, they found the trace of a wild boar and set off after it. Long was the chase before they caught up to the beast. It was a mighty one, silvery-bristled, tusks like curved daggerblades. Tharasmund roared his glee. But the heart in this swine was as great as its body. It did not stand while some hunters got down and others goaded it to charge. At once it attacked. Tharasmund's horse screamed, knocked off its feet, belly gashed open. The chief fell heavily. The boar saw, and was upon him. Tusks ripped, amidst monstrous grunts. Blood spurted.

Though the men did soon kill the brute, they muttered that it might well have been a demon, or bewitched—a sending of Ermanaric's, or of his cunning counselor Sibicho? However that was, Tharasmund's wounds were too deep to stanch. He had barely time to reach up and take the hands of his sons.

Women keened in the hall and the lesser houses —save for Ulrica, who kept stony, and Erelieva, who went off to weep alone.

While the first of them washed and laid out the corpse, as was her wifely right, friends of the second hustled her elsewhere. Not much later they got her married off to a yeoman, a widower whose children needed a stepmother and who dwelt well away from Heorot. Although only ten years of age, her son Alawin did the manly thing and stayed. Hathawulf, Solbern, and Swanhild fended the worst of their mother's spite off him, thereby winning his utter love.

Meanwhile the news of their father's death had flown widely about. Folk had flocked to the hall, where Ulrica did her man and herself honor. The body was brought forth from an icehouse where it had rested, richly attired. Liuderis led those warriors who laid it down in a grave-chamber of logs, together with sword, spear, shield, helm, ring-byrnie, treasures of gold, silver, amber, glass, and Roman coins. Hathawulf, son of the house, killed the horse and the hounds that would follow Tharasmund down hell-road. A fire roared at the shrine of Wodan as men heaped earth over the tomb until the howe stood high. Thereafter they rode around and around it, clanging blade on shield and howling the wolf-howl.

An arval followed that went for three days. On the last of these, the Wanderer appeared.

Hathawulf yielded the high seat to him. Ulrica brought him wine. In a hush that had fallen through the whole glimmering dimness, he drank to the ghost, to Mother Frija, and to the well-being of the house. Else he said little. Presently he beckoned Ulrica to him and whispered. They two left the hall and sought the women's bower.

Dusk was closing in, blue-gray in the open

windows, murky in the room. Coolness bore smells
of leaf and soil, trill of nightingale, but those
seemed distant, not quite real, to Ulrica. She
stared a while at the half-finished cloth in the
loom. "What next does Weard weave?" she asked
low.

"A shroud," said the Wanderer, "unless you
send the shuttle on a new path."

She turned to face him and replied, almost as if
in mockery, "I? But I am only a woman. It is my
son Hathawulf who steers the Teurings."

"*Your* son. He is young, and has seen less of
the world than his father had at that age. You,
Ulrica, Athanaric's daughter, Tharasmund's wife,
have both knowledge and strength, as well as the
patience that women must learn. You can give
Hathawulf wise redes if you choose. And . . . he is
used to listening to you."

"What if I marry again? His pride will raise a
wall between us."

"Somehow I do not think you will."

Ulrica gazed out at the gloaming. "It is not my
wish, no. I've had my fill of that." She turned
back to the shadowy countenance. "You bid me
stay here and keep whatever sway I have over
him and his brother. Well, what shall I tell them,
Wanderer?"

"Speak wisdom. Hard will it be for you to
swallow your own pride and not pursue vengeance on Ermanaric. Harder still will it be for
Hathawulf. Yet surely you understand, Ulrica,
that without Tharasmund to lead, the feud can
have only one end. Make your sons see that unless they come to terms with the king, this family
is doomed."

Ulrica was long mute. At last she said, "You are right, and I will try." Anew her eyes sought his through the deepening dark. "But it will be out of need, not wish. If ever the chance should come for us to work Ermanaric harm, I will be the first to urge that we take it. And never will we bow down to that troll, nor meekly suffer fresh ills at his hands." Her words struck like a stooping hawk: "You know that. Your blood is in my sons."

"I have said what I must," the Wanderer sighed. "Now do what you can."

They returned to the feast. In the morning he departed.

Ulrica took his counsel to heart, however bitterly. She had no light task, making Hathawulf and Solbern agree. They yelled about honor and their good names. She told them that boldness was not the same as foolishness. Young, untried, without skill in leadership, they simply had no hope of talking enough Goths into rebellion. Liuderis, whom she called in, unwillingly bore her out. Ulrica told her sons that they had no right to bring down destruction upon the house of their father.

Instead let them bargain, she urged. Let them bring the case before the Great Moot, and abide by its decision if the king did too. Those who had been wronged were no very close kin; the heirs could better use the weregild that had been offered than they could use somebody else's revenge; many a chief and yeoman would be glad that Tharasmund's sons had held back from splitting the realm, and in years to come would heed them with respect.

"But you recall what Father feared," Hathawulf

said. "If we give way to him, Ermanaric will but press us the harder."

Ulrica's lips tightened. "I did not say you should allow that," she answered. "No, if he tries, then by the Wolf that Tiwaz bound, he'll know he was in a fight! But my hope is that he's too shrewd. He'll hold off."

"Until he has the might to overwhelm us."

"Oh, that will take time, and meanwhile, of course, we shall be quietly building our own strength. Remember, you are young. If naught else happens, you will outlive him. But it may well be you need not wait that long. As he grows older—"

Thus day by day, week by week, Ulrica wore her sons down, until they yielded to her wishes.

Randwar raged at them for treacherous cravens. It well-nigh came to blows. Swanhild cast herself between her brothers and him. "You are *friends*!" she cried. They could not but grumble their way toward a kind of calm.

Later Swanhild soothed Randwar the more. She and he walked together down a lane where blackberries grew, trees soughed and caught sunlight, birds sang. Her hair flowed golden, her eyes were big and heaven-blue in the fine-boned face, she moved like a deer. "Need you always mourn?" she asked. "This day is too lovely for it."

"But they who, who fostered me," he stammered, "they lie unavenged."

"Surely they know you'll see about that as soon as you can, and are patient. They have till the end of the world, don't they? You're going to win a name that will make theirs remembered too; just you wait and see—Look, look! Those butterflies!

A sunset come alive!"

Though Randwar never again told Hathawulf and Solbern everything that was in his heart, he grew easy enough with them. After all, they were Swanhild's brothers.

Men who knew how to speak softly went between Heorot and the king. Ermanaric surprised them by granting more than hitherto. It was as if he felt, once his opponent Tharasmund was gone, he could afford a little mildness. He would not pay double weregild, because that would be to admit wrongdoing. However, he said, if those who knew where the treasure lay hidden would bring it to the next Great Moot, he would let the assembly settle its ownership.

Thus was agreement made. But while the chaffering went on, Hathawulf, guided by Ulrica, had other men going around; and he himself spoke to many householders. This kept on until the gathering after autumnal equinox.

There the king set forth his claim to the hoard. It was usage from of old, he said, that whatever of high value a handfast man might gain while fighting in the service of his lord should go to that lord, who would deal the booty out as gifts to those who deserved it or whose goodwill he needed. Else warfare would become each trooper for himself; the strength of the host would be blunted, since greed counted for more than glory; quarrels over loot would rive the ranks. Embrica and Fritla knew this well, but chose not to heed the law.

Thereupon spokesmen whom Ulrica had picked took the word, to the king's astonishment. He had not expected such a number of them. In their different ways, they brought the same thought forward. Yes, the Huns and their Alanic vassals were foemen to the Goths. But Ermanaric had not been fighting them that year. The raid was a deed that Embrica and Fritla carried out by and for themselves, as they would have a trading venture. They had fairly won the treasure and it was theirs.

Long and heated went the wrangling, both in council and around the booths set up at the field. Here was more than a question of law; it was a matter of whose will should prevail. Ulrica's words, in the mouths of her sons and their messengers, had convinced enough men that even though Tharasmund was gone—yes, *because* Tharasmund was gone—best for them would be if the king was chastened.

Not everybody agreed, or dared admit he agreed. Hence the Goths finally voted to split the hoard in three equal shares, one for Ermanaric, one each for the sons of Embrica and Fritla. The king's men having slain those, the two-thirds fell to Randwar the fosterling. Overnight he became wealthy.

Ermanaric rode livid and mum from the meeting. It was long before anyone got the courage to speak to him. Sibicho was the first. He drew him aside and they talked for hours. What they said, nobody else heard; but thereafter Ermanaric was in a better mood.

When word of this reached Heorot, Randwar muttered that if yonder weasel was happy, it boded ill for all birds. Yet the rest of the year passed quietly.

A strange thing happened in the following

summer, which had also been peaceful. The Wanderer appeared on the road from the west, as ever he did. Liuderis led men forth to welcome and escort him. "How fare Tharasmund and his kin?" the newcomer hailed.

"What?" replied Liuderis, astounded. "Tharasmund is dead, lord. Have you forgotten? You yourself were at the grave-ale."

The Gray One stood leaning on his spear like a man stunned. Suddenly, to the others, the day felt less warm and sunny than before. "Indeed," he said at last, well-nigh too low to be heard. "I misspoke me." He shook his shoulders, looked up at the horsemen, and went on louder, faster: "There has been much on my mind. Forgive me, but I find I cannot guest you this time after all. Give them my greetings. I will see you later." He swung around and strode back the way he had come.

Men stared, wondered, drew signs against evil. A while afterward, a cowherd came home and told that the Wanderer had met him in a meadow and asked him at length about Tharasmund's death. Nobody knew what any of this portended, though a Christian serving-woman at the hall said it showed how the old gods were failing and fading.

Nonetheless, the sons of Tharasmund received the Wanderer with deference when he returned in the autumn. They did not venture to ask what had been the trouble earlier. For his part, he was more outgoing than erstwhile, and instead of a day or two, he stayed a pair of weeks. Folk marked how much heed he paid to the younger siblings, Swanhild and Alawin.

Of course, it was with Hathawulf and Solbern

that he talked in earnest. He urged that either or both fare west next year, as their father had done in his youth. "It will pay you well to get to know the Roman countries, and to cultivate friendship with your kin among the Visigoths," he said. "I myself can be along to guide, counsel, and interpret."

"I fear we cannot," Hathawulf answered heavily. "Not as yet. The Huns wax ever stronger and bolder. They've begun reaving our marches again. Little though we like him, we must agree that King Ermanaric is right when he calls for war, come summer; and Solbern and I would not be laggards therein."

"No," said his brother, "and not only for honor's sake. Thus far the king has stayed his hand, but it's no secret that he loves us not. If we get the name of cowards or sluggards, and then a threat arises, who will dare or care to stand beside us?"

The Wanderer seemed more grieved by this than might have been awaited. Finally he said, "Well, Alawin will be twelve—too young to go with you, but old enough to go with me. Let him."

They allowed that, and Alawin went wild for joy. Watching him cartwheel over the ground, the Wanderer shook his head and murmured, "How like Jorith he still looks. But then, his descent on both sides is close to her." Sharply, to Hathawulf: "How well do you and Solbern and he get along?"

"Why, very well indeed," said the chieftain, taken aback. "He's a good lad."

"There is never a quarrel between you and him?"

"Oh, no more than his brashness brings on every once in a while." Hathawulf stroked his youthfully silky beard. "Yes, our mother has ill will toward him. She was ever one for nursing grudges. But regardless of what some fools babble, she keeps no bridle on her sons. If her rede seems wise to us, we follow it. If not, then not."

"Cleave fast to the kindness you have for each other." The Wanderer seemed to plead, rather than advise or command. "Such is all too rare in this world."

—True to his word, he came back in spring. Hathawulf had furnished Alawin a proper outfit, horses, followers, gold as well as furs to trade. The Wanderer showed forth the precious gifts he carried, which should help win good understanding abroad. Taking his leave, he hugged both brothers and their sister to him.

They stood long watching the caravan trek off. Alawin seemed so small, and his fluttering hair so bright, against the gray and blue that rode at his side. They did not utter the thought that was in them: how yonder sight recalled that Wodan was the god who led away the souls of the dead.

—Yet after a whole year everyone returned safely. Alawin's limbs were lengthened, his voice deepened, he himself ablaze with what he had seen and heard and done.

Hathawulf and Solbern bore news less heartening. The war against the Huns had not gone well last summer. Always made terrible mounted fighters by their skill and stirrups, the plainsmen had now learned to move under the taut control of canny leadership. They had not overrun the Goths in any of the pitched battles that took place, but they had inflicted heavy losses, and one could not say they had suffered defeat. Gnawed down by sneak attacks, hungry, bootyless, Ermanaric's host must at length trudge home over the endless grasslands. He would not try afresh this year; he could not.

It was thus a relief to listen to Alawin, evening after evening when folk were gathered over drink. The fabled realms of Rome awakened dreams. Nonetheless, some of what he told brought a frown to the brows of Hathawulf and Solbern, puzzlement to Randwar and Swanhild, an angry sneer to Ulrica. Why had the Wanderer fared as he did?

He had not taken his band first by sea to Constantinople, as with Tharasmund. Instead, he brought them overland to the Visigoths, where they abode for months. They paid their respects to heathen Athanaric, but were more at the court of Christian Frithigern. True, the latter was not only younger but by now had greater numbers at his beck than did the former, even though Athanaric still harried Christians in the parts over which he ruled.

When at last the Wanderer got leave to enter the Empire and crossed the Danube into Moesia, again he lingered among Christian Goths, Ulfilas' settlement, and encouraged Alawin to make friends here too. Later the group did visit Constantinople, but not for very long. The Wanderer spent much of that time explaining Roman ways to the youth. They went north again late in the autumn, and wintered at Frithigern's court. The Visigoth wanted them to take baptism, and Alawin might have done so, after the churches and other majesties he had seen along the Golden Horn. In the end he refused, but politely, explaining that he must not set himself at odds with his brothers. Frithigern took that well enough, saying merely, "Let the day be soon when things are otherwise for you."

Come spring, mire having dried in the roads, the Wanderer brought the youngster and their men home. He did not remain there.

That summer Hathawulf married Anslaug, daughter of the Taifal chief. Ermanaric had tried to forestall this linking.

Shortly after, Randwar sought Hathawulf out and asked if they two could talk alone. They saddled horses and went for a ride through the pastures. It was a windy day, aboom and aripple across miles of tawny grass. Clouds scudded dazzling white through the deeps above; their shadows raced over the world. Cattle grazed ruddy, in far-scattered herds. Game birds burst from underfoot, and high overhead a hawk was at hover. The coolness of the wind was veined with a smell of sun-baked earth and of growth.

"I can guess what you want," Hathawulf said shrewdly.

Randwar passed a hand through his red mane. "Yes. Swanhild for my wife."

"Hm. She does seem glad of your nearness."

"We will have each other!" Randwar cried. He checked himself. "It would be well for you. I am rich; and broad acres lie fallow, awaiting me, in the Greutung land."

Hathawulf scowled. "That's rather far hence. Here we can stand together."

"Plenty of yeomen there will welcome me. You'll not lose a comrade, you'll gain an ally."

Still Hathawulf hung back, until Randwar blurted: "It'll happen regardless. Our hearts will have it so. Best you go along with Weard."

"You've ever been rash," said the chieftain, not unkindly though trouble weighted his tones. "Your belief that mere feelings between man and woman are enough to make a sound marriage—it speaks ill of your judgment. Left to yourself, what might you undertake of unwisdom?"

Randwar gasped. Before he had time to grow angry, Hathawulf laid a hand on his shoulder and went on, smiling a bit sadly: "I meant no insult there. I only want to make you think twice. That's not your wont, I know, but I ask that you try. For Swanhild."

Randwar showed he could hold his tongue.

When they came back, Swanhild sped into the courtyard. She caught her brother's knee. Her eagerness tumbled upward: "Oh, Hathawulf, it's all right, isn't it? You said yes, I know you did. Never have you made me happier."

The upshot was that a huge wedding feast swirled and shouted through Heorot that autumn. For Swanhild there was but one shadow upon it, that the Wanderer was elsewhere. She had taken it for given that he would hallow her and her man. Was he not the Watcher over this family?

In the meantime Randwar had sent men east to his holdings. They raised a new home where Embrica's had been and staffed it well. The young couple journeyed thither in a splendid company, Swanhild carried over the threshold those evergreen boughs that called on Frija's blessing, Randwar gave a feast for the neighborhood, and there they were.

Soon, however, much though he loved his bride, he was often away for days on end. He rode around the Greutung countryside, getting to know the dwellers. When a man seemed of the right mind, Randwar would take him aside and they would talk about other matters than kine, trade, or even the Huns.

On a dark day before solstice, when a few snowflakes drifted down onto frozen earth, hounds barked outside the hall. Randwar took a spear at the doorway and stepped forth to see what this was. Two burly farmhands came after, likewise armed. But when he spied the tall form that strode into his courtyard, Randwar grounded his weapon and cried, "Hail! Welcome!"

Hearing that no danger threatened, Swanhild hurried out too. Her eyes and hair, beneath a wife's kerchief, and the white gown that hugged her litheness were the only things bright, anywhere around. Joy lilted from her: "Oh, Wanderer, dear Wanderer, yes, welcome!"

He trod nigh until she could see beneath the shadowing hat. She raised hand to parted lips. "But you are full of woe," she breathed. "Are you not? What's wrong?"

"I am sorry," he answered in words that fell like stones. "Some things must stay secret. I kept away from your wedding because I would not cast gloom over it. Now — Well, Randwar, I have traveled a troublous road. Let me rest before we speak of this. Let us drink something hot and remember earlier times."

A little of his olden interest kindled that eventide, when a man chanted a lay about the last campaign into Hunland. In return he told new stories, though in less lively wise than of yore, as if he must flog himself to do it. Swanhild sighed happily. "I cannot wait till my children sit and hear you,"

she said, albeit she did not yet have any on the
way. She was the least bit frightened to see him
flinch.

Next day he led Randwar off. They spent hours
by themselves. Later the Greutung told his woman:

"He warned me over and over of what hatred
Ermanaric bears us. Here we are in the king's
own tribal country, he said, our strength not firm
while our wealth is a glittering lure. He wanted
us to pull up stakes and move away—far away,
clear to West Gothland—soon. Of course I would
have none of that. Whatever the Wanderer is,
right and honor are mightier. Then he said he
knew I'd already been sounding men out about
getting together against the king, to withstand
his overbearingness and, if need be, fight. The
Wanderer said I could not hope to keep this hidden,
and it was madness."

"What did you answer to that?" she asked half
fearfully.

"Why, I said free Goths have the right to open
their minds to each other. And I said my foster
parents never have been avenged. If the gods will
not do justice, men must."

"You should hearken to him. He knows more
than we ever will."

"Well, I'm not about to try anything reckless.
I'll watch for my chance. More may not be
needful. Men often die untimely; if good men
like Tharasmund, why not evil ones like Ermanaric? No, my darling, never will we skulk off
from these our lands, that belong to our unborn
sons. Therefore we must make ready to defend
them; true?" Randwar drew Swanhild to him.
"Come," he laughed, "let's begin by doing some-

thing about those children."

The Wanderer could not move him, and after a few more days said farewell. "When will we see you again?" Swanhild asked as they stood in the doorway.

"I think—" he faltered. "I can't—Oh, girl who is like Jorith!" He embraced her, kissed her, let her go, and hurried off. Shocked, folk heard him weeping.

Yet back among the Teurings he was steely. Much was he there in the months that followed, both at Heorot and widely among yeomen, chapmen, or common fieldhands, workers, sailors.

Even coming from him, that which he urged upon them was naught they were quick to agree to. He wanted them to make closer ties with the West. They did not merely stand to gain from heightened trade. If woe came upon them here— carried, say, by the Huns—then they would have a place to go. Next summer, let them send men and goods to Frithigern, who would safeguard those; and let them keep ships, wagons, gear, food standing by; and let many of them learn about the lands in between and how to get through unharmed.

The Ostrogoths wondered and muttered. They were doubtful about a fast growth of trade across such distances, therefore unwilling to gamble work or wealth. As for leaving their homes, that was unthinkable. Did the Wanderer speak sooth? What was he, anyhow? He was often called a god, and did seem to have been around for a very long time; but he made no claims for himself. He might be a troll, a black wizard, or—said the Christians—a devil sent to lure men astray. Or he might simply be getting foolish at his high age.

The Wanderer kept on. Some who listened found his words worth further thought; and some, young, he kindled. Foremost among the latter was Alawin at Heorot—though Hathawulf grew wistful, while Solbern hung back.

To and fro the Wanderer went on earth, talking, scheming, ordering. By autumnal equinox he had gotten a skeleton of what he wanted. Gold, goods, men to attend these were now at Frithigern's seat in the West; Alawin would go there the following year to push for more trade, regardless of how young he was; at Heorot and numerous other households, dwellers could depart on short notice, should the need arise.

"You have worn yourself out for us," Hathawulf said to him at the end of his last stay in the hall. "If you are of the Anses, then they are not tireless."

"No," sighed the Wanderer. "They too shall perish in the wreck of the world."

"But that is far off in time, surely."

"World after world has gone down in ruin erenow, my son, and will in the years and thousands of years to come. I have done for you what I was able."

Hathawulf's wife Anslaug entered, to say her own farewell. At her breast she suckled their first-born. The Wanderer gazed long upon the babe. "There lies tomorrow," he whispered. Nobody understood what he meant. Soon he was walking off, he and his spear-staff, down a road where lately fallen leaves flew on a chill blast.

And soon after that, the terrible news came to Heorot.

Ermanaric the king had given out that he in-

tended a foray into Hunland. This would not be
an outright war, such as had failed before. Hence
he did not call up a levy, but only his full troop of
guards, several hundred warriors well-known and
faithful to him. The Huns had been wasting the
borders again. He would punish them. A swift,
hard strike should at the least kill off many of
their cattle. With luck, it might surprise a camp
or three of theirs. Goths nodded when that word
reached their steadings. Fatten ravens in the
East, and the filthy landloupers of the steppe
might slouch back to wherever their forebears
had spawned them.

But when his troop had gathered, Ermanaric
did not lead it so far. Suddenly, there it was at
Randwar's hall, while the homes of Randwar's
friends stood afire from horizon to horizon.

Scant was the fighting, as great a strength as
the king had brought against an unwarned young
man. Shoved along, hands tied behind his back,
Randwar stumbled forth into his courtyard. Blood
trickled and clotted over his scalp. He had killed
three of those who set on him, but their orders
were to take him alive, and they wielded clubs
and spearbutts until he sank.

This was a bleak evening, where wind shrilled.
Tatters of smoke mingled with scudding wrack.
Sunset smoldered. A few slain defenders sprawled
on the cobbles. Swanhild stood dumb in the grip
of two warriors, near Ermanaric on his horse. It
was as if she did not understand what had
happened, as if nothing was real save the child
that bulged her belly.

The king's men brought Randwar before him.
He peered downward at the prisoner. "Well," he

greeted, "what have to say for yourself?"

Randwar spoke thickly, though he held his battered head aloft: "That I did not fall by stealth on one who had done me no wrong."

"Well, now." Ermanaric's fingers combed a beard turning white. "Well, now. Is it right to plot against your lord? Is it right to slink about heelbiting?"

"I . . . did none of that. . . . I would but ward the honor and freedom . . . of the Goths—" Randwar's dried throat could get no more out.

"Traitor!" screamed Ermanaric, and launched into a long tirade. Randwar stood hunched, belike not hearing much of it.

When he saw that, Ermanaric stopped. "Enough," he said. "Hang him by the neck and leave him for the crows, like any thief."

Swanhild shrieked and struggled. Randwar threw her a blurred look before he turned it on the king and answered, "If you hang me, I go to Wodan my forefather. He . . . will avenge—"

Ermanaric shot forth a foot and kicked Randwar in the mouth. "Up with him!"

A haylift beam jutted from a barn. Men had already thrown a rope over it. They put the noose about Randwar's neck, hauled him aloft, and made the rope fast. He struggled long before he swung free in the wind.

"Yes, the Wanderer will have you, Ermanaric!" Swanhild yelled. "I lay the widow's curse on you, murderer, and I call Wodan against you! Wanderer, lead him down to the coldest cave in hell!"

Greutungs shuddered, drew signs or clutched at talismans. Ermanaric himself showed unease. Sibicho, perched on horseback beside him, yelped: "She calls on her witchy ancestor? Suffer her not to live! Let earth purify itself of that blood she bears!"

"Aye," Ermanaric said in an uprush of will. He rapped forth his command.

Fear more than aught else gave haste to the men. Those who had held Swanhild cuffed her till she staggered, and booted her out into the middle of the yard. She lay stunned on the stones. Riders crowded around, forcing their horses, which neighed and reared. When they withdrew, nothing was left but red mush and white splinters.

Night fell. Ermanaric led his troop into Randwar's hall for a victory feast. In the morning they found the treasure and took it back with them. The rope creaked where Randwar swung above that which had been Swanhild.

Such was the news that men bore to Heorot. They had hastily buried the dead. Most dared do no more than that, but a few Greutungs felt vengeful, as did all Teurings.

Rage and grief overwhelmed the brothers of Swanhild. Ulrica was colder, locked into herself. Yet when they wondered what they could do, even though tribesmen of theirs had swarmed to them from widely about . . . she drew her sons aside, and they talked until the restless darkness fell.

Those three entered the hall. They said they had decided. Best to strike back at once. True, the king would be wary of that, and keep his guard on hand for a while. However, by the accounts of witnesses who had seen it ride past, it was hardly larger than the band which crowded this building tonight. A surprise onslaught by brave men could vanquish it. To wait would give Ermanaric time he needed and was doubtless counting on — time to crush every last East Goth who would be free.

Men bellowed their willingness. Young Alawin joined them. But suddenly the door opened, and there was the Wanderer. Sternly, he bade Tharasmund's last-born son abide here, before he went back into the night and the wind.

Undaunted, Hathawulf, Solbern, and their men rode forth at dawn.

1935

I had fled home to Laurie. But next day, when I let myself into our place after a long walk, she was not waiting. Instead, Manse Everard rose from my armchair. His pipe had made the air hazed and acrid.

"Huh?" I could only exclaim.

He stalked close. I felt his footfalls. As tall as I and heavier-boned, he seemed to loom. His face was expressionless. The window at his back framed him in sky.

"Laurie's okay," he said like a machine. "I asked her to absent herself. This'll be plenty rough on you without watching her get shocked and hurt."

He took my elbow. "Sit down, Carl. You've been through the wringer, plain to see. Figured you'd take a vacation, did you?"

I slumped into my seat and stared down at the rug. "Got to," I mumbled. "Oh, I'll make sure of any loose ends, but first — God, it's been ghastly —"

"No."

"What?" I lifted my gaze. He stood above me,

feet apart, fists on hips, overshadowing. "I tell you, I can't."

"Can and will," he growled. "You'll come back with me to base. Right away. You've had a night's sleep. Well, that's all you'll get till this is over. No tranquilizers, either. You'll have to feel everything to the hilt as it happens. You'll need full alertness. Besides, there's nothing like pain for driving a lesson in permanently. Most important, maybe—if you don't let that pain go through you, the way nature intended, you'll never really be rid of it. You'll be a haunted man. The Patrol deserves better. So does Laurie. And even you yourself."

"What are you talking about?" I asked while the horror rose in a tide around me.

"You've got to finish the business you started. The sooner the better, for you above all. What kind of vacation could you have if you knew that duty lay ahead? It'd destroy you. No, do the job at once, get it behind you on your world line; *then* you can rest and start recovering."

I shook my head, not in negation but in bewilderment. "Did I go wrong? How? I filed my reports regularly. If I was straying off the reservation again, why didn't some officer call me in and explain?"

"That's what I'm doing, Carl." A ghost of gentleness passed into Everard's voice. He sat down opposite me and busied his hands with his pipe.

"Causal loops are often very subtle things," he said. Despite the soft tone, that phrase shocked me to full awareness. He nodded. "Yeah. We've got one here. The time traveler becomes a cause of the selfsame events he set out to study or otherwise deal with."

"But—no, Manse, how?" I protested. "I've not forgotten the principles. I never did forget them, in the field or anywhere, anywhen else. Sure, I became part of the past, but a part that fitted into what was already there. We went through this at the inquiry and—and I corrected what mistakes I had been making."

Everard's lighter cast a startling *snap* through the room. "I said they can be very subtle," he repeated. "I looked deeper into your case mainly because of a hunch, an uneasy feeling that something wasn't right. It involved a lot more than reading your reports—which, by the way, are satisfactory. They're simply insufficient. No blame to you for that. Even with a long experience under your belt, you'd probably have missed the implications, as closely involved in the events as you've been. Me, I had to steep myself in knowledge of that milieu, and rove it from end to end, over and over, before the situation was clear to me."

He drew hard on his pipe. "Never mind technical details," he went on. "Basically, your Wanderer became stronger than you realized. It turns out that poems, stories, traditions which flowed on for centuries, transmuting, cross-breeding, influential on people—a number of those had their sources in him. Not the mythical Wodan, but the physically present person, you yourself."

I had seen this coming and mustered my defense. "A calculated risk from the outset," I said. "Not uncommon. If feedback like that occurs, it's no disaster. What my team is tracing are simply the words, oral and literary. Their original inspirations are beside the point. Nor does it make any difference to subsequent history . . . whether or not, for a while, a man was there whom certain individuals took for one of their gods . . . as long as the man didn't abuse his position." I hesitated. "True?"

He dashed my wan hope. "Not necessarily. Not in this instance, for sure. An incipient causal loop is always dangerous, you know. It can set up a resonance, and the changes of history that that produces can multiply catastrophically. The single way to make it safe is to close it. When the Worm Ouroboros is biting his own tail, he can't devour anything else."

"But . . . Manse, I left Hathawulf and Solbern bound off to their deaths. . . . Okay, I confess attempting to prevent it, not supposing it was of any importance to mankind as a whole. I failed. Even in something that minor, the continuum was too rigid."

"How do you know you failed? Your presence through the generations, the veritable Wodan, did more than put genes of yours into the family. It heartened the members, inspired them to become great. Now at the end—the battle against Ermanaric looks like touch and go. Given the conviction that Wodan is on their side, the rebels may very well carry the day."

"What? Do you mean—Oh, Manse!"

"They mustn't," he said.

Agony surged higher still. "Why not? Who'll care after a few decades, let alone a millennium and a half?"

"Why, you will, you and your colleagues," the pitying, implacable voice declared. "You set out to investigate the roots of a specific story about

Hamther and Sorli, remember? Not to mention the Eddic poets and saga writers before you, and God knows how many tellers before them, affected in small ways that could add up to a big final sum. Mainly, though, Ermanaric is a historical figure, prominent in his era. The date and manner of his death are a matter of record. What came immediately afterward shook the world.

"No, this is no slight ripple in the time-stream. This is a maelstrom abuilding. We've got to damp it out, and the only way to do that is to complete the causal loop, close the ring."

My lips formed the useless, needless "How?" which throat and tongue could not.

Everard pronounced sentence on me: "I'm sorrier than you imagine, Carl. But the *Volsungasaga* relates that Hamther and Sorli were almost victorious, when for unknown reasons Odin appeared and betrayed them. And he was you. He could be nobody else but you."

372

Night had lately fallen. The moon, while little past the full, was not yet up. Stars threw a dimness over hills and shaws, where shadows laired. Dew had begun to gleam on stones. The air was cold, quiet save for a drumroll of many galloping hoofs. Helmets and spearheads shimmered, rose and sank like waves under a storm.

In the greatest of his halls, King Ermanaric sat at drink with his sons and most of his warriors. The fires flared, hissed, crackled in their trenches.

Lamplight glowed through smoke. Antlers, furs, tapestries, carvings seemed to move along walls and pillars, as the darknesses did. Gold gleamed on arms and around necks, beakers clashed together, voices dinned hoarsely. Thralls scuttled about, attending. Overhead, murk crouched on the rafters and filled the roofpeak.

Ermanaric would fain be merry. Sibicho pestered him: "—Lord, we should not dawdle. I grant you, a straightforward raid on the Teurings' chieftain would be dangerous, but we can start work at once to undermine his standing among them."

"Tomorrow, tomorrow," said the king impatiently. "Do you never weary of plots and tricks, you? Tonight is for that toothsome slave maiden I bought—"

Horns clamored outside. A man staggered in through the entryroom that this building had. Blood smeared his face. "Foemen—attack—" An uproar drowned his cry.

"At this hour?" Sibicho wailed. "And by surprise? They must have killed horses traveling hither—yes, and cut down everybody along the way who might have outsped them—"

Men boiled off the benches and went for their mail and weapons. Those being stacked in the entryroom, there was a sudden jam of bodies. Oaths lifted, fists flailed. The guards who had stayed equipped sprang to make a bulwark in front of the king and his nearest. He always kept a score of them full-armed.

In the courtyard, royal warriors spent their lives on time for their comrades within to make ready. The newcomers bore against them in overwhelming numbers. Axes thundered, swords clanged, knives and spears bit deep. In that press, slain men did not always fall down at once; wounded who dropped never got up again.

At the head of the onslaught, a big young man shouted, "Wodan with us! Wodan, Wodan! Haa!" His blade flew murderous.

Hastily outfitted defenders took stance at the front door. The big young man was first to shock upon them. Right and left, his followers broke through, smote, stabbed, kicked, shoved, burst the line and stamped in over the pieces of it.

As their van pierced through to the main room, the unarmored troopers beyond stumbled back. The attackers halted, panting, when their leader called, "Wait for the rest of us!" The racket of battle died away inside, though outside it still raged.

Ermanaric sprang onto his high seat and looked across the helmets of his bodyguards. Even in the dancing gloom, he saw who stood at the door. "Hathawulf Tharasmundsson, what new misdeed would you wreak?" he flung through the lodge.

The Teuring lifted his dripping sword on high. "We have come to cleanse the earth of you," rang from him.

"Beware. The gods hate traitors."

"Yes," answered Solbern at his brother's shoulder, "this night Wodan fetches you, oathbreaker, and ill is that house to which he will take you."

More invaders poured through; Liuderis pushed them into ragged ranks. "Onward!" Hathawulf bawled.

Ermanaric had been giving his own orders. His men might mostly lack helmet, byrnie, shield, long weapon. But each bore a knife, at least. Nor did the Teurings have much iron to wear. They were mainly yeomen, who could afford little more than a metal cap and a coat of stiffened leather, and who went to battle only when the king raised a levy. Those whom Ermanaric had gathered were warriors by trade; any of them might have a farm or a ship or the like, but he was first and foremost a warrior. He was well drilled in standing side by side with his fellows.

The king's troopers snatched at trestles and the boards that had lain on top. These they used to ward themselves. Those that had axes, having retreated before the inroad, chopped cudgels for their fellows out of wainscots and pillars. Besides a knife, a stag's tine off the wall, the narrow end of a drinking horn, a broken Roman goblet, a brand from the firetrenches made a deadly weapon. As tightly wedged as the struggle became—flesh against flesh, friend in the way of friend, pushing, stumbling, slipping in blood and sweat—sword or ax was of scant more help. Spears and bills were useless, save that from their stance on the benches by the high seat, the armored guards could strike downward.

Thus the fight became formless, blind, a fury as of the Wolf unbound.

Yet Hathawulf, Solbern, and their best men beat a path onward, pushed, rammed, hewed, slashed, stabbed, amidst bellow and shriek, thud and clash, onward, living stormwinds—until at last they came to their mark.

There they set shield against shield, loosed steel upon steel, they and the king's household troopers. Ermanaric was not in that front line, but he boldly stood above on the seat, before the gaze of all, and wielded a spear. Often did he trade a look with Hathawulf or Solbern, and then each grinned his hatred.

It was old Liuderis who broke through the line. His lifeblood spurted from thigh and forearm, but his ax beat right and left, he won as far as the bench and clove the skull of Sibicho. Dying, he rasped, "One snake the less."

Hathawulf and Solbern passed over his body. A son of Ermanaric threw himself before his father. Solbern cut the boy down. Hathawulf struck beyond. Ermanaric's spearshaft cracked across. Hathawulf struck again. The king reeled back against the wall. His right arm dangled half severed. Solbern slashed low, at the left leg, and hamstrung him. He crumpled, still snarling. The brothers moved in for the kill. Their followers strove to keep the last of the royal guard off their backs.

Someone appeared.

A stop to the fighting spread through the hall like the wave when a rock falls in a pool. Men stood agape and agasp. Through the unrestful gloom, made the thicker by their crowding, they barely saw what hovered above the high seat.

On a skeletal horse, whose bones were of metal, sat a tall graybearded man. Hat and cloak hid any real sight of him. In his right hand he bore a spear. Its head, above every other weapon and limned against the night under the roof, caught fire-glow—a comet, a harbinger of woe?

Hathawulf and Solbern let their blades sink. "Forefather," the elder breathed into the sudden hush. "Have you come to our help?"

The answer rolled forth unhumanly deep, loud,

and ruthless: "Brothers, your doom is upon you. Meet it well and your names will live.

"Ermanaric, this is not yet your time. Send your men out the rear and take the Teurings from behind.

"Go, all of you here, to wherever Weard will have you go."

He was not there.

Hathawulf and Solbern stood stunned.

Crippled, bleeding, Ermanaric could nonetheless shout: "Heed! Stand fast where you're up against the foe—the rest of you take the hinder door, swing around—heed the word of Wodan!"

His bodyguards were the first to understand. They yelled their glee and fell on their enemies. These lurched back, aghast, into the reborn turmoil. Solbern stayed behind, sprawled under the high seat in a pool of blood.

King's men streamed through the small postern. They hastened past the building to the front. Most of the Teurings had gotten inside. Greutungs overran those in the yard. Had they no better weapons, they ripped cobblestones out of the earth and cast them. A risen moon gave light enough.

Howling, the warriors next cleared the entryroom. They outfitted themselves and fell on the invaders both fore and aft.

Grim was that battle. Knowing they would die whatever happened, the Teurings fought till they dropped. Hathawulf alone heaped a wall of slain before him. When he fell, few were left to be glad of it.

The king himself would not have been among them, had not folk of his been quick to stanch his wounds. As was, they bore him, barely aware, out of a hall where none but the dead then dwelt.

1935

Laurie, Laurie!

372

Morning brought rain. Driven on a hooting wind, hail-cold, hail-hard, it hid everything but the thorp that huddled beneath it, as if the rest of the world had gone down in wreck. The roar on the roof resounded through hollow Heorot.

Darkness within seemed deepened by emptiness. Fires burned, lamps shone well-nigh for naught amidst the shadows. The air was raw.

Three stood near the middle. That of which they spoke would not let them sit. Breath puffed ghost-white out of their lips.

"Slain?" mumbled Alawin numbly. "Every last one of them?"

The Wanderer nodded. "Yes," he told them again, "though there will be as much sorrow among Greutungs as Teurings. Ermanaric lives, but maimed and lamed, and poorer by two sons."

Ulrica gave him a whetted look. "If this happened last night," she said, "you have ridden no earthly horse to bring us the tale."

"You know who I am," he answered.

"Do I?" She lifted fingers toward him that were

crooked like talons. Her voice grew shrill. "If you are indeed Wodan, he is a wretched god, who could not or would not help my sons in their need."

"Hold, hold," Alawin begged her, while he cast an abashed glance at the Wanderer.

The latter said softly: "I mourn with you. But the will of Weard stands not to be altered. As the story of what happened drifts west, belike you will hear that I was there, and even that it was Ermanaric whom I saved. Know that against time the gods themselves are powerless. I did what I was doomed to do. Remember that in meeting the end that was set for them, Hathawulf and Solbern redeemed the honor of their house, and won a name for themselves that shall abide as long as their race does."

"But Ermanaric remains above ground," Ulrica snapped. "Alawin, the duty of vengeance has passed to you."

"No!" said the Wanderer. "His task is more than that. It is to save the blood of the family, the life of the clan. This is why I have come."

He turned to the youth, who stared wide-eyed. "Alawin," he went on, "foreknowledge is mine, and a heavy load that is. Yet I may sometimes use it to fend off harm. Listen well, for this is the last time you will ever hear me."

"Wanderer, no!" Alawin cried. Breath hissed between Ulrica's teeth.

The Gray One lifted the hand that did not hold his spear. "Winter will soon be upon you," he said, "but spring and summer follow. The tree of your kindred stands bereft of leaves, but its roots slumber in strength, and it shall be green anew—if an ax does not hew it down.

"Hasten. Hurt though he is, Ermanaric will seek to make an end, once for all, of your troublesome breed. You cannot raise as much force as he can. If you stay here, you will die.

"Think. You have readiness to fare west, and a welcome awaiting you among the Visigoths. It will be the warmer for the rout Athanaric suffered this year from the Huns at the River Dnestr; they all need fresh and hopeful souls. Within a few days, you can be leading the trek. Ermanaric's men, when they come, will find nothing but the ashes of this hall, which you set afire to keep from him and be a balefire in honor of your brothers.

"You will not be fleeing. No, you will be off to forge a mighty morrow. Alawin, you now keep the blood of your fathers. Ward it well."

Wrath twisted Ulrica's face. "Yes, you've always dealt in smooth words," shuddered out of her. "Heed not his slyness, Alawin. Hold fast. Avenge my sons—the sons of Tharasmund."

The youth swallowed hard. "Would you really . . . have me go . . . while the murderer of Swanhild, Randwar, Hathawulf, Solbern—while he lives?" he stammered.

"You must not stay," said the Wanderer gravely. "If you do, you will give up the last life that was in your father—give it up to the king, along with Hathawulf's son and wife, and your own mother. There is no dishonor in withdrawal when outnumbered."

"Y-yes. . . . I could hire a Visigothic host—"

"You will have no call to. Hearken. Within three years, you will hear word about Ermanaric that will gladden you. The justice of the gods shall fall upon him. On this I give you my oath."

"What is that worth?" fleered Ulrica.

Alawin filled his lungs, straightened his shoulders, stood for a while and then said quietly, "Stepmother, be still. I am the man of the house. We will follow the Wanderer's rede."

The boy in him burst through for a moment: "Oh, but lord, forebear — will we indeed never see you again? Do not forsake us!"

"I must," answered the Gray One. "It is needful for you." Suddenly: "Yes, best I go at once. Farewell. Fare ever well."

He strode through the shadows, out the door, into the rain and the wind.

43

Here and there amidst the ages, the Time Patrol keeps places where its members may rest. Among them is Hawaii before the Polynesians arrived. Although that resort exists through thousands of years, Laurie and I counted ourselves lucky to get a cottage for a month. In fact, we suspected Manse Everard had pulled a string or two on our behalf.

He made no mention of that when he visited us late in our stay. He was simply affable, went picnicking and surfing in our company, afterward tucked into Laurie's dinner with the gusto it deserved. Not till later did he speak of what lay behind us and before us on our world lines.

We sat on a deck which abutted the building.

Dusk gathered cool and blue in the garden, across the flowering forest beyond. Eastward, land dropped steeply to where the sea glimmered quicksilver; westward, the evening star trembled above Mauna Kea. A brook chimed. Here was the peace that heals.

"So you feel ready to return?" Everard inquired.

"Yes," I said. "And it'll be a lot easier, too. The groundwork has been laid, the basic information collected and assimilated. I just have to record the songs and stories as they are composed and evolve."

"Just!" exclaimed Laurie. Her mockery was tender, and became solace as she laid a hand over mine. "Well, at least you are free of your grief."

Everard's voice dropped low: "Are you sure of that, Carl?"

I could be calm as I replied, "Yes. Oh, there will always be memories that hurt, but isn't that the common fate of man? There are more that are good, and I'm able to draw on them once again."

"You realize, of course, you mustn't get obsessed the way you were. That's a hazard which claims many of us —" Did his tone stumble, ever so slightly? It grew brisk. "When it does, the victim has to overcome it and recover."

"I know," I said, and chuckled a bit. "Don't you know I know?"

Everard puffed on his pipe. "Not exactly. Since the rest of your career seems free of any more disarray than is normal for a field agent, I couldn't justify spending lifespan and Patrol resources on further investigation. This isn't official business. I'm here as a friend, who'd simply like to find out how you're doing. Don't tell me anything you don't care to."

"You're a sweet old bear, you are," Laurie said to him.

I could not stay entirely comfortable, but a sip of my rum collins soothed. "Well, sure, you're welcome to the information," I began. "I did assure myself that Alawin would be all right."

Everard stirred. "How?" he demanded.

"Not to worry, Manse. I proceeded cautiously, for the most part indirectly. Different identities on different occasions. The few times he glimpsed me, he recognized nothing." My fingers passed over a smooth-shaven chin—Roman style, like my close-cropped hair; and when the need arises, a Patrolman has advanced disguise technology at his service. "Oh, yes, I've laid the Wanderer to rest."

"Good!" Everard relaxed back into his chair. "What did become of that lad?"

"Alawin, you mean? Well, he led a fair-sized group, including his mother Erelieva and her household, he led them west to join Frithigern." (He *would* lead them, three centuries hence. But we were talking our native English. The Temporal language has appropriate tenses.) "He enjoyed favor there, especially after he was baptized. That by itself was reason for letting the Wanderer fade away, you understand. How could a Christian stay close to a heathen god?"

"Hm. I wonder what he thought about those experiences, later."

"I get the impression he kept his mouth shut. Naturally, if his descendants—he married well—if his descendants preserved any tradition about it, they'd suppose that some kind of spook had been running around in the old country."

"The old country? Oh, yes. Alawin never got back to the Ukraine, did he?"

"No, hardly. Would you like me to sketch the history for you?"

"Please. I did study it somewhat, in connection with your case, but not much of the aftermath. Besides, that was quite a spell ago, on my world line."

And plenty must have happened to you since, I thought. Aloud: "Well, in 374 Frithigern's people crossed the Danube, by permission, and settled in Thrace. Athanaric's soon followed, although into Transylvania. Hunnish pressure had gotten too severe.

"The Roman officials abused and exploited the Goths—in other words, were a government—for several years. Finally the Goths decided they'd had a bellyful, and revolted. The Huns had given them the idea and technique of developing cavalry, which they made heavy; at the battle of Adrianople in 378 it rode the Romans down. Alawin distinguished himself there, by the way, which started him toward the prominence he achieved. A new Emperor, Theodosius, made peace with the Goths in 381, and most of their warriors entered the Roman service as *foederati*: allies, we'd say.

"Afterward came renewed conflicts, battles, migrations—the *Völkerwanderung* was under way. I'll sum it up for my Alawin by saying that after a turbulent but basically happy life, he died, at a ripe old age, in the kingdom which by then the Visigoths had carved out for themselves in southern Gaul. Descendants of his took a leading part in founding the Spanish nation.

"So you see how I can let that family go from me, and get on with my work."

Laurie's hand closed hard around mine.

Twilight was becoming night. Stars blinked forth. A coal in Everard's pipe made its own red twinkle. He himself was a darkling bulk, like the mountain that lifted above the western horizon.

"Yes," he mused, "it comes back to me, sort of. But you've been speaking about the Visigoths. The Ostrogoths, Alawin's original countrymen — didn't they take over in Italy?"

"Eventually," I said. "First they had dreadful things to undergo." I paused. What I was about to utter would touch wounds that were not fully scarred over. "The Wanderer spoke truth. There was vengeance for Swanhild."

374

Ermanaric sat alone beneath the stars. Wind whimpered. From afar he heard wolves howl.

After the messengers had brought their news, he could soon endure no more of the terror and the gabble that followed. At his command, two warriors had helped him up the stairs to the flat roof of this blockhouse. They set him down on a bench by the parapet and wrapped a fur cloak about his hunched shoulders. "Go!" he barked, and they went, fear upon them.

He had watched sunset smolder away in the west, while thunderheads gathered blue-black in the east. Those clouds now loomed across a fourth of heaven. Lightnings played through their caverns.

Before dawn, the storm would be here. As yet, though, only its forerunner wind had arrived, winter-cold in the middle of summer. Elsewhere the stars still shone in their hordes.

They were small and strange and without pity. Ermanaric's gaze tried to flee the sight of Wodan's Wain, where it wheeled around the Eye of Tiwaz that forever watches from the north. But always the sign of the Wanderer drew him back. "I did not heed you, gods," he mumbled once. "I trusted in my own strength. You are more tricky and cruel than I knew."

Here he sat, he the mighty, lame of hand and foot, able to do naught but hear how the foe had crossed the river and smashed underhoof the army that sought to stay them. He should be thinking what next to try, giving his orders, rallying his folk. They were not undone, if they got the right leadership. But the king's head felt hollow.

Hollow, not empty. Dead men filled that hall of bone, the men who fell with Hathawulf and Solbern, the flower of the East Goths. Had they been alive during these past days, together they would have hurled back the Huns, Ermanaric at their forefront. But Ermanaric had died too, in the same slaughter. Nothing was left but a cripple, whose endless pains gnawed holes in his mind.

Naught could he do for his kingdom but let go of it, in hopes that his oldest living son might be worthier, might be victorious. Ermanaric bared teeth at the stars. Too well did he know how that hope lied. Before the Ostrogoths lay defeat, rapine, butchery, subjection. If ever they became free again, it would be long after he had moldered back into the earth.

He—how blessed that would be—or merely
his flesh? What waited for him beyond the dark?

He drew his knife. Starlight and lightninglight
shimmered on the steel. For a while it trembled
in his hand. The wind whittered.

"Have done!" he screamed. He ruffled his beard
aside and brought the point under the right cor-
ner of his jaw. Eyes lifted anew, as if of themselves,
to the Wain. Something white flickered yonder—a
scrap of cloud, or Swanhild riding behind the
Wanderer? Ermanaric called forth all the courage
that remained to him. He thrust the knife inward
and hauled it across.

Blood spurted from the slashed throat. He
sagged and fell to the deck. The last thing he
heard was thunder. It sounded like the hoofs of
horses bearing westward the Hunnish midnight.